Alexandria Van Kirk has always been a slave to her romantic nature. When a night of liquid courage lands her in bed with one of her best friends, Alex is confronted by a host of feelings that terrify her. Feelings about her friend and, unexpectedly, a barista from her favorite café.

It's a tug of war between heart and body. Desire against all her daydreams of someone to share silence, sunsets, and coffee with.

But Alex's past is also about to catch up with her. Tortured memories and the girl they're all about. It's like fighting the pull of a whirlwind. A surefire losing battle. But embracing a newfound romance amid the return of an old flame is a precarious balance, one not even Alex herself is sure she can manage.

How the hell does she choose between the girl she loves and the one she could never confess loving to begin with?

LIQUID

COURAGE

Stephanie Shea

A NineStar Press Publication

www.ninestarpress.com

Liquid Courage

Printed in the USA

ISBN: 978-1-64890-151-5

First Edition, November, 2020

Also available in eBook, ISBN: 978-1-64890-150-8

WARNING:

This book contains sexually explicit content, which may only be suitable for mature readers, depictions of homophobia, and mention of self-harm.

For anyone who knows what it's like to bleed before learning to be brave.

Part One

Brave

Chapter One

vodka sprite

It had been brewing for weeks.

No.

Months.

Alex supposed it didn't matter how long. Tensions between her and Ryan had reached a boiling point. Her body thrummed with quiet unease as vodka scorched down her throat and seeped through her veins. She shouldn't have been drinking this much. What had she eaten? A few chips and maybe half a dozen gummy bears? No wonder the liquor had gone to her head so fast. It was sort of a nice buzz though—enough for her to feel a little less inhibited but still be aware the creepy guy she'd met earlier had been trying to talk her into a dark corner for the last ten minutes.

She leaned against the doorframe, gaze weaving through the mass of sweaty bodies dancing in the living room to land on Ryan.

Ryan tossed her head back in a laugh, grinding on some random guy who was more than happy to have his hands all over her. Her red, ruched dress rode up her thighs with every move. She flipped her jet-black hair and swept it all to one shoulder as her eyes landed on Alex, a smirk lingering on her lips.

Alex's skin prickled with sweat.

Maybe it wasn't the vodka.

Maybe it was the fact that Dom had crammed more than fifty people into a house meant to accommodate three for the riot he called a birthday party. God knows Alex didn't go to these things for fun, but Dom was her oldest friend. She loved him way too much to not show up for his birthday, even if she was as close as any technology-obsessed millennial to becoming a hermit.

The guy—what did say his name was?—leaned closer, pulling her attention to his gangly, unattractive form. "So, do you want to maybe take a walk down to the park?" He stared at her expectantly, sweaty red strands of hair clinging to his forehead. As if she was going to be lured into the park at midnight to be groped by some guy who resembled a '90s crackhead.

"Do you know what Einstein's definition of insanity is?" she asked.

"No. But being this close to you definitely drives me crazy."

Alex rolled her eyes, pushing him out of her personal space. A spot to herself to wait out the night.

That's all she needed. The one she'd been standing in had been perfect. Until now. Her gaze flittered across the room where Ryan had been dancing only to land on strange faces. "Damn it." She started forward and bumped her way through the teeming living room toward the kitchen.

Nothing.

Doubling back, she tried scanning every five-feet-something girl who had dark hair. It hadn't occurred to her before how many girls fit the criteria. Still, it would only take seconds to process that this girl's hair was a few shades too light; that one's skin wasn't pale enough. Another was wearing a nearly identical dress, but the arch of her back didn't seem quite right. Ry had a bigger ass.

Alex halted at the sight of Ryan sitting hunched over in a loveseat across the living room. She pushed her way through the dancefloor. "Ry?" Alex tilted her head slightly. "What's wrong?"

Ryan peered up, eyes glossy and gleaming as she grinned at Alex. "Nothing." Her head fell to her lap again.

Alex drew her brows together. Nothing really appeared to be wrong with Ry besides her being a little tipsy and possibly playing an adult version of peek-a-boo. She slid into the free space on the couch and shifted at the press of Ryan's thighs against hers. Proximity wouldn't do much to resolve her internal conflict. It sure didn't soothe the thought that even sitting there with this thing between them still simmering was a terrible idea. She forced it down. "Tell me what's wrong."

"I told you. It's nothing."

"Ry...come on." Alex nudged her, pressing her forehead to the side of Ryan's face to provoke her into lifting her head again.

"I got a little light-headed. I'm better now."

"Promise?"

Ryan turned her head, her lips brushing against Alex's. "Promise."

Alex's breath caught, her pulse climbing. The heat... It wasn't the vodka or the party being too crowded. It was them. A million red lights went off in her head. Ryan was one of her best friends. Risking that would be stupid and impulsive, and they'd both had too much to drink.

Ry dragged in a deep breath, and their lips brushed again, and Alex's hesitance burst into spectrums of green. She leaned forward, taking Ryan's lips in a gentle kiss. Slow, timid almost, as if they were both afraid to react too much. To react more than the other.

Was it good or bad that Ryan had kissed her back? Even with all the weird tension between them, she'd never imagined how acting on it would feel. Some lines weren't meant to be crossed. Now that she had, she craved more of Ryan's lips on hers—soft and yielding.

They jerked apart as a girl bumped into them, spilling the last few drops of her drink onto Ryan's lap. The girl giggled and offered a barely coherent "Sorry" as she stumbled away.

Ryan stood, Alex following as Ryan weaved her way through the crowd almost aggressively, forcing people out of the way with her hands to clear a path.

"Ry!" The music smothered Alex's attempt.

Ryan rounded the corner at the end of the hallway leading out of the living room.

Alex quickened her steps. As she rounded the bend too, she noticed Dom's bedroom door had been opened. She took a tentative step inside. "Ry? Are you in her—"

The door slammed, and Alex turned. Ryan backed into it with a thud, pulling Alex against her, their lips pressed against each others. Alex's hands found Ryan's hips, and she squeezed. Everything from her grip to the way her teeth latched onto Ryan's bottom lip was a confession. There'd be no stopping now. Not unless Ryan came to her senses and pulled away. Deep down, Alex was pleading for that to happen before things went too far, before their bodies admitted every word their lips refused to speak.

Ryan pushed off the door and spun to pin Alex against it instead. Something stirred in Alex, something deep in the pit of her stomach and lower. She pressed one of her hands to the left of Ryan's chest and pulled her lips away from Ryan's. Their quick, short breaths mingled, Ryan's heart pounding against Alex's hand. Almost matching hers. Almost. "Ry…"

Ryan's fingers slipped beneath Alex's top and stroked her sides. A gulp slid down Alex's throat, and she dragged in a deep breath, forcing her eyes open. Ryan's lack of hesitance was either the sexiest or most terrifying thing she'd ever seen.

"Tell me to stop." Ryan trailed her fingers higher beneath Alex's top.

"Is that what you want?"

Ryan shook her head, leaning forward until their lips grazed. "No."

"Okay." Alex leaned into the kiss as Ry pulled her closer. Tomorrow she'd mull over the consequences. Tonight, they were both too far gone to care.

Traces of vodka and sprite lingered on Ryan's tongue, her perfume engulfing Alex in a hazy cloud. She sucked on Ryan's bottom lip as Ryan's hand came up to cup her right breast. Ryan moaned, squeezing Alex's breast harder, and Alex bit down on her lip. Hearing Ryan like that, knowing she'd caused it did things to her body she hadn't allowed in years.

Ryan tugged at Alex's top. "Take this off."

The pounding in Alex's chest picked up. The black fabric fell at their feet, and she pulled Ryan closer to kiss her again.

Ryan fumbled with the hook of Alex's bra, groaning at the way her fingers proved incapable of completing such a basic task. Despite all of Ry's confidence and lack of reservation, she wasn't as experienced. Not with girls.

Alex smiled against her lips, switching their positions so Ryan was against the door. She positioned her left leg between Ryan's thighs, causing the dress she'd been wearing to ride up further. Ryan's lips trembled, breaths hot and heavy as Alex unhook her own bra with one hand. In a second, Ryan had tugged it off to cup both Alex's breasts.

Alex forced her leg further between Ryan's thighs, pulling the dress up to her waist for unhindered access.

"*Lexi.*"

There had only ever been a hand full of times when Ryan had called her that, but it had instantly become her favorite variation of her name. Lexi, with precisely that inflection, whimpered and weak. She wanted more than anything to hear it again and again until no other word existed in Ry's vocabulary. Before she'd had time to process her own actions, her hand was between Ryan's legs. She studied the motion as she stroked Ryan over her black thong, fingers brushing the wetness at her core. Then, she barely dipped in, dragging her fingers through Ry's folds up to her clit.

"Oh my God." Ryan wrapped her arm around Alex's neck, grip tight when she kissed her again.

Alex pulled away as she moved her fingers in a circular motion: eyes glued to Ryan's face as if to decipher the knit of her brows, subtle creases on the wings of her tightly shut eyes, her shallow breaths and frustrated groans.

"Kiss me."

Alex shook her head. "Not yet." She wanted to kiss Ry, but the second she'd gotten a sense of how turned on Ryan was, she'd become instantly addicted to the pitch of her moans and shape of her face. If Alex was kissing her, she'd be denying herself the pleasure of seeing how sexy Ryan was when she was hot and bothered and about to be fucked against a door with a party full of people on the other end of it. She slipped a single finger in. Ryan's lips parted, her thighs closing ever so slightly.

"Lexi, please."

Alex adjusted her hand, adding a second finger as she pushed in and out at a teasingly slow pace. The longer the buildup, the harder the crash. She leaned in closer and breathed against Ryan's ear. "You're so close, I can feel it."

"This is"—Ry moaned as Alex curled her fingers—"so not fair."

"Do you want me to stop?"

"Don't you dare."

"Then come for me." She pressed her lips against Ryan's, bringing her thumb down on her clit.

"Oh f—" Ryan sunk her nails into Alex's shoulders and moaned into Alex's mouth. She was so wet—it didn't even seem possible that she could get any wetter—but she was still coming and mumbling things that didn't make sense, and it was the hottest, incoherent drivel Alex had ever heard.

Who knew gibberish qualified as dirty talk?

Alex grabbed Ryan by her hand and pulled her toward Dom's bed. *Fuck it.* She'd do his laundry later. She pushed Ry onto the blue duvet and pulled the dress over her head, Ryan unbuttoning Alex's jeans. Alex stepped out of her boots and quickly got rid of her pants. She settled between Ryan's legs and kissed her as she guided her up the bed.

"That was..." Ryan ran her hands along Alex's stomach, ready to slip her fingers between Alex's thighs.

"The only thing..." Alex grabbed her hand and pinned it to the bed, intertwining their fingers. "I want to hear you say..." She dragged her teeth against Ryan's left nipple, sucked on it and released it with a soft pop. "Is my name."

"Lexi."

"Yeah." Alex nodded, pressing a kiss above Ry's belly button piercing. "Just like that."

She wrapped her free hand around Ryan's thighs as she slid further down the bed to position herself and she gawked down at her. Glistening, blush-red. More than Midnight Sage to her smell now. No amount of liquor Alex had consumed tonight compared to the intoxication of this.

Ryan squeezed their still intertwined hands, using her other hand to sweep a strand of wavy, dark hair out of Alex's face.

Alex ignored the way her heart clenched, taking a tentative swipe through Ryan's folds.

"Lex—" She tossed her head back, squeezing Alex's hand again, burying her other hand in Alex's hair.

And Alex decided...

She *was* drunk. On the vodka, and Ry's taste, her smell, on every ounce of her.

She pinned Ryan's thigh to the bed, dragging her tongue up to her clit as Ryan tugged on a clump of her hair. She wrapped her lips around it, and Ry squeezed her eyes shut, lips parted though she couldn't get enough air.

"Lexi." Ryan's chest heaved, rising and falling in quick, unmeasured breaths. "Lexi, I'm going to come."

From Ry's lips, it almost struck as cautionary, like a warning she was about to hit a climax with her best friend's head between her thighs. To Alex's ears, it was lyrical. Pure poetry. She swirled her tongue and added the subtlest of nips. Ryan squealed, closing her thighs around Alex's head, her body in tremors. Any hint of cool air around Alex cut off, every shallow breath laced with heat, humidity, and *sex*. She forced Ry's thighs open while quickly wiping her own lips and chin before she crawled up for a kiss. Messy and uncoordinated, riddled with moans of desperation.

Alex throbbed with a lack of relief, but she reached between Ryan's legs anyway.

"Lexi, I—" She swallowed, her breaths quick and hot against Alex's lips. "I can't."

"One more."

"You fir—*oh*," she groaned as Alex slipped two fingers inside her, managing to course her fingers between Alex's legs too.

Alex squeezed her eyes shut. "Fuck."

"You're so wet."

"Ry." She was going to come, and Ryan had barely even touched her. The pressure in the pit of her stomach and heat in her core told her as much. It didn't help that her fingers were still knuckle-deep inside Ry with Ry moaning in her ear. It definitely didn't help that she'd begun whispering about how good Alex felt and how close she was to another orgasm.

"Lexi," she whispered, their foreheads pressed together. "Baby, look at me."

Alex clenched as Ryan finally slipped her finger inside her, and it almost hurt because fuck... None of this was fair. It wasn't fair that Ryan was calling her "baby" or coaxing her to look at her while they were naked with their hands between each other's legs. Her eyes opened, and her orgasm barreled into her, knocking the air from her lungs and Ryan's name from the back of her throat. Ryan's body followed, and it felt so good to be close to her, to feel a degree of vulnerability Alex hardly let anyone see.

As she came down from the high, staring at Ryan—skin shimmery with sweat, lips swollen and pupils blown—she tried to remember if Ryan had ever looked more beautiful. But did it even matter? She'd just had the most incredible sex with an incredible girl, who happened to be her best friend. And those things never ended well.

Chapter Two

vanilla chai

They didn't talk about it.

Not after Alex had punctuated the intensity of the last hour with a slow, lingering kiss and rolled onto her back, already reliving it all in her head. Not after Ryan had lain there, catching her breath with the most blissed out expression on her face.

Not the next day.

The one after that.

A week later.

They just didn't talk about it.

Alex wanted to be disappointed, but if she was being honest with herself, she had to admit she wasn't all that surprised. Ry was good at this, fucking up, literally, then pretending like nothing had happened. To her, what they'd done was probably all in good fun. Another meaningless night of partying and drinking. But for Alex, sex was never meaningless, no matter how much she'd had to drink. Then again, she'd always been a little too sentimental, a little too romantic. Wasn't that why everything hurt so much? Why her mind persistently weighed a ton of bricks?

So, since she *was* being honest with herself, she mentally acknowledged the hint of regret at being more vulnerable than Ryan even realized that night, and she admitted, despite the crack in her heart, she'd do it again. Because the truth was, she'd never been quite as guarded as everyone thought. It had always been her nature to put her heart on the line. It's just that no one ever seemed to know what to do with it.

"Vanilla Chai."

Alex glanced up as the barista placed a red porcelain cup on her table. She closed her journal and bound the leather covers with the thin strap. She'd always been driven to pause whatever she'd been scribbling down to look at the barista like nothing was more important. She chalked it up to having a lot of weird quirks and being compulsively attentive to the waitstaff at Brave happened to be one of them. Actually, waitstaff was too inclusive. It had always been the same girl. Daniela.

"Thank you." Alex grasped the cup, taking note of the number four shaped at the center of the foam. A four out of ten seemed about right today. Daniela had always been near flawless at summing up Alex's mood to a single number. Alex scoffed, looking at Daniela again.

"How'd I do?"

"Great." Alex shook her head, almost in disbelief. "I think you're even better at that than I am."

Daniela glanced at the journal set in front of Alex. "I don't know. You seem pretty in touch with your feelings to me."

Alex shrugged, placing an arm over the book and dragging it closer to her chest. "Yeah. It's mostly gibberish."

"I'm having a little trouble believing that, but"— Daniela paused, looking over her shoulder—"I should probably get back." When she faced Alex again, she pulled her bottom lip between her teeth, the dimples in her cheeks taking full effect. "Will you do me a favor though?"

"Uh..." Did they know each other well enough for favors? They'd barely even had a conversation beyond Daniela taking her order and returning with her coffee, stamped with a number for the day. It should've been enough for Alex to come out and say no. When she opened her mouth, the word that came out was, "Sure."

"The open mic thing later...Come."

Alex's face scrunched up.

"Before you say no, I really think you'd like it. Chill vibe, ambient sounds." Daniela glanced skyward for a moment as if to rethink her last words, and then she nodded. "Mostly. Plus, it gives me a chance to turn your four into at least a six."

Lines drew in Alex's forehead. Evaluating someone's mood, let alone without exchanging words with them, then offering an unsolicited result was a strange hobby. Then again, maybe it was Daniela's way of making conversation with her customers, building a rapport of sorts. Reasonable enough, considering Brave tended to be frequented by the same people. Still, making small talk with the customers was one thing, but wanting to make them feel better about their shitty day? Definitely not a part of the job description. "Why would you want to do that?"

Daniela shrugged. "Why not?" She peeked over her shoulder again and huffed at the lengthening line by the counter as Brendan waved her over. "Okay." She faced Alex. "I need to get back. But come. Please." She began backing away, her brows sloped upward as she pouted in what Alex assumed to be her take on puppy-dog face.

Alex rolled her eyes, smiling. Her barista was too adorable.

Too bad she was straight.

*

Alex gazed out the floor-to-ceiling windows at the madness of the city playing out below. Outside, among it all, she hated the chaos—the constant honking of horns, everlasting chatter of people who never seemed satisfied with the volume of their conversations. As if she needed to know that the fortysomething suit, who'd been so fixated on yelling over his Bluetooth headset he almost ran her over, was about to make partner at his firm. Were people in Manhattan loud on purpose, or did they feel compelled to convince every stranger on the sidewalk of their own importance? Then again, everything was louder in the city. After living in New York for all twenty-one years of her life, maybe she should've been more used to that by now, but she wasn't. Her favorite part of growing up in homes set twelve hundred feet above ground had always been the silence of the view, the tranquility of being an observer rather than another bee giving life to the buzz.

"So, are you going to go?"

Alex turned as Dom plopped down in the corner of her bone-white sectional and stuffed a throw pillow under his head. "Probably not. I'm not in the mood to go out."

"When are you ever?" Dom *tsked*, shifting around as he pulled up both sleeves of his brown Henley to his forearms, his skin a deep shade of umber against it. "You need to stop moping over what happened between you and Ry."

"I'm not."

"It's crazy how after knowing each other pretty much our whole lives, you still think you can lie to me."

Alex shook her head, crossing the room to lie next to him. She gazed at the high white ceiling. "When have I ever lied to you?"

"You're telling me you're not fucked up over fucking one of your best friends? Because the Alex I know would never pass on spending time with a beautiful girl unless there was already one on her mind."

Alex closed her eyes, blocking out the images of Daniela that had popped into her mind. "I told you. No falling for straight girls."

Dom scoffed. "Ry can be pretty indulgent, but I don't know if straight describes her anymore. No matter what she says."

Alex sat upright. "Wait, Ryan? I meant Daniela."

"Tell me you don't actually think she's straight."

"She is."

"Oh, come on, VK. The girl has been putting numbers in your coffee for weeks, probably praying for the day you'll ask for hers."

Alex shook her head. "No."

"I'm telling you. She's trying to get you naked."

"You're a pig."

Dom laughed. "Not just that way. I mean, think about it. You go into Brave, hang out for a bit, write, have some coffee, and her every conversation with you starts with her trying to see what's beneath the surface."

"Yeah. She's sweet, rot-your-teeth-sweet, and maybe she needs a crash course in small talk, but that doesn't mean she's into me."

"And yet, you've never said you're not into her."

Alex shrugged. "I never thought I had to."

Dom released a heavy breath, glaring at her.

Alex refused to give him the satisfaction of facing him directly. "What?"

"You're scared."

"I'm not scared."

"Really? Because you haven't let in a single person since—"

"I'm *not* scared."

"Fine." Dom nodded. "I'll drop it. On one condition."

Their eyes met, Alex waiting for him to come out with it.

"We're going to the open mic thing."

*

Alex raked the fingers of her right hand through her hair as she stepped out of Dom's matte-black G-Class. She lifted her gaze to the building in front of her to take in its brick walls and glass windows. She'd always been more taken by the interior, in love with its modern-meets-classic-bookworm aesthetic, its natural shades, wooden bookshelves and industrial hanging lights. Maybe it was a little expensive, but the atmosphere and staff made up for it. The food wasn't bad either.

"Having second thoughts?" Dom moved onto the curb to stand next to her.

Alex pursed her lips. "No."

"Good, because I was going to make you go in anyway."

"Whatever. Are we going or what?"

"You know, you're being pretty time-sensitive for someone who didn't even want to come to this thing in the first place." Dom held the door open for Alex to go in.

She entered the café, already glancing over her shoulder to let him have the first, not-so-polite reply that came to mind, but her brows drew closer together as her ears registered the harmony of someone singing to a slow beat. *Daniela?* She went further into the café and leaned against the closest wall, training her eyes in the direction of the stage. Daniela stood behind the mic, the lyrics flowing from her lips unfamiliar but absorbing.

> *"Slow day but I pass the time*
> *Coffee and a half a pack*
> *Said I'm thinking about you and I*
> *Took a while but you hit me back..."*

Alex kept her eyes locked on Daniela, almost relieved she clearly hadn't been noticed yet. It presented the opportunity to take her in in more detail than Alex had ever given herself permission to do before. Daniela's hair brushed her shoulders in perfectly done waves. A complete makeover from the endearing curls Alex had become accustomed to seeing in a messy bun. Everything about her seemed more done up—the arch of her brows, liner around her eyes, glow to her skin. Although, her skin always glowed like that. Like warm caramel being kissed by sunlight. The off-one-shoulder knit crop top she wore didn't exactly scream risqué, but as Alex took note of her exposed collar bone, chest, toned stomach...

Alex glanced down at her own boot-clad feet, silently scolding herself for letting her gaze wander too long before looking up at Daniela again. This time, she allowed the melody of Daniela's voice to be her focus. Had she always been able to sing like that?

Dom leaned closer. "She's good."

Alex nodded. "Yeah."

He mumbled something else too, but her mind had already written it off as unimportant before bothering to process the words.

Daniela clearly loved singing. She didn't seem interested in the power of being on stage in front of a room full of people, how enchanted they all were by her haunting melody, by her. Too trapped in the beat and lyrics. An unknowing slave to her passion. The last word had left her lips before her eyes even opened.

The audience broke out into a generous applause, and Daniela laughed, then mumbled a shy "thank you" over the mic, hand across her chest as if the nerves had only slipped in when it was all over. She glanced around the room, taking a quick inventory before settling in the corner where Alex and Dom had been standing, replaced the mic, and started toward them.

Dom nudged Alex with his elbow. "She was looking for you."

"She invited me."

"VK—"

"Don't even start. Here she comes."

Daniela beamed, stopping in front of Alex. "You came."

Maybe it was in Alex's mind, but when she smiled like that—all dimples and teeth—her eyes shined brighter. Tiny specks of lime swimming in honey. Alex turned away, clearing her throat. "Yeah. He talked me into it."

Daniela glanced up at him. "Dominic, the friendly giant."

Six four was hardly giant, but Dom accepted graciously. "That's me. Full-time giant, part-time cupid."

Alex rolled her eyes.

Daniela laughed. "Shooting any arrows tonight?"

"I don't know." Dom shrugged. "I guess we'll see. Right, VK?"

"Sure. Would you mind shooting them somewhere else? Like, *way* over there."

Dom breathed a laugh, shaking his head in Daniela's direction. "I'm going to get a drink. I hope she's a lot nicer to you than she is to me." He started to weave through the crowded café.

A light grip on Alex's hand stole her attention.

"Come on." Daniela pulled her in the opposite direction.

She creased her forehead but went willingly. When she noticed the reserved sign set on the table of her favorite corner booth, it occurred to her where they were headed. Daniela dropped her hand, then slid onto the seat as she tucked away the sign somewhere under the table.

Alex shrugged out of her leather jacket and threw it across the back of the chair. "So, you just knew I'd show?"

Daniela smiled. "No. But I hoped you would."

Why? Why the numbers in her coffee, why invite her to the open mic, why reserve her favorite booth in hope that she'd show? Alex was pretty sure she'd get another answer like the one Daniela had given her earlier. *"Why not?"* So, she didn't bother. "You were amazing up there."

Daniela glanced up from picking her nails. "Thank you."

"Is that what you do? Sing?"

"God, no." She shook her head, laughing. "I study photography at RISD."

Alex's eyes widened. "Wow. You must be pretty talented. RISD is competitive."

"It is, but I'm hanging in there."

Modest. About her singing, most likely her photography. Alex was already dying to ask about her portfolio. Maybe that way, she'd get to know Daniela better than all the words they were about to exchange would allow. But a lot of intimacy went into artist's craft, and they'd barely begun talking, so she didn't press. "Okay. So, school's in Rhode Island. What brings you to New York?"

Daniela swept a strand of hair behind her left ear. "I still live here during break. Here, meaning New York, but not Manhattan."

"Where?"

"Brooklyn. Two years before I was born, my mom came to visit her sister. She'd never even left the Dominican Republic before, but she hadn't seen my aunt in years, so she was super excited. It was only supposed to be for a month. Two, tops. But her first week, she walked into a bodega on Bushwick Ave, and the boy at the checkout counter went stupid trying to ask her name."

Alex laughed. "Don't tell me. Your dad."

"Yup. It's funny, because he'll swear from now until forever that he was so smooth, but every time my mom gets to the part where he dropped her change and accidentally slammed the cash drawer on his finger, I can't even imagine him as anything but super awkward."

"Maybe he was, but clearly he did something right if you're here."

"Yeah," Daniela agreed through a chuckle. "He chained her in the basement and wouldn't let her loose until she developed a bad case of Stockholm's."

"Romantic."

"Completely. Seriously though, he always says it was love at first sight. That he saw her, and everything else he felt was pure compulsion. She just happened to want him too."

Storybook romance. The only kind Alex recognized. She didn't think less of them; she didn't think that kind of thing only ever happened in books or movies. But few people would ever be lucky enough to experience it. Still, there had never been a time when she hadn't wanted the kind of love she wrote or read about. She just didn't think she'd ever have it.

"Do you believe in that? Love at first sight."

Daniela glanced down, playing with her hands again. After a moment, she shrugged. "I believe that...I believe a person can be so taken by someone else's beauty, or demeanor, or just their existence at precisely the moment they first lay eyes on them, that they feel drawn to the other person in a way that's entirely inexplicable. I mean, we can force our minds to rationalize it, but I don't think we'll ever be satisfied with the answer. So, we call it something we've never been able to explain either. Love."

Alex's forehead creased. "That's uhm—" She shook her head. "Interesting."

Interesting wasn't the word she'd been looking for. It wasn't even the one that had come to mind. *Beautiful.* Daniela was beautiful—mind and body. The type of person Alex might talk with for hours and never get bored because she'd never shy away from conversations many people were too facile, or too afraid to have.

"I don't know," Daniela replied. "Sometimes I feel like having parents who've been married for quarter a century made me too sentimental."

"What do you mean?"

Daniela cocked her head a bit to the right, her expression laced with amusement. "Why do I feel like this entire conversation has been about me?"

"Because you're more interesting,"

"Right," she answered skeptically. She didn't argue though. Instead, she dipped into the right pocket of her jeans and came up with her cellphone. "Here. Tonight, I answer as many questions as you have, and in exchange, I get to text you one a day."

Alex laughed, keying in her number without overthinking it. "That doesn't seem like a good deal for you. I mean, who says I won't ghost you after I leave here tonight?"

"I know where you drink your coffee." Daniela beamed, taking her phone back. "Besides, I don't think you're the ghosting type."

"I guess we'll see."

"We sure will."

Chapter Three

tequila sunrise

Alex's heart hammered inside her chest, working frantically to fill her lungs with the air they'd been craving for the last fifteen minutes. Her legs, tense with fatigue, were on the edge of buckling any second and forcing her face to become acquainted with the running belt beneath her feet. She was on the last stretch of her workout though, so she wasn't about to quit, no matter how much her limbs whined. Thoughts plagued her. Thoughts about Ryan. About Daniela. Since writing about it would only leave her brooding for hours, she decided to take control of her body and concede to her mind.

She decreased the speed of the treadmill as her countdown timer hit two minutes. To distract herself a little further, she tuned into the music pouring through her earphones and focused on Kelly Jones's raspy tenor. "Maybe Tomorrow," still her favorite Stereophonics song.

Once the timer hit zero, she allowed herself a few more minutes to sit and take gulps of her water. If she was to make going to the gym a regular thing again, she'd do it at precisely times like these when she had it all to herself. Her phone chimed, and she glanced down to see two texts. One from Ryan, the other from Daniela, both stamped about half hour ago. *Great.* Exactly what she needed. More reasons to have them both on her mind. More reasons to wonder why Ry was set on pretending things were normal between them after what had happened at Dom's party. More to wonder why Daniela went out of her way to be so nice, minus Dom's she's-not-straight theory. Taking another sip of her water, she swiped her thumb across the screen of her phone.

> *Ryan: Guessin yoir bpring, hipster karapke tghind is ovr by now. This party sux!*

One look at the message and Alex knew. Ryan was drunk. She stood and crossed the room to exit the gym, fingers tapping a response as she entered the long hallway leading to the elevator.

> *Alex: Where are you? I'm coming to get you.*

> *Ryan: Way ahead if you.*

> *Alex: Tell me that means you're on your way home.*

Alex entered the elevator and hit the button to the penthouse, barely looking away from her phone. She didn't like to admit it, but she had an active protective instinct, and moments like these—knowing Ry was intoxicated and out with God knows who—was like sprinkling gasoline on the wildfire of her thoughts.

The number one to the top left of her screen reminded her Ryan wasn't the only person who had messaged her earlier. She quickly opened Daniela's message, welcoming the distraction.

Daniela: So, did we make it to a six?

Alex's lips stretched in a smile. Two seconds ago, she was exhausted from her workout and worried about Ry. She was still both, but her mind had drawn a strange correlation between Daniela and being at Brave. So much, a mere text from her was almost like being there. Warm. Comforting. Her fingers made their way across the screen before her mind even consented.

Alex: Definitely.

Maybe she was being naive by insisting Daniela wasn't into girls at this point, but how else would she stop herself from feeling anything more than she should? Besides, she didn't consider herself primed for romantic involvement right now. Not until she managed to make sense of her feelings for Ryan, and she hadn't the first clue what those were beyond friendship and sexual attraction. Was it even possible for those two to coexist? Despite it all, seeing Daniela's text, feeling the unexplained concern laced into her words, did make Alex feel better than a four. A lot better. Her phone went off again. Twice, almost simultaneously.

Ryan: Yes. On my wsy.

Alex: FaceTime when you're there. Gonna hop in the shower.

She walked into her room, pulling her drenched sports bra over her head before dropping her shorts and underwear. Then, she switched message threads again.

Daniela: I hope that means you had as much fun as I did tonight. Good night, Alex.

Alex grinned.

Alex: Good night, Daniela.

She pulled her AirPods out of each ear and tossed them onto her messy, California king. Once she'd made her way to the bathroom, she placed her phone on the counter, paired it to the speakers mounted on the opposite wall, and hit shuffle. When she finally made it into the shower, it took maybe two minutes of feeling the warm water against her skin before she even remembered to free her hair from its messy bun. She should have gone for a bath if the ache in her legs was any indication, but she ignored it and reached for her shampoo. She wasn't planning on a long shower anyway.

The music stopped, and Alex frowned, hand glued to the spot where she'd been getting the last remnants of suds off her right shoulder blade. A new beat streamed through the speakers as the intro to "Hypnotic" picked up. Alex slowly withdrew her hand from her shoulder and leaned forward to clear a portion of the fogged-up glass for a glance at where her phone laid on the counter.

The door slid open, and Alex jerked against the wall, heart hammering inside her chest. She shook her head, blinking as her eyes adjusted to the image in front of her. It was a dream. All she had to do was close her eyes and when she reopened them, she'd be awake. Because of course this was a dream. It had to be.

Ryan stepped in and turned to close the door, water from the shower head catching her hair and cascading down her back. The pounding in Alex's chest picked up as she forced her gaze higher only for Ryan to face her, breasts now in full view instead.

Higher.

Ryan smirked, gray eyes dark, intentions clear.

"Ryan." Alex paused. This really, really shouldn't happen again. "What are you doing?"

"You mentioned you were hopping into the shower, and I guess it sounded"—her eyes drifted to Alex's feet then up again—"inviting. So here we are."

"You were supposed to be headed home."

"I was, but I missed you." Ryan took a step forward, and Alex took one back, more grateful than ever for the capacity of her shower. "Lexi—"

"Don't." Alex squeezed her eyes shut, repelling the effect Ryan calling her that while they were both naked and wet had on her.

"Why not?"

It hit Alex, the same instant the liquor on Ryan's breath did, that closing her eyes wasn't very smart because now Ryan was standing way too close. "You're drunk."

"Not as drunk as you'd like me to be."

"What's that supposed to mean?"

"It means..." Ryan's gaze fell as she pressed one hand against Alex's tense stomach. "You want me to be drunk enough to give yourself an excuse to not do anything about me being naked in your shower right now." She leaned in closer and their lips grazed. "And I really don't want you to do that."

"Wha—" Alex creased her forehead. "How did you even get in here?"

"The receptionist. New guy that started working here last week. I think he's hot for me."

"He's fired."

Ryan laughed, tequila and oranges on her breath as she brushed her lips against Alex's. "Stop fighting."

A chill crept through Alex causing her toes and fingers to curl. "Damn it, Ry." Her hand shot to the back of Ryan's neck, and she kissed her hard. Ryan stepped closer—their bodies flush against each other—and her tongue slid across Alex's in the same instant her hard nipples brushed against Alex's breasts.

Ryan hummed, squeezing Alex's hips. "Isn't it so much more fun when our bodies do the talking?"

There it was. Not conjecture. Not Alex hypothesizing what it all meant to Ryan. She'd confirmed it, and once again, Alex had let herself get too far to turn back. Maybe deep down she'd been hoping she was wrong. Or maybe, there was something so familiar about this thing between them, she didn't know how to say no to it yet. Because no matter how fucked up the situation was, her body wanted it even if her heart didn't.

She pushed off the wall and quickly stepped behind Ryan to press her against it. A groan escaped Ryan's lips, dragging out into a moan as Alex swept her dark hair to one shoulder and kissed her neck. She wrapped one hand firmly around Ryan's waist and pulled her closer as the other hand rested lightly on her ass.

Ryan's breathing quickened.

Alex's lips trailed her neck. "What do you want?"

"Isn't it obvious?"

Alex's hand slowly made its way between Ryan's legs. "How?"

"Wh—what?"

Alex smiled, sliding her fingers through Ryan's hot, wet folds. She dragged them up and stopped on Ryan's clit, gently pressing her index and middle finger against it in slow, teasing circles. "Like this?"

Ryan nodded a bit too ardently. "Yeah."

"Or..." Alex coursed the hand she'd wrapped around Ryan's waist up to her neck, gently wrapping her fingers around it before shifting to Ryan's hair. She took a clump in her grip and pulled, pressing harder on Ryan's clit with her other hand. "Like that?"

"*Lexi!*"

"Sounds like a winner."

"Enough"—Ryan swallowed—"with the teasing."

"Say please."

"As if."

Alex laughed, tightening her grip on Ryan's hair as she slowly slipped two fingers inside her. "Say..." She leaned in, touched her lips to Ryan's ear, and pulled.

"Fuck."

"Please."

"Lexi, please."

Alex dragged her fingers in and out slowly. "Please what, Ry?"

"*Harder.*"

Alex slipped her fingers out of Ryan to enter her from behind instead. She slid them knuckle-deep, reveling in the needy moans escaping Ryan's lips before pulling them out to repeat. Harder. Deeper. She let go of Ry's hair and rolled her nipple.

"Oh my G—" Ryan's thighs closed in on the hand between her legs, a telltale sign she wouldn't last. Not much longer.

Alex removed her fingers, reflexively glancing down at how wet they were as Ryan groaned in disapproval.

"Don't—" Ryan shook her head. "Don't stop."

"Shut up." Alex grabbed her arm, forcing her against the wall so they were face-to-face again. She palmed Ryan's left thigh and loosely wrapped it around her before sliding two fingers of her other hand inside Ryan and bringing her thumb to Ryan's clit.

Ryan tossed her head back. "Lexi, yes—" Her body shook, clenching around Alex's fingers like they belonged to her now, like her body had claimed them with no intention of return. But she was also twice as wet as she'd been thirty seconds ago, and eventually, Alex's fingers sort of just slipped out, clear signs of Ryan's crash all over them.

Alex lifted her gaze to Ryan's face as it relaxed, and she came down from the intensity of it all. After how rough she'd been, she wanted to lay the softest of kisses on Ryan's lips, but Ryan's word echoed in her mind. *Isn't it so much more fun when our bodies do the talking?* And more than anything, the idea of kissing Ryan felt too emotionally draining to waste on something that would cease to exist once the sun rose.

Chapter Four

french vanilla

It was a mistake.

Alex's first thought when she rolled over in her bed and opened her eyes the next morning was that having sex with Ryan again was a mistake. It took a few days to set in anyway. A few days for Alex to realize the night in her shower had to be the last time. Exploring the physical dimensions of their relationship every time Ryan felt propelled by a little liquid courage was dangerous. No matter how good the sex was. Besides, Alex wasn't built for it. Something so one-dimensional. There were things she wanted in a relationship she didn't imagine sharing with Ryan.

Long talks bordering on philosophical.

Sunsets shared in silence.

Slow kisses that burned right through her veins.

Her heart, in all its fire and ice.

And her art. All the gibberish that broke free of her chest and flowed straight into her fingers, day after day.

And coffee.

She stared into the mug of french vanilla set in front of her. One of her favorites. Yet, something about this brew didn't sit quite right. Maybe the taste. Too sweet. Not sweet enough. Maybe no matter how long she allowed it to sit, it wouldn't get to the right degree of warm, and this coffee had come with a generic foam design that did nothing to measure her mood. She sighed, sliding it further across the wooden table.

Her father glanced up at her, his eyes shifting enough to watch her over the rim of his cup. "Something wrong with your coffee?"

"It's fine."

"Is that why you took one sip and barely touched it since?"

"I don't know." Alex shrugged. "Maybe I'm over it. Coffee."

Her dad chuckled, lowering his cup to the table. "Your mother almost had you put in rehab because you're pretty much hooked on the stuff, and I'm supposed to believe you're suddenly over it?"

Alex stared across the lobby of the café, half to avoid her father's gaze, half-focused on the fact that it wasn't nearly as warm as Brave.

"Does this have anything to do with my walking in on Ryan in your bed last Saturday?"

"Ry and I are friends. She's slept in my bed plenty of times."

"Does she always do it so..." he trailed off, clearly trying to think of the most appropriate word for naked, barring the word itself.

She rolled her eyes. "Dad, why are we even talking about this?"

His eyes shifted to the Italian sausage lying in his plate, and he used his knife and fork to slice it into smaller pieces before looking up at Alex again. "I like to know who you're dating."

"We're not dating."

"So, you two are—"

"Jesus, Dad." Alex huffed. "Things between us got a little messy at Dom's party. Ry and I...We had a bit too much to drink and a few lines were crossed. We've been having some trouble reestablishing boundaries."

"Hmm. That's not like you."

"Yeah."

For a while, they both allowed the silence to spread—just the hissing of machines behind the counter, baristas bustling from table to table, businesswomen and men having obnoxiously loud conversations over their phones while ignoring the person seated across from them. It reminded Alex even more of why she hated this coffee shop, and why she loved her dad. Xander Van Kirk was a billionaire hotel mogul, who all but lived in overpriced, designer suits, but he would never be a typical Wall Street zombie. He insisted on things like breakfast with his daughter three times a week, asked invasive questions about her love life and valued the importance of being present when sitting at the same table as someone else.

Alex dropped her fork, giving up on picking around the waffle on her plate.

Her father shook his head. "I don't see why we didn't go to Brave. You know how picky you are."

"I'm not picky."

"Would you prefer spoiled?"

Alex grinned. "Whose fault is that? Not that I'm confirming anything."

"Of course you aren't." He grasped the cotton napkin on the table and wiped his lips, reclining in his chair. When his smile faded, one hand smoothing over the silk tie he wore, Alex steeled herself. He was so damn obvious sometimes.

"I've made arrangements for you to have dinner with your mother tomorrow night."

"Dad—"

"The divorce shouldn't affect your relationship. Whatever differences your mother and I have are between me and her."

"It's not the divorce."

"Then would you mind telling me why you won't even willingly sit in the same room as her anymore?"

A few reasons why she didn't want to sit through a meal with her mother had readily come to mind. Neither of which Alex wanted to discuss. Not with her dad, nor anyone else. She picked up her napkin, wiping her fingers as if she'd even touched her food, before tossing it against the table with unnecessary force. "I'll go."

"Alex, if there's something I need to know—"

"Dad"—she met his gaze, brown eyes the same shade and intensity mirroring each other—"I said I'll go."

He sighed, watching her for a few more moments before nodding. "Okay."

Alex had always been in constant conflict about this quality of his. He never pushed her too hard—never forced her to talk when she didn't want to, go to school whenever she wasn't feeling well, or take any interest in things that simply weren't interesting. There were times when she loved this about him, especially since her mom had always been pretty much the opposite.

Annalise Van Kirk was all push and pull and pressure. So much fucking pressure Alex could compress into nothingness from just being in her presence.

Then, there were times when Alex didn't love this about her dad, where she just might float away on all the air he gave her to breathe. He didn't know about all the stuff with her mom because he never tried hard enough to find out. It wasn't about the divorce. She didn't mind them being apart. Maybe she even preferred it. The problem was, between them, there had never been any fucking balance. Nothing to keep her grounded. Maybe that was a part of the reason her love life had always been such a mess. Because she was constantly getting lost, trying to find her anchor in all the wrong places.

*

Daniela: Is it weird that I woke up with a smile on my face, thinking about last night? We should do that again.

Daniela: Missed you at the café today.

Daniela: You okay?

Daniela: Alex?

Daniela: Can you just let me know you're okay?

Daniela: Okay. You're reading these, so it's probably safe to assume you're fine.

Daniela: I get it.

Daniela: Guess you are the ghosting type.

Alex reread the thread of unanswered messages Daniela had sent her since the night of the open mic. A part of her wanted to think, like what happened with Ryan later, going had been a mistake. Going and hearing Daniela sing, letting herself admit how beautiful Daniela was inside and out was something she should never have done. She'd yet to decide which had been worse—sleeping with Ryan again or going to the open mic. Though she hadn't taken a single sip of alcohol that night, she'd woken with a pounding headache and thoughts that were overwhelmingly sober. And regrets.

Regrets and guilt.

She didn't expect Ryan to still be there when she woke, or the ache in her chest as she took in Daniela's text. Never mind the sense of misplaced loyalty she now felt toward a barista from her favorite café.

So, it hit Alex like a slow rolling boulder, coming to terms with the idea that maybe she did have feelings for Daniela.

Maybe she'd had them all along.

And maybe, just maybe, Dom had been right about Daniela not being straight. Maybe by some twist of fate Daniela felt things that weren't entirely platonic for Alex too. Except Alex had gone and fucked everything up before either of them had gotten a chance to figure it out.

She adjusted, then pulled her legs against her chest as she leaned against the wooden bench. Sunset approached—bright golden beams casting a glow through the plush pink hues in the sky. Her obsession with the sunset had always been a bit cliché, but some time ago, her mind had rationalized it as a metaphor of sorts. A revolving door of beginnings and ends, light and dark, the beauty in the irony of it all, how the sun wasn't most stunning at its peak, but every time it was saying goodbye.

Sure, Alex enjoyed the subtle splendor of the night sky, but there wasn't too much of it to admire in the city. The sun set the world on fire through its very existence, and somehow, she couldn't help feeling like that's what she'd been waiting for. Something, or someone, to set her world on fire.

Someone passed in the peripheral of her gaze, and she casually turned her head in their direction. Curly golden-brown hair, slender frame hugged in a red T-shirt and jeans, skin like butterscotch candy. The beat of Alex's heart faltered. Before she even processed what she was doing, she stood. "Daniela?"

She didn't stop, didn't even flinch, but it was her.

Alex started after her, not even attempting to make sense of why she was desperate for her to stop or what she'd even say if she did. "Daniela!"

Daniela kept going, quickening her pace a bit.

Alex grabbed her arm. "Dani, wait."

Both stopped.

Daniela's shoulders rose in a slow, considerate breath. "Look, I was just taking a walk. I don't know why I even came here. Maybe I was hoping you wouldn—" She shook her head. "Of course you're here."

Alex frowned. Why was Dani trying to explain herself? "Dani—"

"I get it. Really." Dani pressed her lips together. "Actually, that's a lie. I don't get it. At all. But that's okay. You don't owe m—"

"Dani, shut up." Alex closed her eyes, dragging her hand through her hair. "Sorry." She sighed, reopening her eyes to Dani's creased forehead.

Alex didn't know what she wanted to say, or what to do. She didn't know what it meant that her heart hadn't stopped racing, or that she was still holding Dani's arm because a part of her was terrified once she let go, Dani would turn and leave. It didn't matter that she'd been avoiding Dani all week, or that simply the idea she had feelings for this girl had all her heartbreak faculties already on standby because Dom was right. Maybe she was scared.

Maybe she was terrified.

She released Dani's arm and took a step back. When their eyes met again—the last remnants of golden shine bright against Dani's skin, lighting the shades of green in the honey of her irises—Alex said the first thing she'd somehow managed to not overthink. "Do you want to watch the sunset?"

*

The sun disappeared behind the high trees of Central Park and beneath the horizon. Being there with Dani helped. But it also didn't. This was what Alex wanted. Sunsets shared in silence. She'd never given much consideration to the silence bit, always assumed not talking would make it easier to appreciate the beauty of the moment. And it did. It was the sunset that had her lips wired shut and her limbs paralyzed. But it also wasn't. It was the girl.

Maybe she'd tried to block Dani out for as long as she had because everything about Dani, even before the open mic, told her Dani was fearless. Truly fucking fearless. And in that regard, Alex was a fraud. Everything scared her. Everything.

Dani faced Alex, lips parted as she gently shook her head. "I don't get you. I really don't. You spent two hours basically learning any and everything about me, and then you screened my texts for a week. Not a single word in reply. We run into each other, you chase after me, tell me to shut up, and then you"—she scoffed—"ask me to watch the sunset. I don't get you, Alex. But I want to."

"Why?"

"Why, what?"

"Why do you want to get me?"

Dani narrowed her gaze to Alex's, angling her body to face Alex fully. "Do you honestly need me to say it?"

Alex did. She needed to hear it from Dani's lips. Otherwise there was no believing it—what Dom had said, what she herself was starting to think was true.

"I like you, Alex. God, isn't it completely obvious?"

"So, you're not straight?"

Dani laughed. "I've never been straight. I can't even remember ever thinking I was."

Alex's brows twitched. Had she genuinely misread the situation, or had Dani told her something she'd always subconsciously hoped to be true?

"Sometimes," Dani started. "You look at me, kind of like you are right now, and I can't help but wonder what you're thinking, what you're trying to figure out. And then sometimes, you glance over when I'm behind the counter, and it's like you don't even know you're staring. Sometimes I think you do know, but you don't want to stop. Sometimes I think you like me too, Alex. But mostly, you're exactly like your fucking coffee, hot and cold, and I know what to do when you show up at Brave and sit in your booth and write for hours, but I don't know what to do now. So, you have to tell me."

Alex stared at her, sort of processing everything she'd said, sort of finding it crazy how she still managed to be so damn adorable when saying the word *fucking*, sort of randomly wondering if she was fluent in Spanish. Somehow, it hadn't come up the other night though they'd talked about both Dani's parents being Latino and Alex had probably asked her a hundred questions about herself.

"I do," Alex whispered.

"What?"

"Like you, Dani."

Dani furrowed her brows. "Then why? Why not text me back? I've heard of the waiting three days rule or whatever, but you don't strike me as the type to play games."

"I'm not." Alex shook her head. "I promise I'm not. It's just..." She raked one hand through her hair. "Things are a little messy right now, and by a little, I mean a lot, and the last thing I want is for you to get caught up in it."

"I'm not afraid of messy."

"Something tells me there's a lot you're not afraid of." It was difficult to explain, but it wasn't just the thing with Ryan. There was something about Dani that felt so inherently good, and whole, and untainted by bullshit. Alex didn't want to be the one to change that.

"Are you seeing someone? Is that it?"

"No. I mean—No. It's just—"

"But there is someone else." Dani shifted to angle her body away from Alex's.

Alex's stomach sank, but she grabbed Dani's hand, making her face her again. She wanted to say what she had with Ry—though special and aged in a way her relationship with Dani wasn't—didn't compare. She wanted to say although she and Ryan had been friends for almost three years, there were things she wanted to share with Dani that she'd never wanted to share with Ryan. She wanted this. Silent sunsets and talks, real talks, on park benches where their eyes never left each other's, and her heart never stopped racing. She wanted to say no one— only one person, in fact—had ever made her feel as terrified as Dani did, but that Dani was completely worth facing her fears.

She wanted to say she tried. She tried to be the way she was with everyone else. Guarded and indifferent. But with Dani, it was pointless. With her, Alex had always felt transparent anyway. Wasn't that part of the reason she had held back as long as she had, part of the reason she was still holding back? Because most times, it was like Dani saw right through her, and surely someone like Dani had better, less complicated options.

Why waste her time trying to get to know someone who only kept pushing her away?

Even so, Alex had already resolved to admit that she *did* have feelings for Dani. Maybe, subconsciously, she'd even decided that a week ago when she woke up and read Dani's text. That's why she felt so bad. Because her mind, her body, her heart had already decided who she wanted and being with Ryan completely betrayed that.

Alex didn't say any of that. Instead, she lifted her hand to stroke Dani's cheek and confessed the one thing that had been revolving in her brain as she sat across from Dani at the open mic. "You're so beautiful."

Dani glanced down at her lap. "Alex."

"No. You are. And I was an idiot for not saying that sooner and for not replying to your texts. I'm sorry, Dani. I'm sorry I'm so inexplicably impulsive, and cowardly, and annoyingly broody. And I'm sorry I made this, whatever it is, messy before even acknowledging it exists. But I'll fix it. In fact, it's already fixed."

Dani leered, her gaze seeming to flitter along every inch of Alex's face. Then, she locked eyes with Alex again, curling her lips wider as she swept a strand of hair behind Alex's ear and kept her hand there. "I don't think you're annoyingly broody. I love how much goes on in here. I just wish I didn't have pry you open with a crowbar to get a glimpse of it."

The irony—Dani thinking she'd been trying so hard, when to Alex, everything she did was entirely effortless. "I'll work on that."

"Good."

Alex's gaze drifted to Dani's lips, and the boom-clap of her heart echoed in her ears. She was ready. She was so ready for whatever this meant—sitting on a bench in Central Park with Dani next to her; cool night zephyrs, indistinct chatter, and city buzz around them. But instead of leaning in and kissing her, she forced her eyes to the honey of Daniela's because she was so done screwing things up. And she didn't want anything hanging in the background when their lips touched for the first time. All she wanted was the flip in her stomach, frightening race of her pulse, fire and just...

Wow.

"What are you doing tomorrow?"

Dani's nose twitched. "Just work. Why?"

"Work's great." Alex nodded. "Work's perfect, actually, because I'd really like to have coffee with you."

Chapter Five

cortado

Alex rolled over with a groan at the chime of her phone. She fumbled her free hand around the empty spaces of her bed in search of it, her other hand carefully rubbing the sleep from her eyes. The cool hard surface of her screen materialized beneath her fingertips, and she brought the phone up for a look. Her lips stretched in a dopey grin.

Daniela: I can't wait to see you later.

Alex had already decided honesty was one of the things she liked most about Dani—her fearlessness in expressing her feelings. Everything about her just felt so pure and real and right. Alex typed out a quick reply.

Alex: Me too. I miss the coffee and my booth...And my barista.

Daniela: Your barista, huh?

Alex: Yeah.

Not sure if you guys have met.

Average height, dark hair, gorgeous eyes, smile that hits like a heart attack. Super chatty though. She can never just bring me my coffee and get back to work.

Daniela: Doesn't sound like anyone I've met. She must be new. You'll have to introduce us when you come by later. Assuming you even notice me. You sound pretty into this barista of yours.

Alex: I mean, she does make awesome coffee.

Daniela: And nothing's more important than that, right?

Alex: Not a single thing.

Daniela: I'll keep that in mind.

Alex laughed, gazing down at their message thread. She hoped somewhere in Brooklyn, in a bedroom of a quaint, cozy apartment, Dani sat on her bed just the same, smiling at their ridiculous banter with butterflies in her stomach and nothing but anticipation buzzing through her veins. Alex couldn't wait to see her at Brave. Better to make the most of it too. She still had dinner with her mom later, and those had only ever gone so well.

*

Alex peeked up from the black scribbles in her journal, absentmindedly shifting her pen between her fingers. Dani beamed at her from behind the counter, and Alex returned the gesture. They'd been at this game for at least an hour, and she still wasn't over it. She wasn't over the confession of their feelings last night, or Dani being equally distracted by her presence, sometimes being more attentive to Alex than customers who were standing in front of her. But they promised they'd wait for Dani's break to spend some time together. The last thing Alex wanted was for Dani to get in trouble with Brendan, who'd been paying attention to their exchanges since Alex had walked into the café. She'd made a conscious effort to keep the staring at a minimum. Failed mission, safe to say.

Everything had shifted so quickly. A week ago, she'd been screening Dani's texts, guilt-ridden and confused over waking with Ryan naked in her bed. Next, she was in her favorite coffee shop, thinking Dani was the girl she'd wanted for weeks. Admittedly, she'd refused to acknowledge it—besides convincing herself Dani was straight. Dani was the first person in four years who seemed worth the risk of truly getting to know someone's mind and body in all the intimate detail she craved. It was exactly why she wanted to take things slow.

No dates. No kisses. Minimal touching.

Glances over melting numbers in her coffee, talks between breaks, morning texts that bordered on too honest, too soon.

Dani faced the counter again, a plain cup and saucer tight in her grip as she carefully stepped forward and handed it to the middle-aged woman in waiting. Her lips parted, eyes bright as she laughed and said something indiscernible to the woman, and Alex got what Dani had meant last night about her staring—sometimes unknowingly, others, more mindful. She didn't have much of a choice but to keep looking, especially when Dani smiled like that. And it wasn't just her smile. She was genuinely the sweetest person Alex had ever met, and strangely, that degree of politeness wasn't something Alex had ever found to be attractive. But here she was, equally taken by the honey of Dani's eyes and her soul.

Dani wiped her hands in a checkered towel, smile still on her lips as she rounded the counter and started across the wooden floor.

Alex glanced at her phone. *3:37 p.m.* Definitely not break time.

"Hey."

Her gaze instinctively trailed Dani from the pair of worn sneakers, jeans, and Brave T-shirt she wore, to the curly brown strands framing her face. "Hi."

"Can I sit?"

"Um..." Alex narrowed her eyes. She surveyed the counter where Brendan was still focused on them, despite the man standing in front of him, then regarded Dani again. "Is that a good idea?"

Dani raised her brows, glint in her eyes. "Is that a no?"

"Of course not. I just don't want to get you in trouble."

"Don't worry about it." She slid into the booth and rested both elbows on the table, her focus on the leather diary still open in front of Alex. "What are you working on?"

Alex shook her head, shrugging as she closed the book. "Nothing important."

"That a book title?"

Alex laughed. "How's your shift going? I figure Brendan isn't hovering as much today. He's too busy watching our every move."

"He's not going to say anything unless he needs help. He thinks the only reason you tip so well is because you have a crush on me."

"You don't seem convinced."

"I'm not."

"You're not convinced I have a crush on you?"

"I don't think it's the reason you tip well." Dani glanced at the journal again. "Is that what you study at Columbia? Writing?"

Alex shifted in her seat, taking a sip of her cortado. "Creative writing and film. Double major."

"Really?" Dani's face lit up with interest. "That sounds amazing. It's probably more work than excitement though, right?"

"Probably."

Dani hesitated, staring at the empty space in front of her. When she finally looked up again, she held Alex's hand, her gaze steady. "Why do you always do that?"

"Do what?"

"Try to make everything about you seem uninteresting and mundane the second the conversation shifts. I like you, Alex, and if we're going to do this, I'm going to want to spend our time talking about more than just me."

"I know. And I like you too. I meant that. I guess—" She sighed. "The writing's a weird topic for me. Besides"— she adjusted her hand in Dani's and squeezed a little tighter—"I kind of like just listening to you talk."

Dani rolled her eyes, biting down on her bottom lip. "That's not what you were saying this morning."

Alex tilted her head in feigned ignorance, relieved Dani hadn't pressed the writing topic. "This morning?"

"Yeah." Dani nodded, free hand dipping into the pocket of her jeans to come up with her phone. She unlocked it and swiped her thumb against the screen for a few seconds. "According to you I'm 'super chatty.' Can never just bring you your coffee and get back to work."

Alex tossed her head back, laughing. "As if you can trust anything I say before I have my morning dose of caffeine."

"That's your excuse?"

"It's not an excuse. I have a problem. Full-blown addict."

"Is that why you're in here almost seven days a week? Because you're addicted?"

"Yeah." Alex nodded, holding Dani's gaze. "To the coffee."

"Right." Slowly, Dani's smile faded, dimples in her cheeks disappearing to Alex's dismay. Her gaze roamed Alex's face in an almost identical way to yesterday. When she settled it on Alex's lips, fortunately, or not, there was a table between them. Yet, a vision of the moment flashed in Alex's mind—both of them leaning in, Dani's skin smooth and warm beneath the tips of her fingers, the brush of their lips, coffee on both their breaths.

"Dani!"

Both their heads snapped in the direction of the counter where Brendan stood, his eyes wide and palms open.

"Yeah." Dani nodded. "I'll be right there!" A visible gulp slid down her throat, and she turned to face Alex again, clearly jolted from her own reverie. "My five minutes are up." They both stood, Dani's hand slipping from Alex's.

"I think maybe I should've waited until you were on lunch to stop by."

Dani laughed. "It probably would've been less distracting."

"Which is why...I should probably go."

"That's not what I meant."

"I know, but I have a thing later, and I promised Dom we'd hang out before."

"Okay." Dani took Alex's hand, gently holding it as she took a few steps away. "Can I call you later?"

"How's ten?"

"Perfect."

They released hands, but kept her eyes locked with Dani's, ignoring the pounding in her chest, tingles in the tips of her fingers until Dani finally turned away with one more flash of her dimples and semibashful bite of her lip. Alex clung to the promise she'd made to herself. Slow. But maybe getting used to this sooner rather than later wasn't the worst idea. Something told her Dani was more than ready for it too.

Chapter Six

caffè macchiato

Alex stepped out of her closet and crossed her bedroom to the mirror.

"Damn." Dom leaned forward in the bed to rest on his elbows. "Didn't you say you're going to dinner with your mom?"

Alex rolled her eyes, adjusting a few strands of her hair. "I *am* going to dinner with my mom."

"Really? Because I think Dani will appreciate that dress a lot more than your mother will."

"Yeah, well, I don't have anything that says, 'I honestly don't want to be here, but Dad insisted,' so this is what I'm wearing."

"And all I'm saying is Dani may not mind the opportunity to get you out of that later."

Alex turned and shook her head as she grabbed her shoes and sat at the edge of her bed. Dom was more serious than his words suggested, but she pushed them to the back of her mind. It was way too soon. She pulled on one of her heels, then wrapped the strap around her ankle. "D, we haven't even had our first kiss yet."

Dom scoffed. "You're fucking with me."

Alex put her other shoe on, letting the silence speak for itself.

"VK"—he sat upright—"you're fucking with me. Right?"

"No." She crossed the room back to her closet and briefly ran her index finger along her collection of black leather jackets before settling on her favorite Yves Saint Laurent. She'd just begun searching for a purse to match when she heard Dom enter the closet too.

"You're telling me you spent hours talking last night, and had a lunch date at Brave tod—"

"It wasn't a date."

"Whatever, and neither of you even tried?"

"I mean, I think she wants to because—" Alex sighed, grabbing a purse from the rack. "I don't know, D. We just haven't, okay?"

"When are you going to stop being so afraid of this?"

"It's not about that."

"Then what's it about?"

"Can you not make me any more stressed out than I already am over this fucking dinner?" She started toward the stairs, Dom following close behind.

"I don't mean to, but I can see how into her you are. And I'd hate to see you screw this up because you can't get out of your head."

Dom was right. Of course he was right. Still...

"The timing hasn't been the best. And before you ask when the best time will be, I don't know."

A beep echoed to signal the front door to penthouse had just been opened. Alex narrowed her eyes as she walked toward the entrance—her dad hadn't mentioned anything about coming over, and it was way too late for housekeeping. The door swung open and Ryan stepped in, smiling as she scanned Alex from head to toe.

Alex turned to the end table nearby and grabbed her key fob. "We agreed you weren't going to do that anymore."

"Do what?" Ryan pushed the door closed. "Hi, Dom."

"Sup, Ry?"

"Flirt your way into getting my key. It's like you want that kid to get fired. Why not just use the doorbell or text me that you're on your way up?"

"What's the fun in that? Besides, we both know you're not going to fire him."

Alex sighed. "What's up, Ry? I'm on my way out."

"Clearly. Hot date?"

"Not even close, but I do need to go. So?"

"I just wanted to hang out. Maybe get a few drinks?"

Something in her last words resonated so unassumingly, yet equally suggestive. Maybe it was because they were words she'd spoken to Alex lots of times before. A few weeks ago, Alex would think nothing of them. But drinking and hanging out had taken on a new meaning for them lately, one it should never have in the first place, and Alex was done with it even if Ry wasn't. There would be a time to talk to Ryan about that where they'd both have to consciously and soberly acknowledge what had happened between them. Alex just didn't think it'd be tonight.

Still, the sooner she got it done, the better she might feel about promising Dani there was no one else. And Alex wanted nothing more than to reassure Dani, 100 percent, that their thing—coffee, sunsets, and talks—was all she wanted. Dani was all she wanted.

She glanced up at Dom.

"So...I'm going to get out of here. VK isn't the only one with a hot date tonight." He closed the gap between them to wrap Alex in a one-armed hug, lips lowered to her left ear. "Good luck. With your mom too." Then, he headed toward the door. "See you, Ry."

"Bye, Dom."

Alex's lips parted. "Ry..."

Ryan went deeper into the apartment. "One drink!" she called back. "You're already late, right?"

Alex sighed, going after her. "Can't. I'm driving."

"One drink won't stop you. You're a heavy weight. Me, on the other hand... One drink and I can barely think straight."

"Ryan, we need to talk."

"About what?" She placed a bottle of brandy and two glasses on the counter.

Something simmered in Alex's veins, just waiting. She didn't know what for. But if Ryan's next words were that she didn't remember pushing Alex against Dom's bedroom door or showing up in Alex's shower naked, their conversation probably wouldn't end well. Even if Ry did blame those on the liquor, she was sober last Saturday when she woke naked in Alex's bed. So sober, she'd stuck around for breakfast before flashing Alex a smirk as she left. She was more than sober when she walked in tonight and blatantly checked Alex out.

"We had sex, Ry. Twice."

"Yeah." Ryan met Alex's gaze. "And we had fun, right? What's the big deal?"

"That is the big deal."

"Alex, it's just sex. It doesn't have to mean anything. Just two single girls, having f—"

"I'm seeing someone." She was getting sick of hearing Ryan use that word. Fun. Maybe it was perfectly apt. Maybe it was exactly what sex was supposed to be, but without all the other stuff—without the meaning and emotion—all it felt was empty. "It's new, but it's serious. At least, I want it to be."

Ryan slowly lowered her glass back to the counter. "What's his name?"

"*Her* name. Daniela."

"That barista from Brave?"

Alex nodded.

"But you told Dom you weren't into her."

"I think I just didn't want to be, Ry."

"Why?"

"Because I like her, okay? A lot. And maybe Dom was right. Maybe I was scared."

Ryan scoffed. "Come on, Alex. How much can you like her? A week ago, you had me pinned to your bathroom wall."

Alex let her gaze fall. Ryan had a point. If she liked Dani as much as she claimed she did, why had she slept with Ryan in the first place? Shouldn't these feelings she supposedly had for Dani have stopped her before she kissed Ryan, before she'd put her hands on her? Shouldn't she have known exactly what to say to Ryan now? But Alex didn't know. She didn't know what to say or how to rationalize the mess of thoughts Ryan had just caused in her mind.

Ryan downed the rest of the brandy in her glass, rounded the counter, and left a kiss on Alex's cheek. "Have fun on your date. Text me later."

*

Alex handed her key fob to the valet and entered Gabriel. She'd never minded the food, and the service was impeccable, but the air reeked of artificial purity and aristocracy. Just the idea of having to sit through three courses with her mother had her airway constricted. Nothing had changed. White walls, delicate detailing, fine dining layout, and menus with dishes she only ordered with ease because her mother insisted being semifluent in Italian and Dutch wasn't enough. She needed French too.

She followed her escort in the direction of the table—a corner setup by a wooden stand topped with peace lilies.

Her mother glowered, resting her phone on the table. "You're late, Alexandria."

"I know. Sorry."

The server who had escorted Alex turned to her. "May I take your jacket, Miss Van Kirk?"

"Sure." She shrugged off the jacket and handed it over. "Back of the chair is fine."

"Very well." He pulled out Alex's chair and hung the jacket on the back as she slid into it. "Might you be ready to order Mrs. Van Kirk? Or would Miss Van Kirk like a few minutes to settle in?"

"Alexandria?"

"It's fine." The sooner it was over, the better. "I'll have the perdrix rouge to start and the...sériole to follow."

Her mother shook her head disapprovingly, barely glancing at the menu herself. "I'll have the foie gras as well as a bottle of your Chandon Dom '85."

"Will that be all for now?"

"Yes."

The waiter nodded. "I'll be back shortly."

Her mother scrutinized at her again, less discreet in her disapproval now that the waiter had gone. "Must you wear those things everywhere?"

Alex sighed. "It's just a jacket, Mom. I'm wearing a dress, aren't I?"

"Yes. One that barely covers everything it's supposed to."

"You're exaggerating. As usual."

"Is it too much for me to expect you at least be properly dressed after showing up here—"—she glanced at the elegant gold watch on her left wrist—"all of thirty minutes late? No call or explanation."

"I don't want to talk about it." Was this—savoring cuisine dishes while she chewed through her only child— what Annalise Van Kirk classified as bonding?

"Excuse me?"

"I said I don't want to talk about it, Mom."

Alex didn't want to talk about why she was late. She didn't want to talk about her conversation with Ryan, how upset it had left her, and how she wished having dinner with her mom was comforting instead of exaggerating her anxiety. She wished it did. She wished being with her mom was what she imagined it should be. Soothing and safe. Just something other than *this*. Maybe then, she would want to talk about it. Maybe then, she would feel like she could.

"Alexandria—"

"How was your day? Can we have a normal conversation? Ask me how I've been, considering we haven't seen each other in a month. Ask me if I'm ready to go back to school in few weeks. Or just talk about you. What's going on with you, Mom?"

Her mother regarded her, allowing the silence to drag out between them. Then, she sighed. "I've been well. Busy with work."

Alex stifled the *what else is new* wanting to leave her lips, offering an emphatic nod instead. "I guess that's supposed to happen when you're successful." If anything, Alex had always respected that about her mother. In business, she was strong and stern, and she got shit done. It wasn't her job Alex resented or that she was good at it. It was everything else.

"Which might be you one day. But I'm assuming you still want to be a writer."

"Yes, Mom. I still want to be a writer."

"Alexandria," she said evenly. "You know I have no objections to your hobbies but writing...It's just not practical. Have you considered what we talked about?

Business or medicine. Medicine would make your grandparents so proud."

This conversation again. How many times did she have to say it before the words took root in her mother's brain, before she accepted that Alex didn't want to be a fucking doctor or spend her days in power suits? Her grandparents were amazing—both being surgeons—and her mom was brilliant at what she did, but that didn't mean Alex wanted it for herself. Why was that so hard to understand?

"Mom—"

"Perdrix rouge." The waiter placed the dish in front of Alex before turning and announcing the foie gras to her mother in a similar manner.

Alex took his interruption as the diversion she needed and directed her attention to the partridge on her plate almost the second it had been set in front of her. Thankfully, her mother had done the same. They ate in silence, only the light clink of cutlery hitting the plate between them, but this was the best part. The food and the quiet. At least now, she didn't feel so anxious she was pretty much choking on all her unsaid words. At least now, she wasn't being told what she was doing wrong or how it should be done right. All hushed tension and unresolved feelings, but this was exactly how Alex preferred to deal with them anyway. By pretending they didn't exist. It's what her mom had always done. It would've been okay. Alex would've made it through the meal that way.

Ten minutes into the quiet, barring a mumbled exchange about how the food was, her mom stopped eating, gaze locked across the room, lips curled in that distinct way they would whenever her distaste would take shape on her face only seconds before rolling off her tongue. Alex turned too, trying to pinpoint the reason for her mother's reaction.

Annalise Van Kirk was all proper etiquette and manners, reserved expressions, and carefully crafted sentences except when lecturing her daughter or staring at a perfectly content pair of men, who were clearly smitten with each other.

The blond reached up with a napkin and wiped something from the corner of his partner's lips.

"They're everywhere in this city."

Alex dragged her gaze back to her plate with her jaw clenched, reminding herself not to feel the least bit affected by her mother's words. But this had always been one of, if not the thickest, wall between them—why she would never know who her daughter truly was, why Alex would never willingly tell her, why she made her dad promise not to. She didn't know how he'd been married to her mom for over twenty years and not seen how ugly she was sometimes. Actually, maybe he was starting to. Maybe that was precisely why they'd separated. They rarely seemed in love anyway.

"They don't even have the decency to tone it down."

"Enough, Mom. They're not bothering anyone."

Her mother shook her head, reluctantly picking up her knife and fork. "To think I was worried about you. All the soccer, all that time you spent with Dominic and his friends. I was glad to see you grow out of all that boyish nonsense."

Alex wanted to say that was the stupidest thing she'd ever heard, that there was no actual correlation between those things. But she'd gotten good at listening while her mother grumbled about *them* being everywhere—all over the city and the TV.

"I don't know what your father and I would do if you turned out to be one o—"

Alex dropped her utensils and pushed back her chair from the table. She stood and grabbed her jacket.

"Alexandria..."

Alex *wasn't* good at this. Not as good as she wanted to be. Her mother's words still tore through her. Every time. And it wasn't just this. It was everything. But mostly, it *was* this because it was the one thing about herself Alex wasn't capable of changing. She didn't know how. She wished she did. She couldn't remember how many times since she'd turned fourteen and had set out to have more female friends, like her mother wanted, that she'd wished she didn't think girls were beautiful in more than just a general sense.

Maybe she did remember.

At least once every day. At least once a day, she'd wished she wasn't something her mother would never love. But she was. Women were beautiful—their bodies crafted with all the intricacies imaginable. Lips and hips and thighs that curved like lines literally drawn by an artist. She loved the softness of their skin and inflection in their tone and discovering all the things that made them so sensitive. Mentally and physically.

She tried everything to make it go away. Blood and tears, and some nights, whispers into the dark of her room to whatever God was supposed to be listening. When morning came and she opened her eyes, she never felt any different. So, she learned to accept who she was, as much as possible anyway. But that didn't change the fact that her mom still had this power. She still had the power to rip Alex open and leave her bleeding every fucking time.

She dragged the back of her hand across her face, trying to dry her eyes while she squeezed the steering wheel with her other hand. It didn't surprise her that she was crying or that she couldn't remember when the first tear had hit her cheek—back at the restaurant when she'd stepped out on the curb and demanded her car from the valet, when she'd gotten in and started the engine, or when she peeped up and realized she was in front of Brave.

She got out and slammed the door behind her. She'd parked in a no parking zone, and though she'd made an effort to wipe her face, it was probably all runny mascara and dried tear marks. It didn't matter. It didn't matter that it was after eight on a Saturday night, and Brave was teeming with its late crowd. There was only one person she wanted to see anyway, one thing she needed to do. She pulled the door open and frantically scanned the lobby for Dani. Searching, searching, searching...before she noticed Dani, back turned as she took an order from a table by the cluster in the center. Alex's legs moved before her brain had given them permission, heels clicking through the muffled chatter and hissing machines.

"Two caffè macchiatos and a—"

She grabbed Dani's hand, muttering a barely audible "Dani."

"Hey, what's wr—"

Alex kissed her. Dani hesitated, held back by surprise or reservation, before she finally kissed back with all the certainty Alex needed. Lips delicate, but sure, hands gripping Alex's hips like she never wanted to let go. Alex's heart hammered in her chest, but her mind slowed, blocking out everything to focus on the way Dani's lips tasted like vanilla caffeine, and her skin smelled like... It didn't matter. She wasn't anxious that she was kissing Dani in the middle of a room full of strangers. Because here, in this café where she could show up in her pajamas and no one would even bat an eye, with this girl—this beautiful, invasive, very feminine girl—was where she felt safe, warm, and completely all right.

Slowly, Dani pulled away. "Okay...Wow." She opened her eyes, lightly stroking Alex's cheek. For a while, she just did that—stroked Alex's face, watching her. Then, slowly, she leaned in again and gently placed another kiss on her lips. "Ten minutes and I'm yours. Okay?"

Alex nodded. She didn't know what she wanted when she'd shown up, apart from to kiss Dani, but the second Dani had offered, it occurred to Alex that both of them getting out of there to go do whatever—it didn't even matter—was exactly it.

This was what Alex wanted. No matter what her mom or Ryan thought.

Chapter Seven

espresso

Alex let Dani pull her out the door and unto the curb outside of Brave. She'd never get used to having Dani's hand in hers. She'd never get used to the feeling of being with Dani period. Unlike before when she'd show up at the café and Dani just happened to be there with numbers in her coffee, there was nothing subconscious about it anymore. Alex hadn't been there for just the coffee and the ambience for weeks now.

The way she'd always set aside whatever she'd been working on the second Dani came by her table... Maybe it's because somewhere in the back of her mind that was precisely what she'd been waiting for. Maybe Alex would stare when Dani was busy behind the counter because just the possibility she wasn't going to stop by disappointed Alex in ways she hadn't been ready to come to terms with yet.

Dani turned to face her and took a step closer. Their eyes locked, Alex's heels creating an unnecessary difference in height she didn't appreciate. But going barefoot on a sidewalk in the middle of lower Manhattan didn't seem like an option.

Dani raised her free hand, then gently brushed her thumb under Alex's left eye. "Where should we go?"

"Wherever you want." A small part of Alex meant that too literally, meant right now she would go anywhere with Dani even if they would have to hop on a plane to do it.

"Somewhere quiet?" Dani glanced around them. "Where do you go to escape all this?"

The ordered chaos of the city. The laughter and chatter and uncensored arguments brushing by them on the sidewalk. The zooming cars and persistent honks. The thickness of the air weighted with dirt and unfulfilled dreams.

"My rooftop," Alex answered.

Dani nodded. "Okay. Take me to your rooftop."

*

Alex never welcomed someone she'd just met into her most intimate spaces. Maybe to half the world a luxury penthouse didn't seem too intimate, but it was her home, and maybe to half the world Alex was just another trust-fund kid, who was so fucking privileged, she didn't have any *real* problems, so she went out of her way to seem like she did. What qualified as real problems anyway? What was enough of a reason for someone to consider maybe things would be simpler if they weren't *here*?

She'd always been an introvert. By choice, sure. Also, because having wealthy parents came with notions of exclusivity extending beyond A-list parties and networks of affluent associates. One such idea—hotel heiresses weren't allowed to cry. What could Alexandria Van Kirk possibly have to cry about anyway?

Isn't that exactly the kind of thing that would cross Dani's mind?

Though Dani hadn't said anything when they slipped into Alex's car back at Brave, she hadn't missed the way Dani hesitated before getting in or the way Dani had been scanning the interior so intensely for the first few minutes of the ride. While Alex didn't feel particularly chatty, it still bothered her that their drive was pretty much all silence and apprehension.

"Hey." Dani touched the hand Alex had rested on her own lap.

Alex glanced at her then switched back to the view of the road. She tightened her one-handed hold on the steering wheel and fought her impulse to lock eyes with Dani again, humming a response instead.

"Is everything okay? I mean, not everything. Obviously. But I'm pretty sure it's the third time we've rounded this block."

"I know. It's just..."

Dani added a gentle squeeze to Alex's hand before wrapping it in hers as she waited.

The quiet dragged out, save Arctic Lake playing from the radio, until Alex came up on a short line of traffic and rested lightly on the brake. She sighed, glancing down as she adjusted her hand to intertwine her fingers with Dani's. "I don't know what, or who, you see when you look at me. I just know I don't want anything to change that."

"And you think taking me to your rooftop will?"

"I don't know." Alex shrugged. "Maybe?"

"I could try to tell you how impossible that feels, and I could tell you why, but you probably wouldn't believe me, or it would make you want to—" She broke off, shaking her head. "Just let me show you, Alex. Let me show you that nowhere we go tonight and nothing you tell me, or don't tell me, will change what I see when I look at you tomorrow. Okay?"

Alex was terrified of how amazing Daniela was. It was unreal. As she redirected her attention to the road, waiting for the light to change, she squeezed Dani's hand a little tighter just to assure herself that it *was* real. This was as real as it gets.

*

It took less than two minutes to get to the hotel once Alex had stopped stalling. She was still apprehensive, but there was a part of her that had never wanted to let someone in more than she did now. So, she ignored the thought of how much it would hurt if something suddenly happened to ruin this thing that was growing between them, how terrified she was of how quickly her feelings for Dani were clawing free of wherever she'd buried them. There was no stopping them anyway.

After pulling up in front of The Van Kirk, she shifted into park and opened her door before the valet staff had even managed to properly react to the sight of her car. If she sat there any longer, she'd wind up driving away and circling the block again, maybe going to the park. As nice as that would be, home was where she wanted to take Dani.

Alex held the passenger side door open as Dani stepped out, her gaze locked on the large illuminated letters naming the building.

As one of the valets, Jack, approached Alex, she turned to him and ignored the urge to tell him *Alex is fine* when he called her Miss Van Kirk again. "Please park it in the usual spot and leave the key with the desk."

He nodded. "Yes, Miss Van Kirk."

"Thank you."

She dragged in a breath as she turned to face Dani in search of signs in her relaxed expression and gentle eyes. Something besides patience. She wasn't sure what she'd been anticipating, but after a few moments of being unable to find it, she extended a hand to Dani, who accepted without hesitation.

Alex started into the building, taking slow steps across the lobby toward the elevator. She wanted Dani to have time to process any thoughts or questions she might have. There had to be a few. She loved the way Dani kept close to her anyway, how their hands never separated even for a second. It was reassuring. Comfortable. So, this time, the silence was too. It didn't even bother Alex that they'd gotten to the penthouse and onto her balcony—to the stillness and cool air where she could *actually* breathe—before the first words were said between them.

"I always wondered why Dom calls you VK."

"Yeah? Well now you know." Alex kept her gaze locked on the skyline, bright beams from the high-rises lighting the night, water shimmering in the distance. She'd stood there so many nights, taking it all in with a cup of espresso keeping her warm. Tonight, she didn't need the coffee. Tonight, she had the girl. At least, she hoped so.

"Alex"—Dani touched her arm—"you know I don't care, right? Not about any of this. I mean, sure. It's insane that you drive a Maserati, and your name is on a five-star hotel, and this—" She released a breath, glancing in the direction of the city again. "I bet you're so used to views like this. It probably doesn't even phase you anymore."

It did still phase Alex.

"Maybe I'm slow at processing. Because we're here, but a part of me is still stuck back at Brave with your lips on mine, and it was perfect. It was *so* perfect, but I also can't ignore the fact that you were really upset back there."

"Dani..."

"Talk to me. Please."

Alex sighed. "I was at dinner with my mom. It's this thing we do every month since my parents separated a year ago. I hate it. Fuck," she breathed, running a hand through her hair. "I really hate it, Dani."

Dani took Alex's free hand and gently guided her in the direction of the pool. Alex followed, doing the same when Dani sat on the ledge and folded one leg in front her while the other dangled in the water.

When they were face-to-face again, their fingers loosely locked, Alex parted her lips. "Remember when you told me having parents who've been married for quarter a century made you too sentimental?"

Dani nodded.

"My parents made it to twenty, and I've never gotten even a hint of the kind of love your parents must have. I don't even think they're capable of it. At least not with each other. They never talked. Not really. And whenever they did, it was either to argue or about business. Budgets and the stock market, mergers and public appearances. I wasn't even surprised when they told me about the divorce. I was kind of happy even. How fucked up is that?"

"Do you think they still love each other?"

Alex scoffed, shaking her head. "I don't think they ever did. They got married when my mom was a month pregnant. If I know my dad, he was probably trying to do the right thing by asking. And if I know Mom, she accepted for appearances."

Annalise Van Kirk would never be caught dead pregnant out of wedlock. It wasn't the proper thing to do. Not what was expected from the golden child of affluent, Catholic parentage. There was an order to things for people like her. Private education from pre-K through to undergrad. Grad school. Fiancé. Wedding. White collar job at a good firm. Then kid. She just had to accelerate the last few. Thanks to Alex.

Alex closed her eyes, willing back the tears welling behind them. It had the opposite effect, but she didn't bother wiping them away when she opened her eyes again. "She hates me, Dani."

"Alex—"

"No. I'm nothing like she wanted me to be, and we're both reminded of that every time I cave and go to one of those fucking dinners. I'm too impractical, too moody and disrespectful, too edgy, too much of everything that bugs her and not enough of the things that don't. And even if I did become everything I'm supposed to—"

"Alex—"

"Even if I transfer to med school tomorrow and change my wardrobe, and my friends, there would still be this. There'd still be you. And I'd still be too ga—"

Dani grabbed Alex's face. "You're not too much. Of anything." She swept both thumbs under Alex's eyes. "You're perfect. Just like this. And your mom"—she scoffed—"your mom's ideals can go screw themselves."

A noise escaped Alex's lips. Half sob, half laugh. Then, pure laughter. She closed her eyes for a second to adjust to the dose of emotional whiplash Dani's words had sent her way. "Did you just say my mom should go screw herself?"

"Your mom's *ideals*."

"Semantics."

When the moment passed, Alex placed one hand over Dani's and held it against her cheek for a moment before pulling it toward her lips for a gentle kiss. A simple gesture of thank you for Dani leaving her shift early to come to Alex's rooftop and listen to Alex ramble about her mess of a relationship with her mom, and for so effortlessly turning her shit days—and nights, apparently—into better ones. She wouldn't be over all the stuff with her mom because Dani said she was perfect, but she felt lighter somehow. Freer. On her rooftop, above the noise and bullshit.

"I'm sorry our first kiss tasted like tears and drama."

Dani shook her head, her eyes filled with tenderness. "I'm not. I'm not sorry I got to see you like this. It makes me feel close to you, and all I've wanted for weeks is to feel close to you."

What was the precise date stamp on that? How long had Dani wanted to get to know her? Since the first day she started working at Brave two months ago? And what exactly did Dani mean by "close to you"?

The question seared deeper into Alex's mind as Dani leaned in and joined their lips. Alex's eyes fluttered closed, the pounding in her chest intensifying by the second. Hesitantly, she rested one hand just above Dani's hips, reminding herself to not squeeze too tightly, no matter how good Dani felt. Lips, hands, everything. Dani shifted one of her hands, moving higher to tangle ever so gently in the hair just above Alex's neck. Alex tensed, and she tried to stifle the hum settling low in her stomach. Dani grazed Alex's bottom lip with her teeth, almost like a test, and Alex's grip tightened on her hips. Both hands, though she struggled to remember how the other one had gotten there. Dani bit down harder, sending a shiver straight through Alex's body.

"...all I'm saying is, Dani may not mind the opportunity to get you out of that later." Dom's voice echoed in Alex's head, and brushed her hand against Dani's cheek. They locked eyes again, Dani's a darker shade of honey than Alex had ever seen, and Alex almost pulled Dani right back against her. But that would only make it harder for them to stop. "Can you swim?"

Lines drew in Dani's forehead. "What?"

Alex smiled, pulling away from Dani as she slid into the pool. "It doesn't even matter. Come in with me. I won't let anything happen to you."

"Should you even be swimming in that dress?"

"Forget the dress." Alex bit her lip, fighting the image of a late-night skinny dip with Dani out of her mind. "It's heated."

Dani rolled her eyes. "As if I couldn't tell from having my feet in it for the last ten minutes." She splashed some water in Alex's direction. "And stop looking at me like that!"

"Like what?" Alex laughed. "I'm not even doing anything!"

Dani glanced skyward as she playfully shook her head. Then, she shuffled into the pool too. She drifted to the surface, already close to Alex, so close, a whisper was enough when she said, "That's the scary part. You didn't have to do single thing for me to drive myself nuts, thinking of ways to get your attention."

"What do you mean?"

"Did you think I went around putting numbers in everyone's coffee? God, just the time it takes."

Alex swept a strand of hair behind Dani's right ear. "I'm sorry you thought you ever had to try. It's not like I could walk into Brave and not notice you."

Dani laughed. "Smooth."

"I mean it. Do you know how hard it is to think straight and look you in those eyes at the same time?"

"Yeah, you're not doing too much to convince me you aren't smooth."

"Fine. I'll stop." Alex bit her bottom lip, suppressing her amusement. The effects of their last kiss still buzzed all through her. She wanted nothing more than to lean in and pick up where her mind had forced them to stop, but she called on all the restraint she had to prevent herself. She didn't want to ruin things by moving too fast. "Can I drive you home?"

"Right now?"

Alex shook her head. "Later, if that's okay."

"Yeah." Dani nodded. "Later would be great."

Chapter Eight

black russian

Alex shifted, trying for what felt like the hundredth time to get comfortable. This never happened. Not on her couch. Usually, once she plopped down onto it and leaned into the backrest, she could stay for hours. Tonight, everything got under her skin. She wasn't sure if it was because Dom had been over earlier, and because every time he was, he just had to fuck with the thermostat. Now the penthouse was too cold. The shiver that had run down her spine five minutes ago probably had more to do with the way Dani was obviously not paying attention to the movie anymore, which kind of sucked because Alex loved *White Bird in a Blizzard*. She loved every Shailene Woodley movie ever.

Dani kept her eyes fixed on Alex. Not even casual about it anymore. Blatantly staring. Alex parted her lips, trying to keep her gaze steady as the pounding in her chest picked up. Why was she so nervous? She'd done this before. She was even good at it. Getting a little hot with girls in dim lit rooms—making *their* hearts race, *their* skin heat up, and *their* minds go crazy over what her next move would be.

"Alex."

In the glow of the TV, Dani's features appeared softer. The natural arch of her brows and glimmer in her eyes. The edge to her low cheekbones. Teasing flare of her lips. "You don't like the movie?" Alex asked.

Dani shook her head, moving closer, limiting all the space Alex had purposely put between herself and the crop top Dani had decided to show up in. Never mind the goddamn shorts.

"Because it's okay if you don't. I can put something else on, or we can go ou—"

"Alex." Dani paused, closing the last few centimeters between them.

The second their thighs touched Alex wished she hadn't banked on the fact that they'd be staying in. At least then, she would've gotten dressed in something less casual than fleece lounge shorts. She swallowed and tried to stay still. No screwing it up that way. All she had to do was sit there. Maybe Dani was just cold, and she wanted to cuddle. Alex could totally do cuddling. Nice, clothes on, perfectly PG cuddling.

Dani lifted her hand to Alex's cheek. Her thumb stroked Alex's skin as the rest of her fingers curled gently through the hairs at the back of Alex's neck.

Alex's eyes fell shut. "Dani."

"What?"

"You can't, you shouldn't—"

"Why?"

"Because if you keep doing that, I'm going to—"

Dani leaned in, waves of warmth from her skin coated in that subtle-sweet smell Alex was forever trying to place. Their lips brushed. "You're going to what, Alex?"

Alex squeezed her eyes shut tighter, fisting both hands to keep them grounded at her sides. "Maybe we shoul—"

Dani pressed their lips together, and it was just like Alex remembered. Soft, but so fucking sure, with a hint of vanilla coffee. And then they were gone. She opened her eyes to find Dani already staring at her, and she was sure Dani could hear her heartbeat, even with the movie still running in the background.

"I don't want to go anywhere. I don't want to watch any movies." Dani sat up on her knees, adjusted her weight to hook one leg over Alex, and straddled her. "I just want to kiss you. I want you to stop being so afraid of wanting to kiss me. Unless..." She trailed off, her expression turning doubtful.

"You have no idea what you do to me, do you?"

"Might help if you'd show me."

Alex rest both hands on Dani's legs, brushing her lips against Dani's, relishing the feel of her skin as she dragged them higher. Midthigh, fingers tingling at the tips of the frayed edges on Dani's shorts, she stopped and squeezed.

Dani's breath caught. "Are you going to kiss me or what?"

Alex leaned in as Dani's eyes closed in anticipation. With one finger, she tilted Dani's head up and presssed a kiss to the underside of her jaw.

Dani groaned, her grip tightening in Alex's hair. "Now you're just being a tease."

Alex moved her lips lower, parting them to breathe against Dani's neck.

"Alex."

"What?" The pressure on her lap and Dani's fingers in her hair, her hands threading higher on Dani's thighs, her name intoned in what almost sounded like a moan... It was the kind of thing that provoked Alex's most dominant side. So while she probably seemed perfectly in control, she was tethering on the edge of flipping Dani onto her back and discovering all the ways to make her scream so loud people on the ground floor would hear. She pulled her lips away from Dani's neck and met her gaze again in hopes that would help, in hopes for some flash of her sweet adorable barista, only to be met with dark eyes, almost daring her to do her worst.

"Don't overthink it." Dani leveled a light kiss on Alex's lips. "Okay?"

Alex nodded. "Don't overthink it."

*

Alex had lost track of how long they'd been at it. Somewhere after Dani had straddled her in the first half of the movie, they'd switched positions, so Dani was reclined on the sofa, and she was on top of her. It was taking all of Alex's will power to not grind down on Dani's thigh so hard, she'd come right then and there.

Dani tugged Alex's bottom lip between her teeth and Alex groaned. "Fuck."

"You were doing it again," Dani mumbled.

Alex pulled back to look at her. "Doing what?"

"Thinking too much." Dani's gaze fell as she leaned in and soothed Alex's bottom lip with her tongue.

Alex's toes curled.

"Not that I wouldn't have bit you anyway. I think you like it."

Alex breathed a laugh. "Yeah?"

"I think you like it a lot." She stroked Alex's hair while analyzing her face. "I keep trying to figure these out. Your eyes. I keep failing. But your body"—she trailed one hand under Alex's shirt—"I like that you can't hide from me when we're this close. I like that I can feel your heart beating. Racing. I like that you shiver, almost unnoticeably, when I do this—" She broke off, teasing the hairs along Alex's neckline.

"Dani."

"I like that too. The way you say my name like a warning every time you feel something that makes you want to lose control."

Alex licked her lips and swallowed as she edged one hand closer to Dani's ass, the other steady at the back of her neck.

"When I bite you, you tense up. It's like you're literally fighting a battle in there." Dani bobbed her head toward Alex's. "One you're on the edge of losing."

Alex's chest heaved, and she squirmed, forcing her leg further between Dani's. She didn't miss the way Dani's breath caught, the perfect O of her lips, the way her grip tightened.

Dani leaned in again. "So, I'm going to keep doing it. I'm going to keep trying to find ways to make you feel even half as weak as I do right now. Until you tell me to stop." She brushed their lips together. "Do you want me to stop, Alex?"

Alex's mind followed the race of her heart. Ruining things between them terrified her, but she was beginning to think maybe fighting it—the attraction, the tension—might be the thing that did. The last thing she wanted was to somehow give Dani the impression she didn't want to be with her. Physically, or otherwise. If Dani could be brave and honest about what she wanted, wasn't it time Alex started trying too? She lowered her lips to Dani's then kissed her. "I don't want you to stop. I don't think I ever want you to stop."

Dani's eyes rolled back as Alex peppered kisses along her jaw. "You're so sexy like this. All open and honest."

"Good," Alex breathed against her ear as Dani's nails dragged lightly across Alex's back. "Then you won't mind it when I tell you to shut up." She pressed her hips against Dani's, muffling her moan as she brought their lips back together. Liking the reaction, she finally surrendered to the urge to slide her hand higher and grab Dani's ass as she ground down against her again.

Their lips separated.

"Ah—Alex."

Alex wondered if this was what it sounded like when Dani was close. Breathless and pitchy with a hint of an accent somewhere in the midst. Maybe it was only in her head. Dani couldn't suddenly sound more Latina because she was about t—

"*Se siente tan bien.*"

"I don't speak Spanish."

"Sor—" Dani's hips jerked as Alex dragged her teeth against her neck. "God, sorry."

"Don't be." She moved her lips to Dani's collarbone, fingers of one hand trailing the edge of Dani's bra, down her stomach to the waistband of her shorts. She wanted it, the top and whatever other completely unnecessary pieces of clothing Dani was wearing out of her way. Her fingers, lips burned against every inch of Dani's skin. And then realization hit. As much as she wanted to undress Dani right there on her couch, she couldn't. If she did, Dani would want to do the same, and she wasn't sure she was ready for that, for Dani to see.

Dani touched her cheek, and their eyes met. "What's wrong?"

Alex glanced away, shaking her head. "It's nothing."

"Babe..."

Her gaze snapped back to Dani's. She half thought it an accident, that Dani was still caught up in the haze of their bodies pressed against each other's with an entirely different level of intensity only seconds ago. But there was no hesitance in the dark of her eyes. Nothing but patience.

Alex shifted so they were at eye level again. She wrapped an arm around Dani's lower back, sat upright, and held Dani against her lap. She smoothed the edges of her own shorts into place, covering her upper thighs.

Dani took Alex's hands in hers. "Talk to me."

"Before we uh—" Alex's phone buzzed against the coffee table.

"Do you need to get that?"

She shook her head, letting it ring. "No. I uhm— Maybe there's something we should talk about before things go any further. It's nothing you need to worry about. I just don't want you to feel blindsided or weirded out."

Dani squeezed Alex's hands a little tighter. "Okay."

"I haven't always had—" The doorbell rang, and Alex glanced in its direction.

"Are you expecting someone?"

"No. It doesn't even matter. Dani, I us—"

The door beeped, signaling it being open. Alex clenched her jaw, shifting Dani to the couch as she stood. "I'm sorry. Just—" She held her hand up, silently asking Dani not to move. "I'll be right back."

This was it. That receptionist was definitely fired.

Alex got there just in time to see Ryan step in and push the front door closed behind her.

"Don't be mad. I used the doorbell. You didn't answer."

"Yeah, and the normal thing to do would be to either wait until I did answer, or I don't know"—Alex shrugged—"just leave?" The blood in her veins had gotten to a boil before she'd even realized how upset she was. She didn't know if it was because Dani was literally a few feet away and Ryan had interrupted a conversation she wasn't sure she'd get the nerve to have again, or because she'd had it with Ry continuously doing something she'd asked her not to.

Ryan rolled her eyes. "When have I ever been normal?"

"Ryan."

"What?" With a sigh, she dropped the grin on her face and handed the swipe key to Alex. "Fine. I'll stop, I promise. Just..." She grasped the hem of Alex's shirt—Alex following the act with her eyes—as she took a step closer. "You never texted me. After your date. That was three days ago."

Alex narrowed her gaze at Ryan's dark dilated eyes. "Have you been drinking?"

"What?" Ryan's expression blanked before realization appeared to set in. "Just coffee with like, a single shot of vodka. So?"

"Damn it, Ry." Alex glanced skyward as she dragged a hand through her hair. "Just let me get my phone, and I'll call you a car."

Ryan grabbed her hand. "Wait. Why are you so mad at me?"

"I'm not." Alex sighed. "But you should probably just get some sleep."

"Fine, but why can't I do it here?"

"Because I al—"

"Alex?" Dani called. "Your phone's still ringing!"

Ryan's expression shifted in confusion. Perhaps realization.

Alex ignored it anyway, answering Dani. "It's fine! Just leave it!"

"It's Dom. Maybe you should just pick up." Her voice had softened, as if she'd left the couch and was headed toward them. Before Alex had even begun to register the possible consequences of all three of them being in one room, Dani spoke again.

"If he's calling this much, it might be impor—" Dani stopped a few inches away. Her brows hung low as her eyes locked in on Alex and Ryan.

Alex gently retracted her hand from Ryan's, not wanting to offend either of them. Too late. She didn't know what to do about it either way.

"Dani, this is Ryan. My best friend." Alex nipped her bottom lip as something stirred inside her. In her chest and stomach. She didn't know what it was, but the words had never felt more offbeat leaving her lips. Maybe there was even something in them that resonated vaguely untrue now. She forced the thought away. "Ryan, this is Daniela. My..."

Dani smiled, meeting Alex's gaze as her expression relaxed. "Her barista."

"Right." Ryan stepped forward. "You're Lexi's best kept secret. She never talks about you. Clams up every time Dom so much as mentions your name. I don't know why. You're hot."

"Ryan."

"What? She is. I don't get why you're so shy about it." Ryan laughed, glancing at Dani again. "She's never shy. She's literally the most alpha person I know. In everything."

Alex clenched her jaw. "Ryan, that's enough."

"See? It just comes out."

"Yeah." Dani twisted her lips into a closed smile, shifting her eyes from Ryan's to Alex's. There was something foreign about the look in them, about her whole demeanor—her right arm stretched across her chest to grip her left, the way her eyes never stayed with Alex's for more than two seconds, the way her tone resonated duller than Alex had ever heard it when she spoke. "I think I'm going to go."

"Dani..."

She shook her head. "It's fine. We've been hanging out all night."

Ryan smirked. "You can stay. I don't have a problem with sharing."

Another closed-lip smile followed from Dani as she turned in the direction of the living room. "Don't worry about it. She's all yours."

"Dani!" Alex started after her, shrugging off Ryan's attempt to grab her hand. "Don't, okay?" She closed her eyes as she made a conscious effort to keep her breathing steady. When she reopened them, Dani was already headed back from the living room and past them with her eyes averted.

"Good night."

Alex followed, catching her by the hand the second they'd both gotten out the door. She pulled it closed behind them, wanting to block out Ryan and all the unnecessary tension of the last couple of minutes. It didn't work like that. There was no erase or reverse button. She kind of wished there was anyway, kind of wished they were back on her couch with Dani on her lap and their fingers intertwined. It didn't have to be sexual. Every moment they'd spent together felt so intimate.

"Hey." She tugged on Dani's hand—soft, more of a plea than demand that Dani face her. Dani turned but kept her gaze low. If Alex didn't know something was wrong before, that was all the confirmation she'd need. She raised her other hand to Dani's chin and tilted her head up. "What just happened?"

"I don't know, Alex. You tell me."

"Please come back inside."

Dani shook her head. "I can't do that."

"Dani—"

"How long have you been sleeping with your best friend?"

"Just give me a minute. I'll make her leave and we can tal—"

"Are you going to tell me that's not what she meant by you being an alpha in everything? Because it wasn't very subtle of her. Although, subtlety doesn't really seem like her thing. In fact, I think she just went out of her way to mark her territory."

"I'm no one's territory, Dani. Definitely not hers."

"Does she know that?"

"Yes! She said it herself. It was just sex."

Dani scoffed, shaking her head. "It's never just sex, Alex! God, how does someone like you not know that?"

"What does that mean? Someone like me."

Dani dragged in a long breath. "Look, I know I said I'm not afraid of messy, and I'm not. At least, I didn't think I was. But that was when I thought you had a crazy ex or something. Maybe they call too much after a rough break up, maybe they stalk you on Instagram. I didn't think you meant I'd have to compete with your best friend."

"You don't."

"She has a key to your apartment, Alex! And I can't"—she gulped as tears gathered in her eyes—"I can't be the girl in the movie, hanging around 'til the end just for the star to realize she's in love with her best friend."

"Dani—"

"No." She pulled her hand from Alex's, wiping away the first tear as it fell. "This already hurts too much. Don't follow me."

Dani disappeared into the elevator, and Alex dug her toes into the carpet beneath her feet to keep herself from doing the exact opposite of what Dani had asked. It's what she wanted, but the longer Alex stood there, the more it occurred to her she wasn't sure what *it* was. For her to let Dani go tonight? Tomorrow too? A week? How long was she expected to not go chasing after her? Something about their conversation felt so final. Maybe it was the ache in Alex's chest, the pounding in her head, or the way as Dani left she hadn't turned to look at Alex. Not once. Tears welled behind her eyes, her blood boiling again. She forced away the hurt—she'd never been any good at managing it anyway—and let the anger surface.

When she reentered the penthouse and slammed the door shut behind her, Ryan was no longer in foyer. She rounded the high columns toward the living room. There, she found Ryan stretched out on the couch, watching as the last few minutes of *White Bird in a Blizzard* played out on the plasma. Alex grabbed the remote to turn off the TV.

"Okay. Clearly I wasn't watching that."

"Ryan," she gritted out. "Go home."

"I'm guessing your talk with Daniela didn't go well."

Alex narrowed her gaze at Ryan—jet-black hair splayed over a throw pillow, gray eyes glossy, legs crossed at the ankles. She'd seen her like this countless times. All cavalier. Zero demure. Her way of not letting anything weigh on her too much. If she told herself she didn't care about something enough, eventually she'd convince herself she didn't. Like her dad taking her to school when she was seven, then just never coming back to get her. Alex got it. It was one of the reasons they'd become good friends. Mommy issues. Daddy issues. Neither of them liked to acknowledge anything that hurt. They both had different ways of ignoring, of masking. Ryan and her liquor. Alex and her razors. The truth was, both were manifestations of people they already were. Ry was a party girl. She drank as much when happy as when she wasn't. Maybe even more. And Alex had always been a little too attached to her own brokenness. Still, it had always been difficult to tell the difference. Ry drinking for kicks or to forget. This felt like the former though. A lot like it.

"Are you sure you only had one shot of vodka in that coffee? Because usually it takes a lot more for you to be this much of a bitch."

Ryan rolled her eyes and sat upright. "I get it, okay? You're hot for your barista."

"No, Ry! You don't. Otherwise, you wouldn't have taken one look at Dani and decided to let the claws out like I'm some fucking tree that needed marking!"

"You think I was jealous?" Ryan breathed a humorless laugh. "What would I possibly have to be jealous about, Alex?"

"Exactly! Two single girls having fun. Isn't that what you said? That it was just sex?"

Ryan got to her feet. "It's always just sex with you, Alex! Isn't that why you've never actually been in a relationship with a girl? Why are you so set on pretending Daniela's any different?"

Alex didn't view her relationships with women as purely physical. At all. She just hadn't gotten the voices— hers and her mother's—out of her head long enough for anything realer. Maybe the reason she and Ry had never talked about that was because those kinds of talks had never been their thing. They hardly ever sat still long enough. Ry always had to be on the move, and Alex didn't mind that that was who she was. They'd built their friendship on the common knowledge that being in constant motion wasn't Alex's thing. They'd never be the kind of friends that spent every waking moment together. Still, Alex didn't understand why Ryan would assume she only wanted casual sex with women. Didn't Ryan know her better than that?

"I never said it was just sex. You did," Alex clarified.

"So, what are you saying? That you do have feelings for me?"

"Don't be ridiculous."

"Oh, so now it's ridiculous?"

"What do you want me to say, Ry? Why are you so set on making this so fucking hard?"

Ryan pursed her lips, grabbing her phone from the coffee table. "Forget it." She took a few steps forward and stopped to look Alex right in the eyes before adding, "Oh, right. You already have."

Chapter Nine

espresso con panna

Alex didn't text Dani. She didn't call. She didn't show up at Brave the next day. Dani hadn't called or texted either. So, Alex figured this was what she wanted.

Space.

Was it supposed to hurt so much to be apart from someone she'd only known for little over two months? She and Dani had spent half of that barely talking anyway. A week of Dani leaving Alex's coffee with a foam-shaped number, and Alex not having the slightest clue what it meant. Another two of Alex pretending to ignore them even after she did know. One more of staring across the room in between scribbles in her journal. Then, subtle smiles and brief talks where Dani would bite her bottom lip—all dimples, light peeking through the spectrum of her eyes, igniting a warmth Alex had made every effort to shut out.

Today, I think the reverse had always been true. It wasn't that I'd been trying to freeze her out. A part of me had always been cold, that part that most needed reaching. And the warmth I'd attributed to my corner booth at Brave—to the strudels, and the coffee—was her, melting me from the outside in with her patient eyes and radiant skin and fearless affection... With her entire way of being. Today, I think it hurts this much because in her absence, I sense the changing air. Summer giving way to autumn. The leaves will wilt, and the cold will return.

Alex closed her journal and wrapped the leather straps around it. She'd only recently begun writing about Dani, but the more she did, the more she realized on paper was the only place her feelings ever made sense. With Dani, there was a lot Alex needed to make sense of, starting with the day they'd met.

She had some figuring out to do with Ry too. She was just as responsible for everything that had happened between them since Dom's party. Until two nights ago when they'd fought about it, she hadn't realized how much. She'd been too content to brood in their lack of communication, lick her wounds over crossing a line few friends came back from, to blame it on Ryan's free spirit and her own hopelessly romantic nature. She forgot that as much as Ryan was supposed to know her, she was supposed to know Ry too. She hoped it wasn't too late to remember, hoped it wasn't too late for one of their incredibly rare but needed talks. And she wasn't big on faith, on defying odds or anything, but she hoped she and Ry were the kind of friends that would come back. She couldn't lose what was starting to feel like her first real chance at love, and one of her closest friends all in go.

Even Alexandria Van Kirk wasn't that much of a screwup, right?

*

Alex stood on the Manhattan waterfront, taking in the East River as the rotor blades of the nearby helicopter thrummed. She glanced at the time on her phone. Five minutes ago when she'd called Ryan to find out where she was, Alex still heard the hesitance in Ry's voice about agreeing to spend the day together when they hadn't exchanged a single word since their fight two days ago.

It was only a second that their eyes had met just before Ryan walked out, but it was enough for Alex to see that she'd been wrong in her assumption that Ry was just being a bitch for the sake of it. She was actually hurt. Alex had just been too caught up in her own feelings to see it.

Marcus beamed, moving forward. Alex turned to trace his steps with her eyes, only for them to land on Ryan, dressed in a tank top, shorts, and sandals as she pulled a small carryon along with her.

"Always fashionably late, huh, Ry?" Marcus extended a hand, offering to take her bag. Unlike most of the men on her father's payroll, he wasn't terrified of being casual with her and her friends. Only six years older than them, Alex didn't see any reason why he should be calling them "Miss" anything.

"It's not on purpose, I swear." Ryan laughed, sweeping a strand of black hair behind her ear as the wind whipped around them. "My internal clock just happens to be set like twenty minutes behind everyone else's."

"I take your word for it." Marcus shook his head, wheeling her bag toward the helicopter.

"Sorry I'm late."

Alex shrugged. "Just glad you came."

"As if I'd pass on a day of perfect weather in the Hamptons."

Alex smiled though something about Ryan's expression felt artificial. Ry was so fucking good at being okay, it was always difficult to tell when she wasn't.

Marcus reemerged at their sides. "All set?"

"Yup."

"Perfect." He clapped his gloved hands before rubbing them together. "Let's get out of here."

*

Forty minutes over some of the most spectacular views in New York and a ten-minute drive to the beach house from the Southampton heliport, Alex still hadn't broached the topic of her and Ryan's fight. She clung to the excuse it was a conversation they should probably have in private, out of the earshot of pilots and chauffeurs, which had gotten her through the traveling bit. Still, it had been a while since they'd both disappeared to their own rooms to slip into bathing suits for lunch by the pool, and that reasoning would no longer hold up. She stood in front of the full-length mirror, tying the strings of her all-black bikini around her neck when there was a knock on her door. She glanced toward it. "Ry?"

"Can I come in?"

"Uh..." Alex fumbled with the other set of strings on her bikini, quickly tightening them around her back. "Yeah. It's open."

Ryan stepped in, scanning Alex's room from the ceiling of one end to the open deck doors of the other. Wind from the ocean picked up, whipping the white curtains back, nothing but cool salted air ripping through the tension.

"Why does it feel like forever since we've been here?" Ryan leaned against the doorframe. "Fourth of July was barely a month ago."

Alex took a few steps back to sit on her bed. "You love it here. It always feels like you've been away for too long."

"Yeah, well, until you met me this place was way underused. Dom lets you get away with the broody shit too often. I don't mind being the one to pull you out of your hole every now and then."

"Except this time, I was the one to pull you out of yours."

"I don't have a hole. I prefer to live on top of the world instead of under it, remember?"

"Ry..." Alex trailed off. For the first time since Ryan had opened the door, Alex allowed herself to take her in—

all black hair, piercing eyes, and pale skin covered in nothing but a blue, geometric print bandeaukini. A part of her had been afraid to truly look at Ry, the same part that was second guessing inviting her to spend the day hanging out, half-dressed so as to work past all the weirdness between them.

Ryan sighed, crossed the room only to plop down on the bed and toss her head back against it.

The weight on Alex's chest shifted. Sure, Ry was wearing minimal clothing, and they had been intimate, but this version of her best friend was so familiar. An exasperated Ryan Pierce throwing herself into bed next to Alex because she hated talking about her feelings even when there was no avoiding them. Last time, Alex remembered, it was the morning after Ry had drunkenly admitted to the football captain of the Columbia Lions that she kind of, maybe, thought he was a little hot even though she'd spent half the semester telling him she was way out of his league.

"I'm sorry, okay?" Ryan breathed. "And I know you are too, so can we just fast forward to lunch?"

Alex was at least tempted to let it be that simple. The more mature thing to do, the better thing to do, was to talk about all the hard stuff. Even if neither of them wanted to, there were things she needed Ry to know anyway.

"Ry." Alex tugged on Ryan's hand to force her upright, but after an exaggerated groan and nothing but pure resilience, Alex lied back next to her. "Can you please look at me?"

Ryan huffed, jaw clenched as she turned her head to face Alex. "I know what you're going to say."

"Do you?"

"Yes." She shook her head, shifting her gaze skyward as her lips parted again. "You want to talk about the fact that I totally acted like a jealous ex on Tuesday even though I said I wasn't, and the feelings thing, whether it was more than just sex and I—" She eyed Alex again.

Alex dragged in a deep breath, half preparing herself for the question lingering on her tongue, half bracing herself for the answer that would most likely make things worse between them. If she was right though, they'd be okay. "Was it? I mean..." She glanced down, her heart racing, echoing all her anxiety. "Did you feel something?"

"Besides the constant tremor in my legs?"

Alex laughed, shooting Ryan a look. "Come on. Be serious."

"I am."

Alex rolled her eyes, moving to sit upright only for Ryan to grip her by the arm and pull her back.

"Okay." She released another breath. "I know you don't think I understand the seriousness of what we did, but I do, Alex. Believe me, I do. And sure, the sex was great. It was amazing, but I think a part of that was because you're my best friend. And it's weird because I guess that's what should've stopped me, but I also think that's what made it so good. Because I know you and you know me, and it was easy to let myself be open to this whole idea of being with another woman." Amusement traced her lips. "Remember the first girl I told you about? The one that went down on me after that keg party at Lambda Phi?"

"Yeah?"

"It was terrible. It was clumsy and awkward and just...so not good." She shook her head. "The second was the same. Only, we didn't even get that far because her nails were like, really sharp, and I didn't even know girls who liked girls kept their nails that long. It just leaves scratches in places you don't want to have scratches, you know?"

Alex laughed. "What's your point, Ry?"

"You were the first girl that did it for me, and I guess it's three years too late because I feel like you were checking me out that day at freshman orientation. I was never sure though because you never even hit on me. Not once. I thought I was straight anyway." She sighed. "After spring break, when Dom dared me to kiss Ash, it's like I opened my eyes, and I looked at you, and suddenly, it was freshman orientation all over again."

That's when it had started for Alex too—the feeling of sometimes sexual that had invaded purely platonic. In Alex's mind, it was because she *had* checked Ry out that day at freshman orientation, but she had also decided early in their friendship that Ryan was only interested in men. She only ever talked about men. After the dare, after

Ryan had willingly kissed a girl and liked it, the possibility Alex had ignored the day they'd met had slipped back in, plaguing her until they'd had way too much to drink on Dom's birthday.

"That doesn't mean I want to marry you or have your babies." Ryan teased. "Maybe...Maybe what happened at Dom's party was just residual tension or something, and I admit that it felt good, so I wanted to do it again. Like I said, it was fun, and I thought it was for you too. I mean, you're no stranger to being with girls that way, but then it was over before I even knew it was. I could feel you slipping away, especially after that night in your shower, and I didn't want to lose you because...despite everything, I'm not sorry we went about this backward, Alex. If we didn't, we would've never become friends first, and I love being your completely opposite, totally inappropriate friend. I pushed too hard when you started seeing Dani. I know I did. And it's not that I wouldn't have respected your decision to stop what we were doing. I just hated feeling like—"

"The other girls."

"You never talk to your exes, if you can even call them that." Ryan grimaced. "They all seem so disposable to you."

Alex shut her eyes. "Ry, you're my best friend."

"Would it have mattered?"

"Jesus, Ryan. Of course it would've mattered!" Alex sat upright, shaking her head. "I can't even believe you just said that to me." She stood, forehead creased as she locked eyes with Ryan, who'd sat up almost the second Alex had. "Is that what you think? That I have some kind of fuck-and-forget MO? How many girls do you even think I've been with?"

"I don't know, Alex. It's not like you ever talk about it. Not to me anyway."

"So, why didn't you just ask, Ry?"

"Would you have told me? Because you're pretty selective about who you drop your guards for."

Alex bit her bottom lip. "That's not fair. We're the same like that and you know it."

"Maybe. But I still told you about my dad."

"And I still showed you my scars."

"Yeah, but you never told me why you ever felt like you needed to do that." Ryan shook her head, gaze unwaveringly set on Alex. "We say we're best friends, Alex, but you keep me at this"—a gulp carried down her throat—"this distance. You tell me things, but never why. And knowing things never helps someone understand why it happened. Maybe that's what keeps my mom haunted, what keeps *me* haunted. It's not that he drove me to school, kissed me on the forehead, went home, and packed his shit. It's that I never got why he did it."

Alex closed her eyes, raking a hand through her hair. "I'd never do that to you." She reopened them and crossed the room to sit next to Ryan again. "I meant what I said that night. I'm not him, Ry. And this thing with

Dani...It's new and intense, but you were never going to lose me because of it." Alex nodded. "You're right. I should've talked to you about how messy everything felt once we had sex and I started realizing how I felt about her. I wanted to do the right thing by her, and I forgot to remember this, but you're not—Fuck." She licked her lips, shaking her head again. "You're not...*disposable*, Ry. I didn't mean for it to feel like I was dropping you for the next girl. The girls you're talking about—" She dragged in a breath. She really fucking hated talking about it. "It never went anywhere with any of them. And it wasn't about sex. It was never about sex. I only ever got there with two other people before you, and I hated myself for it. I hated what my mom would think of me."

"So, you hurt yourself?"

"Sometimes." Alex shrugged. "I guess it kind of felt like I deserved it."

"Alex—"

"I know. I know everything you're about to say to me. I've told myself a million times."

Ryan sighed. "Do you still do it?"

"It's been a long time since."

"Okay. Promise me something?"

"Yeah."

"I know you think I'm not here for this stuff, the real stuff, because you know how much I like to push it away, but let me try to be, okay?"

Alex nodded. "Okay."

Ryan breathed in and laid back on the bed. Alex did the same—both enjoying the ocean breeze and the comfort of the silence. "How badly did I screw it up? Your chances with Dani."

"I don't even know, Ry."

*

Alex pulled up along the curb outside of Dani's home in Bushwick and parked. She'd had a great time in the Hamptons with Ry, almost good enough for her to want to stay more than just the day they'd planned, so they'd only gotten back just over an hour ago. Ryan had all but insisted they leave after noticing how Alex would mentally check out at points in the day, her thoughts drifting off to Dani, wondering if she was at work, or walking through the park late afternoon, if her mind and heart felt just as unsettled because of how they'd left things a few nights ago.

Still, it was almost ten o'clock at night, and Alex hadn't spoken to Dani. Maybe that's why she'd been parked outside for the last ten minutes, just staring at the old Victorian she'd imprinted in her memory after dropping Dani off almost a week ago when they'd spent half the night on her rooftop. An image of them crept to the forefront of her mind—both soaked head to toe from being in the pool, Dani in her Brave sweatshirt and jeans, Alex in a designer dress her mother didn't think was the right level of conservative.

Tears.

Laughter.

Slow kisses.

Fear and fascination.

The front door swung open, giving way to the silhouette of a woman—roughly Dani's height, fuller hips and more defined curves.

"Shit." Alex bit down on her bottom lip, fingers desperate to start the engine of her car and speed out of there. The small, wrought-iron gate opened. The woman stepped onto the curb, and Alex froze. She barely managed to reach the button on the arm of her door, retracting the window as the woman hunched by it. Not opening the window at least would be downright offensive, and Alex wasn't about to be discourteous to a woman with low cheekbones and a butterscotch complexion just like Dani's. The woman's lips curled upward. *She has her smile too.*

"You must be Alex."

Alex opened her mouth but hesitated. "You...know my name."

The woman extended her hand. "Lucia. Daniela's mom."

Alex gulped, staring. It was all so strange—the mother of a girl with whom she'd been romantically involved standing just inches away, introducing herself with an open smile and literally open arms.

"Don't leave me hanging, mija."

"Oh. God." Alex's hand shot up to shake Mrs. Ramírez's. "I'm sorry. Can I just—" She pulled her hand away to open her car door and step out. Having Dani's mom stand outside her window felt just as rude as not opening the window for her at all. She slammed the door shut, rounding the hood to stand in front of the woman and offer her hand again. "Sorry. I'm Alexandria." Her eyes squeezed shut as she inwardly cringed. "You already know that."

Mrs. Ramírez chuckled and took a step forward to wrap her arms around Alex. "Nice to meet you, Alex."

"Ye—You too, Mrs. Ramírez."

"Lucia." The woman pulled away, the look of pleasant interest never leaving her face. She shifted a hand to Alex's and gave a light tug as she turned in the direction of the house. "You have to come in. Javi has been dying to meet you. And lock up that nice car of yours."

Alex glanced behind her and hit the lock button on her key fob before facing forward again, feet following Mrs. Ra—Lucia as her mind raced to process. On one hand, this wasn't how it was supposed to happen. She was supposed to sit outside the house for a bit, working up the nerve to call Dani and ask her to come downstairs. She'd probably say no, and Alex would beg, with no reservations because she desperately needed to talk to Dani. Maybe she still wouldn't agree to come out, and Alex would be forced to drive home, fighting back tears to the melody of a sad playlist. But maybe, Dani would say yes, and Alex would do everything to explain that she was in this, that the thing with Ryan was so completely over. She just needed a chance to prove it. Neither scenario included meeting Dani's parents. If Dani and her parents were as close as Alex imagined, they'd probably hate her by now anyway. She couldn't be any good for their daughter, who was nothing short of fucking incredible. So, as they crossed the threshold into the Ramírez's home and Alex stepped out of her boots to leave them at the door, the only rational explanation was that Marcus had lost control of the helicopter on their way back to Manhattan, and they'd crashed into an alternate universe.

Obviously.

"Javi!" Lucia called, closing the front door behind them.

A smile tugged at Alex's lips as she scanned the small entrance way. They continued deeper into the house. White walls, wooden floors, and lemon-yellow curtains. Family portraits Alex desperately wanted to stop and stare at for more than the few seconds it took to walk by, especially when the little girl in most of them was clearly a young Dani, missing her front teeth in one instance but irrefutably adorable all the same.

A wave of Spanish mumblings travelled to Alex's ears as they rounded a corner into the living room—two all-white sofas and a blue one set on top of a red carpet, throw pillows of varying patterns and colors all over. She noticed that the kitchen took up the other half of the room as the muttering persisted, and the man responsible, back turned, stretched to put some drinking glasses in a cupboard. Like Lucia, he wasn't very tall, and his dark hair was thinning on top. He turned and relaxed his thick brows, grin replacing a frown as he shifted his light-honey eyes, like Dani's, to his wife's.

"Alex?"

"Yes," Lucia answered. "I saw her waiting outside, and I couldn't let her go without saying something."

"Go?" Mr. Ramírez rubbed his chin as he made his way toward them, shirt only half-buttoned, shorts maybe a size too big. "Daniela hasn't come down all night."

Alex glanced at her feet, taking a distinct interest in the outer-space theme of her socks. This was such a bad idea.

"Ahhh." Mr. Ramírez nodded. "You two are still fighting." He raised a hand to Alex's shoulder and pulled her a few inches from his wife.

"Javi, don't be scaring her off with all your foolishness."

He scrunched up his face as he waved his free hand. "Luci, please. Alex and I are talking."

Lucia shook her head and started toward the kitchen.

Mr. Ramírez's eyes locked with Alex's again. "My wife likes to talk, but I won't let her keep you down here when there will be plenty of time for that later. Daniela is in her room. Upstairs. First door on the left."

"Mr. Ramírez, I don't know if that's a go—"

"Call me Javi. Listen, Daniela is just like her mother when she's upset. The only thing you have to do is be open with her. Nothing more. Nothing less." He started to walk again, the hand on Alex's shoulder guiding her along with him until they stopped at the foot of a wooden staircase. "Go on," he added with a wink.

Alex hesitated, only mounting the first step once she realized Javi didn't have any intention of moving until she did. Her heart pounded, but she kept going. It was so easy to understand how Dani had come to be the way she was from being in her parents' presence for barely five minutes. They were everything she was: warmth, comfort, and degrees of patience and understanding that were out of Alex's world. Not that her dad wasn't all those things because he was, and she loved him for it. But she'd never been able to enjoy that about him without it being tainted by the belief that her mother was just the opposite. She stopped in front of Dani's bedroom door and dragged in a breath as she brought her knuckles to it, then knocked twice. If she waited even a second too long, she'd lose what nerve she'd managed to conjure from Javi's pep talk. Glancing at her feet, she anxiously wiggled her toes and slid both hands into the front pocket of her jeans. Then, the door swung open and bright honey eyes were trained on her. The pounding, the ache, everything in her chest just stopped.

"Hey," Dani mumbled softly, her hair damp and curlier than Alex had ever seen it, leaving the straps and chest of the tank top she wore damp.

"Your parents let me up."

Dani stepped aside, holding the door open in offering for Alex to come in. As Alex entered the room, she scanned the framed Polaroids neatly arranged over the single bed against the opposite wall. The door closed behind her, and she pulled her gaze away from them. She'd been so anxious to see some of Dani's work ever since she mentioned being a photographer. She hadn't quite imagined the moment, how it would happen, but something about this one didn't feel right.

"Dani"—Alex shook her head as the ache crept back in—"I'm so sorry."

Dani took Alex's hand and started toward the bed. Alex clutched on to it, intertwining their fingers, not breaking the contact even when Dani climbed onto the bed and stared at her expectantly. Especially not then.

"It happened twice," she went on. She fixed her eyes on their hands and ran a thumb over the back of Dani's. "The first time we were drunk. Not that we didn't know what we were doing because we did. It was a lot of built-up tension, and the liquor just...made it worse, I guess. I knew it wouldn't be anything more, so a part of me was kind of terrified that I might lose her because of it. Then, we never talked about it, so I figured maybe it would just go away. The night of—" Alex closed her eyes, chest rising and falling. She squeezed Dani's hand and made herself meet her gaze when she opened her mouth again. "The night of the open mic was the second time."

Dani shifted her eyes and pursed her lips.

"I'd just spent three minutes listening to you sing and ten seconds feeling your hand in mine for the first time. More than an hour sitting across from you and being unable to stop myself from asking you a million invasive questions." Alex knit her brows. "It was, like you said. Compulsion."

Their gazes met again.

"I didn't think about a single thing but you and how you're so fucking beautiful. Inside and out. Then I got home, and I had too much room to think about it, and it started to set in how terrifying the whole thing was. You terrify me, Dani." Alex shrugged "So, I pushed it away. Told myself what I'd been saying since the day I laid eyes on you. You're straight. That way, there was nothing to be afraid of. Nothing I felt for you would ever turn into anything, so what was the point of even acknowledging it?

"When Ry showed up at my place and started talking about how fun it was to just be with each other like we were, I let myself buy into it. Something about it didn't feel right anyway, besides the fact that having sex with each other isn't something best friends do, but I didn't know why. And then you texted me the next morning, and she was still there, and I felt sick." Tears prickled her eyes. "I've never cheated on anyone." She forced herself to keep talking, to not think of the one instance that could classify, the one thing that had probably defined her relationship history for the last four years. "The rational part of me kept saying that's not what happened with Ry either, but after being with you at Brave that night, being with her felt exactly like that. Like I cheated on you."

The tears fell, and Dani squeezed Alex's hand.

"I didn't know what to do with that, so I just didn't text you back. I should've. Dani, I'll say it a million times that I should've texted you, and I shouldn't have slept with Ryan that night. I should've talked to her before Tuesday. I should've told her how badly I want *this*. How much I want *you*." Alex took Dani's other hand, daring to shift closer to her. "It's over. We talked about it, about everything. But I get it. If you need time to reevaluate me or us, whatever. It won't change the way I feel about you. I don't think anything will."

A silence spread between them, Dani just looking at Alex and Alex looking back. When it became too much, when the possibility that Dani hadn't replied because everything Alex had just told her changed nothing, Alex broke and glanced down at their hands again. If this was the last time she would get to hold Dani's hand like this for a while, or forever, she wanted to remember it. The smoothness of Dani's palm, the beauty mark just beneath her knuckles.

Dani let go and reached up to dry Alex's cheeks before sweeping a few strands of hair behind Alex's right ear. Alex peered up just in time for her eyes to fall shut when Dani's lips touched hers. It was like her lungs were tasting fresh air for the first time in two days, the first time since Dani had gotten onto that elevator. Crisp, clean air she only breathed late at night, twelve hundred feet above ground on her rooftop. Except, she was on the other end of the city in a quaint Brooklyn two-story. This is what

Dani did to Alex. Her barista was a persistent illusion of all her favorite feelings in the world. Her alternate universe. Her dreamland. Her fairytale. Smack dab in all the bullshit of reality.

Dani pulled away, shifting her hand to back of Alex's neck. "Say it again. That it's over."

"It is. Completely over."

"And you guys are staying friends?"

Something faltered in Alex. "Is that okay?"

Dani shook her head. "It's fine. Just…"

"Tell me."

"Her key to your apartment."

"That's over too. She promised. She doesn't want to mess things up between us. And I know you have no reason to believe that after what happened on Tuesday, bu—"

"I don't know her." Dani brushed their noses, then leaned forward on her knees before shifting to hook her leg around Alex's waist. "But I trust you."

Alex took Dani by the hips and pulled her as close as possible, though just doing that sent her emotions into a riot of fearful, anxious, relieved, and turned on all at once.

Dani closed her eyes, pressing their foreheads together. "I don't want to scare you, Alex. I don't want to push too hard, and what I'm about to say will probably sound too possessive, but I want to be the only one who's allowed to do this, who's allowed to be this close to you. Just the thought of anyone else—"

"You are." Alex pulled back, reaching up to hold Dani's face and confirm her gaze. "There's only you."

"Then no more running away." Dani leaned in and took Alex's bottom lip between her own. Her fingers threaded the hair at the back of Alex's neck, making Alex's grip tighten on her waist.

Alex's breath caught as Dani kissed her way across her jaw. "Dani."

"No more holding back." Dani kissed her way down Alex's neck, nipping at her skin before soothing it with her tongue. "I missed you."

Alex shifted, tempted to cross her legs. Not that it would work in her current position. Dani pushed Alex to lie against the bed, and Alex had to conjure every ounce of resistance she had. She widened her eyes at Dani's amused expression. "Your parents are downstairs."

"We're being quiet. It's not like we're doing anything anyway."

"Yeah, but if you keep doing what you were doing, I'm going to want to"—Alex dragged in a breath—"do some things, and then it won't be so quiet."

"Is that so?" Dani joined their lips, one hand drifting under Alex's shirt. She dragged her nails against Alex's abs.

A moan echoed.

"Okay, baby. Wait."

Dani smiled into the kiss. "I like baby," she whispered, looking Alex in the eyes before closing the gap between them. "I like that other sound too. Let's see if you can make it again."

Laughing, Alex wrapped her arms around Dani and squeezed tightly. "God, I missed you." She leaned in for a slow kiss, taking the opportunity to flip Dani onto her back. "But there's no way we're having our first time like a pair of horny teenagers inside these paper-thin walls with your parents downstairs."

"I know." Dani stroked Alex's cheek. "You're too much of a romantic, but I do love watching you squirm."

"I bet you do. Is that so bad though? That I'm a romantic. Apart from the fact that it makes me terribly cliché sometimes."

Dani shook her head. "I don't think you're cliché. I love that you're passionate."

"Does that mean you'd be okay with it if I say I really want to take you on our first date?"

"We already had our first date."

"We did?"

"At Brave. The day after we watched the sunset. Then there was the movie at your place."

"Those weren't dates." Alex leered. "We didn't even watch that movie."

"Right." Dani bit her bottom lip, dimples in full effect. "We *could* watch it now. If you want to."

"Whatever you want," Alex mumbled. She was just happy they were back, that she was lying with Dani, between her legs in this completely intimate position, debating their dating history with their eyes locked and their lips touching every few seconds and her heart beating too fast for normal.

Dani flipped them and landed on top again. It was probably exactly what it would be like once they were physically intimate. A constant battle for the top. She leaned in and kissed Alex briefly before standing. "I'll be right back."

Alex caught her by the arm, pouting. "Where are you going?"

"Coffee. My dad's kind of addicted to the stuff too. I got him an espresso machine last Christmas. The two things we never run out of are coffee beans and whipped cream."

Alex grinned. "Espresso con panna."

Dani furrowed her brows.

"It's Italian. For espresso with cream."

"I know what it means, babe." Dani smiled. "I do work in a coffee shop. It's just the way you said it sounded very...authentic?"

"Oh. Yeah." Alex shrugged. "My dad taught me. Italian and Dutch. My French isn't as good though, probably because my mom forced me to learn."

Dani shook her head, her lips parted in awe.

Did Alex mirror that expression every time Dani opened her mouth? In the spur of the moment, she asked, "Do you want to meet him? My dad." She snapped her lips shut. "Uh, I mean—"

"I'd love to." Dani stepped back, still beaming. "I won't be long. Don't think too much, okay?"

Alex nodded. "Okay."

Chapter Ten

aquavit

Alex squeezed Dani's hand as they continued up the bustling sidewalk, their comfortable silence overpowered by the constant buzz and zoom of the city. Not her preferred choice to the start of their date, but the museum was only a five-minute walk from The Van Kirk, and although she'd driven to pick up Dani earlier, she didn't want to have to go through the trouble of finding parking when she had a spot with her name on it so close by. Besides, it was nice out tonight—not too warm or cold— and as long as she ignored the near collision with random strangers every few seconds, the walk was pleasant enough.

Alex glanced at Dani—Dani fidgeting with her top again. She didn't see what Dani was so anxious about. Jeans and a nice pair of heels was exactly what she imagined her wearing tonight. The white top with a cutout neckline hadn't exactly entered Alex's imagination, but it was her favorite part of the whole ensemble. She grinned as she leaned closer to whisper in Dani's ear. "Stop. You look amazing."

Dani rolled her eyes. "I'd know if you just tell me where we're going. What if I'm underdressed?"

"You're not underdressed." The currant-colored crop tank, black jeans, and suede booties of the same color Alex had settled on put them at equal levels of casual. "It's not like there's anything you can do about it now anyway," she added, gaze shifting as the facade of the building came into view. "We're here."

"What?" Dani's head snapped up.

Alex laughed.

Dani peered up at the building before facing Alex with a look of subdued excitement. "The Museum of Modern Art?"

Alex shrugged. "I know it's cheesy, and I figured you've probably been, but I thought it would be nice if we toured it together anyway. I also made reservations at The Modern, but if you want to go somewhere el—" Her eyes fell shut as Dani gave her a quick kiss.

"You're so cute." She turned toward the museum and pulled Alex through the spinning doors.

Alex scrunched up her face. "Take that back."

Dani laughed. "You are, which is funny because you're kind of intimidating from the outside. Actually, you're very intimidating."

"Intimidating?"

"I don't think you even know how bad it is. You're naturally stunning, your lips just happen to be perfectly pouty, then..." She shook her head smiling. "Then there's the fact that every time you walk into Brave in your dark leather jackets with your hair just falling on your shoulders, you do it like you own the place."

Alex creased her forehead. "What are you even talking about?"

"Don't even get me started on the way you run your fingers through your hair."

"That's a bad habit."

Dani stopped in front of Alex as they got to their first piece. Claude Monet's *Water Lilies*. "It's sexy." She stepped closer and rested her free hand on the exposed skin of Alex's waist, then grazed her ear with her lips, voice low when she muttered, "You're...*sexy*."

Alex released a measured breath, giving her mind time to adjust to the effect the combination of Dani's words and their being so close had on her. She willed the pounding in her chest to slow and the tingle in her fingers tempting her to pull Dani even closer to settle. She had always considered herself to be a physical person, so this happened to be one of her favorite things about Dani. She was bold and brave. But it also made it difficult for Alex to determine the pace of their relationship. Maybe it was old-fashioned, but she wanted to woo and romance Dani. The urge to get her out of every piece of clothing she owned just happened to be strong too.

"If you keep talking to me like that, we're never going to make it through this exhibit."

Dani simpered. "Sorry. Must be the art. Total turn on." She let go of Alex's hand before glancing over her shoulder and stepping closer to *Water Lilies*.

*

Surreal.

There was no other way to describe it all.

Maybe Alex still hadn't gotten used to the feeling of having Dani near her and not having to suppress all the feelings her presence provoked. Maybe it was that they'd spent last night snuggled in Dani's bed, watching one of Alex's favorite movies then one of Dani's, and vice versa until Alex had fallen asleep. She still hadn't gotten over how she'd slept through the night in a strange place, how the next time she'd opened her eyes it was with Dani hovered over the bed telling her it was time to go. Alex was more than happy to drive Dani to Brave, then leave her with a kiss on the cheek before heading home herself.

Now, only twelve hours later, they were making their way through some of the most significant pieces in modern art. Dani's face lit up with fascination every time she pulled Alex in the direction of a painting or sculpture she'd either come across in her contemporary arts module last year, or had just read about somewhere. Alex found it too endearing. Still, as they came to a stop in front of one of her personal favorites, a Boccioni, her mind from drifted off to the only other time she'd visited MoMA.

"I love this one." She stared at the gold, armless sculpture. "It's one of the only pieces I got to see when I came here with my mom."

Dani backtracked a bit and turned to look up at Alex. "Your mom took you here?"

Alex nodded. "Little over three years ago. Summer too. A Sunday. I was sitting around at home, texting Dom, and she just popped into the living room and said, 'Get dressed, Alexandria. We're going to the Museum of Modern Arts.'"

"Just like that?"

"Yup. It's kind of the Annalise Van Kirk way. She says everything like a demand." Alex hated the feeling of nostalgia that had snuck up on her, drenching her words in sentimentality—moments like this were always hell, moments when she reflected on the better days with her mom without being able to pause the persistent undercurrent of resentment she also felt toward the woman.

Dani shifted closer to her.

"I didn't even care how random it was. That was kind of the best part. The fact that she'd made an unscheduled effort for us to do something together. Something I'd enjoy. She got a business call twenty minutes into us being here, but it was still a good twenty minutes, you know?"

Dani nodded. "What do you love about it? The *Unique Forms of Continuity and Space*."

Alex glanced away from the sculpture. "I've read about it symbolizing the dynamics of a body in motion. Divisionism and all that. But"—she shrugged—"I just thought it was striking. That's one of the reasons I'm so into art, to be honest. For the beauty. Not that I think there's anything wrong with analyzing or interpreting. I just think it's amazing that we can do this. Turn whatever we feel, however positive or fucked up, into something real and beautiful."

Dani didn't say anything. She just stood next to Alex, as if lost in contemplation, not frowning or smiling either. There was something comforting about the light in her eyes, but Alex had to ask, "What?"

"I'm just glad I went taking pictures in the park that day."

"When we watched the sunset?" Alex tilted her head. "You didn't have your camera with you."

Dani leaned in and kissed Alex softly on the lips before turning away. "Come on. I want to see Oppenheim's *Object*."

*

Alex slid into the black, armless chair as she and Dani settled into their reservation at The Modern. In the back of her mind, she hoped it wasn't too much. A fine dining restaurant, most formal of the three offered at MoMA. The other two were cafés, which were closed by now anyway, and while Alex loved that she'd met Dani at Brave, she wanted to try something kind of different. To make sure it wasn't too over the top, she even rejected the restaurant's offer for an upgrade when she'd presented her name. A table in the main area was more than okay, especially since theirs was by the window and directly overlooked the Abby Aldrich Rockefeller Sculpture Garden. They'd seen enough of the museum for the night, but the garden offered a nice backdrop for dinner.

She set aside her menu. "See anything you might like?"

"The salmon," Dani answered, lowering hers too. "Kind of more excited for this banana bread pudding though."

Alex pushed her menu aside too, then reached across the table to take Dani's hand in hers. "We can skip straight to it if you want."

Just then, a waiter—a blonde woman, hair swept in a neatly groomed bob—stopped by their table. "Are you ladies ready to order?"

Alex glanced at Dani, having already decided what to eat herself. "Are we doing dessert, or do you want to be stuck with me for consecutive courses?"

"I mean"—Dani scrunched her nose and let her eyes wander playfully—"being stuck with you doesn't sound like the worst idea in the world."

Alex smiled, shaking her head as she glanced up at the waiter, only to catch the woman in an almost identical act. "Sorry."

The waiter waved off the apology. "Don't worry about it. You guys are adorable."

"Thank you." Alex's cheeks burned. She faced Dani again, ignoring the amusement on her face too. "Want to order?"

Dani nodded. "I'll have the salmon and a martini, then the banana bread pudding later."

"Good choice." Mason turned to Alex. "And for you?"

"The grilled lobster, a glass of aquavit and the uhm—" She broke off, using the hand not holding Dani's to shift her menu into view. "Apple crème fraiche mousse for dessert."

"Awesome. I'll be back with your orders in a bit."

"Thank you." Alex turned to Dani, who appeared to be scanning the restaurant, glancing over the suit and ties and hipster crowd alike. It wasn't too packed—one of the upsides of coming this late at night—but maybe something about being there bothered Dani anyway. She squeezed Dani's hand, and Dani faced her. "Is everything okay? Is this"—she took a casual glance at their surroundings—"okay?"

"It's great, babe. I was just looking."

"Okay." Alex lifted their hands, then leaned forward to kiss Dani's fingers.

"Alexandria?"

She glanced right to see a tall Asian man dressed in a navy suit approaching their table. The smile on his face suggested she was supposed to know him, but her memory refused to yield a where or when they'd met.

He took the final steps to close distance between them. "I apologize." Then, he chuckled a bit and brought one hand to his chest. "Edward Chung. I work at the Garvey Group with your mother."

"Uhm…" Alex's chest tightened. "Hi?"

The man laughed again. "You must feel completely blindsided. I was just walking by, and I recognized you from that picture on her desk. Although, I must say, you look a lot more like her in person."

"Right."

The man's smile faltered. "Well…" He shifted his gaze to her and Dani's linked hands, to Dani's face, then back to Alex's. "I'll let you get back to your dinner. It was nice seeing you. She talks about you all the time."

Alex registered his awkward nod and mumbled goodnight as he walked away, but her mind had already begun drifting off. She couldn't decide where to focus—on the anxiety creeping through her since someone, who was apparently acquainted with her mother, had seen her on a date with a woman, or on the fact that her mother kept a picture of her at work. She talked about her too, and from Edward's reaction it wasn't about all the reasons Alex was such a disappointment.

Dani tugged on her hand. "You okay?"

Alex nodded, making a conscious effort to relax her expression. To relax, period. "Yeah."

She'd never felt bad about being with Dani. Never been anxious about being seen holding her hand or kissing her out in the open, at Brave, outside the hotel, here at the museum. All places where she could've easily been seen by people like Edward Chung. People familiar with her mom. Out in her city, among the bustle she hated and loved all at once, she didn't know what it was like to be in the closet. No one seemed to care. It was at home she'd always felt the need to hide. Then, she got the penthouse for her eighteenth birthday and the hiding got less. She still hadn't brought any women home, but that was hardly because she couldn't. It'd been almost four years since she'd come out to her dad, and she hardly ever saw her mom now anyway. The whole concept of being closeted was practically nonexistent.

The idea that her mother would probably hear about her being at dinner with Dani from Edward come Monday morning was scary, but she couldn't bring herself to succumb to that. Not if it meant giving up date nights at museums and public dinners with the woman seated across from her. She wasn't about to damage her relationship with Dani to salvage a shard from all the broken pieces between her and her mom. Every time she tried, she'd wound up cut and bleeding anyway.

Maybe this was the universe's messed up gift to her—its way doing something she had never been brave enough to do her own. Give her mom the main reason for all the space between them. Would she try rebuilding the bridge, or set fire to what was left of it?

*

It was perfect.

Minus Edward Chung's drop in, the date had gone exactly how Alex had hoped.

Somewhere after ten, they'd decided to head back to The Van Kirk—the five-minute walk being more pleasant considering half the city's population was no longer out. Alex was already reliving her and Dani's conversation over how interesting Andy Warhol's *Brillo Box* concept was, "despite the fact that he's portrayed as a complete asshole in this season of *American Horror Story*." And Alex still found *Object* creepy in appearance "because it's a goddamn cup and saucer covered in fur," but Dani found the juxtaposition of warm and soft with cold and hard sort of cool.

They'd definitely have to eat at The Modern again because, while Alex had had better lobster, they both agreed that the dessert was absolutely spectacular, and their waiter was the sweetest. Halfway through her second flute of aquavit, Alex had made a silent decision to not finish it. The last thing she needed was to be buzzed while driving Dani home. It was making her insides all warm anyway, and she'd had enough of that from being with Dani all night.

She glanced at Dani as they entered the elevator. Her finger itched to hit the button to the penthouse, but maybe Dani was tired and ready to go home. "Do you want to come up for a bit, or should we head straight to the car?"

"I want to come up, if that's okay."

Alex smiled, pressing the button. "Of course that's okay."

The elevator started its ascent and Dani turned to face her, eyes somewhat wary. She swept a lock of hair out of Alex's face as Alex pulled her closer. "Are you sure you're okay?"

"What do you mean?"

"I mean...You seem okay, although a bit quiet. But I was just wondering because of that guy at the restaurant. You've never explicitly mentioned your mom doesn't know you date girls, but based everything else, I get the impression she doesn't."

Alex leaned in and joined their lips. "I'm fine, babe."

The elevator stopped, and the doors slid open, but Dani kept her gaze locked on Alex's. "You are?"

"I am." Another brief kiss followed. Alex pulled Dani toward her suite. She reached into the pocket of her jeans and took out her keycard to hand it to Dani. Dani didn't question it, just slipped the key into the lock as Alex wrapped both arms around her waist from behind and pressed a kiss to the exposed skin of her shoulder. A beep followed, signaling the door had been opened, and Dani's lips parted in a smile.

"Is this what it feels like to be romanced by a hotel heiress? Picked up in a Maserati, whisked off to fine art and fine cuisine, then taken back to a penthouse?"

Alex shook her head. "No. That's when we jet hop to Buenos Aires for a week." Her arms fell from Dani's waist as she spun, eyes wide. Alex laughed, pushing the door closed behind them. "I'm kidding."

Dani rolled her eyes, releasing an audible breath as they both stopped to take off their shoes.

"Unless you want to go." Alex started through the foyer. "Then we can totally go."

"Alex..."

She paused, turning to look at Dani who'd just gotten her other shoe off. After taking a few steps back toward the nearby pillar, Alex leaned against it and furrowed her brows as she took note of the frown on Dani's face. "What?"

Dani took both Alex's hands and moved closer until they were all but breathing each other's air. "I had a great time tonight. I always have a great time with you. And I want to see as much of your world as you want to show me. But you know we don't have to do stuff like that, right? Fancy restaurants and trips to Argentina."

"I know," Alex replied. It was just banter. Not that she didn't mean it. There were moments in the short time she'd been with Dani when she felt she'd go anywhere in the world with her. She didn't mean tomorrow, next week, or even in a month. But someday. She was ready to hold out for someday.

She stroked Dani's cheek. "It won't always be like that. Sometimes, I'll want it to be just like it is at Brave. I write in a corner while you do whatever else. I'll be okay just knowing you're close by. Sometimes, I'll just want to do what we did last night. Cuddle and watch a movie, your place or mine." She cracked a smile. "Maybe one night, I'll make you one of the, like...four dishes I can cook, and it won't be five-star cuisine, but it'll taste good."

Dani laughed.

"And just the idea of it scares me, but maybe one day I won't drive you home. We'll take the subway instead. I hear it's faster anyway."

"Sounds like you plan on being stuck with me for a bit."

Alex shook her head. "I'm just kind of hoping it takes you a while to realize how much better you can do."

Dani leaned into her and lifted one hand to the back her neck to press their lips together. "I hate it when you talk like that."

"Sleep with me tonight. We don't have to do anything but sleep. I just"—Alex sighed—"I don't want you to go." Maybe she wasn't as okay as she'd hoped. Maybe she was afraid the second she dropped Dani off and walked into the penthouse, her airway would constrict, and she'd spiral straight into a panic attack at the mere idea of Edward Chung telling her mother what he'd seen.

The resulting conversation was one she didn't want to have. With Dani here, it mattered less. A lot less.

"Then I won't," Dani answered.

"There's one more thing."

Alex's chest rose then fell again as her pulse quickened. Dani fixed her eyes on her, patient but curious. Instead of saying anything else, she started toward the stairs with Dani's hand in hers. A silent minute later, she opened her bedroom door, faced Dani, then took backward steps toward her messy California king. When the back of her knees hit the duvet, she dropped Dani's hand.

Dani peered around the darkened room for a few seconds, and then she settled her gaze in Alex's direction again. Alex breathed in and reached for the button of her jeans. She snapped it open and slipped out of them. Lines drew in Dani's forehead. It would make it a lot easier on her if Alex turned the lights on, but she wasn't sure if she would be able to handle Dani's initial expression in vivid detail. So, this is where they were—in the dark of her room, light from the city peeking through the drapes. She took Dani's hand and guided it toward the rows of horizontal scars on the uppermost portion her right thigh.

Dani spread her fingers, trailing each mark individually, and even in the dimness, hurt visibly crossed her features. The crease of her forehead, light leaving her eyes, downward turn of her lips as she asked, "Where are the lights?"

"Dani—"

"Tell me."

Alex glanced at her feet and took a slow gulp. "By the door."

Without another word, Dani started toward it, and in a few seconds the room was all bright, florescent beams bouncing off white walls. She adjusted the brightness to a subtler, more pleasant intensity, and she started toward Alex again.

Alex forced herself to not look away when Dani stopped in front of her. Comforted if only by the fact that Dani wasn't merely staring at her scars.

"I won't ask you to talk about it. Not unless you want to." Dani shook her head. "But don't hide from me, okay? You never have to hide from me."

Alex brought her lips to Dani's. Nothing but a slow brush to begin with. A show of gratitude for making it easier than it had ever been to let someone see her. She leaned in, adding more pressure as Dani held her face in both hands. An admission of how good this felt, how good Dani felt. She clutched onto Dani's hips, maybe a little tighter than she'd intended based on the way Dani's breath caught, but she held her closer, then turned to gently lie her on the bed. An act of surrender...to the realization that the only thing Alex's denial had done was robbed them of all the time they could've spent together since the day they'd met two months ago.

In two weeks, Dani would be heading back to Rhode Island for school, and what they had wouldn't have to end, but the ability to see each other as much as they did now was about to become a luxury Alex already missed.

She separated their lips, one hand pressed against the mattress to hold her weight as the other brushed the hair back from Dani's face.

"What happened to sleeping?" Dani asked.

"There can still be time for sleep later." Alex released a steady breath, then joined their lips while Dani's fingers trailed down Alex's lower back. "Preferably a lot later."

Dani smiled into the kiss. "Are you sure?"

"So sure." Alex placed her legs alongside Dani's hips and sat upright. She tugged on Dani's blouse and pulled her to sit up too. "I like this top." Her gaze trailed all the places where Dani's skin—soft and glowing—had been left on display. Her shoulders and collarbones, upper chest. "But I'm dying to get you out of it." Alex lifted the hem of the blouse and slowly brought it over Dani's head. Dark hair fell in waves against her shoulders, and Alex glanced at the delicate, gold detailing of her blush-pink bra. She leered, bringing one hand to the center clasp and let it rest there. "Coincidence?"

Dani laughed, her chest rising and falling with each breath. "Yes, actually." She pulled Alex's crop top off and carelessly dropped it on the bed, eyes widening at the unlined demi bra. "I think you lied to me." She shook her head. "This is why you wanted me up here. To seduce me wearing *that*."

Alex brought her hand to Dani's chin and tilted her head up. "I always wear matching underwear."

"Weirdo."

"Are you telling me"—she broke off, her hand trailing Dani's stomach to hook two fingers under the waistband of her jeans until they met the soft material of her underwear—"these aren't the same pink as that really nice bra?"

A breath escaped Dani's lips, one-part humor, one-part something else. "No. They are. But this is date underwear. The kind you wear in case things like thi—" Alex pressed a kiss to her neck while undoing the button of her jeans and pulling the zipper down. "You're good at this, aren't you?"

Alex slid her hand under the jeans again and reveled in the feel of Dani's skin against her palms. "Good at what?" She took one part of what she discerned to be a double strap V-string between her fingers and tugged before letting it snap back into place. A breathy moan fell on her ear. She slid off Dani's lap, gripped her jeans by the sides and tugged them off. Back on the bed next to Dani, both more comfortably settled in the middle of it, she pulled Dani closer, ready to join their lips again when Dani rolled on top of her and did it instead. *Okay.* Alex didn't care who was on top as long as she got to have Dani's body against hers like this, with her hands on

Dani's hips, and Dani's threading the edge of Alex's bra. Nothing but warmth and want.

Dani broke the kiss, quick breaths mingling with Alex's. "You're so..."

Something about Dani's stare made her feel naked. Not undressed. Naked, like earlier when she'd stripped herself of her pants to show Dani the marks on her thighs. The pounding of her heart picked up, and she made a move to switch their positions, but Dani shook her head. A barbed tingle shot from Alex's chest to her stomach to settle at the apex of her thighs.

"It's okay," Dani whispered. "It's just me."

Alex nodded, incapable of doing anything else. She willed her onset of paralysis to pass sooner rather than later. Was this what performance anxiety felt like? Sure, it was Dani, and Alex felt things for her she couldn't even begin to explain, but talking with her body was still something that came naturally, especially with women. She'd studied the art of moving her hands and lips along their bodies, feather-light kisses to set their skin on fire, make them hold her tight. And yet—

Her eyes snapped open and she bit her bottom lip as Dani slipped one leg between her thighs. "Dani."

Dani dropped a hand to Alex's hip and gently rocked forward. "Yes, baby?"

Alex's eyes rolled back. "Fuck." She was so focused on the pair of soft lips making their way across her cleavage, she almost missed her bra being opened. Dani slipped the left strap off her shoulder then the right. Her nipples had only seconds to adjust to the cold air in the room before Dani took one between her lips, fingers around the other. "Oh-kay." Alex slid further up the bed.

Dani shifted too, teeth gently grazing Alex's hardened nipple.

Alex's toes curled, and she exhaled through her nose.

It wasn't anxiety over possibly not being good at pleasing Dani. It was another version of Alex dropping her pen and bounding her diary in its straps to give her barista all her attention whenever she'd stopped by Alex's table at Brave. Alex sitting on a park bench then chasing Dani to ask her to watch the sunset. Driving through tears to get to the café just to kiss Dani for the first time. Going to her rooftop, showing up at Dani's house at ten o'clock at night to say, "I'm sorry."

Surrender.

Compulsion.

Alex opened her eyes as Dani's lips disappeared from her breast. It gave her a second to catch her breath. Then, Dani's eyes—honey almost completely swallowed by the black of her pupils—were locked on Alex's. She used one hand to undo the front clasp of own her bra, and Alex's jaw went slack, trapping all the air in her lungs. The paralysis lifted, overcome by her urge to touch, to kiss Dani everywhere. Dani forced her to lie back the second she'd tried to sit up. She tossed her head back, groaning. "*Babe.*"

Dani leveled a kiss on her lips, slowly grinding against Alex's thigh, coating it in her arousal. "Do you feel that?"

"Yes." Alex dropped her hands lower and grabbed Dani's ass to grind their hips together, but Dani caught both hands and pinned them against the bed. "Dani."

"I want you," she breathed against Alex's lips. "I know you feel how much. But if you start touching me, really touching me, I'll never want you to stop."

"I won't."

"You spent all night taking care of me." Their lips met. "Now let me take care of you."

Alex glanced up at the ceiling, breathing through parted lips as Dani kissed a trail back down her neck, breasts, stomach, and along her panties. The hammering in her chest turned violent when Dani lifted the hem, pulling them down, lips against her inner thighs. She swallowed hard as Dani parted her legs, and kept her gaze locked on the ceiling.

"Look at me, baby."

Alex's chest and core clenched as her gaze fell to Dani's and she struggled against the urge to close her legs.

This was compulsion.

Dani, dark hair wavy and wild, leaned in and pressed a kiss to Alex's center, eyes falling shut a fraction of a second before Alex's.

"Oh my God." She was wrong. Nights ago, she and Dani nothing but lips and teeth and moans on her couch, she thought she'd never be more turned on. She was so fucking wrong.

Dani took a tentative swipe through Alex's folds, the hum from her lips sending a chill through Alex. She clutched onto the duvet beneath her and her chest heaved as she struggled to hold onto any semblance of control. Dani's lips wrapped around her clit, and she fought the urge to not tremble. Fought and lost. All she could do was shudder and burn and feel. Her breaths quickened. She squirmed, trying to ward off the pressure in her stomach, a coil twisting and twisting lower. "Da—Dani—" She closed her eyes tighter. "Fuck. Dani, I can't."

Dani gripped Alex's thighs tighter, lips letting up for a second, and then they were back on Alex's clit.

The coil snapped, and a moan tumbled from the back of Alex's throat, louder, completely unrestrained. Her body tensed and a tremor passed through her as Dani's lips made their way back up her body. She slid her hand between Alex's thighs, threading through her wetness like this was all they knew—their bodies against each other, burning through all the cold and oxygen in the room, her lips in a constant whisper of "Don't stop."

Alex's second orgasm barreled into her before she'd even come down from her first, and she latched onto Dani's command—*don't stop*—as if she had any control over her body's response to anything, everything Dani was doing to her. She pulled Dani closer, mumbling Dani's name as her legs quivered.

This was compulsion.

Or maybe...

This was everything Alex had imagined sex and love to be. Something so overwhelmingly blurred she doubted the distinction.

Dani stilled her fingers, and Alex's breath caught as she slipped them out, her body left to process their absence like they'd always been a part of it. She opened her eyes to Dani's, breathing in and out as Dani admired her, brushing back a few strands of hair clinging to the light layer of sweat on her face.

I love you.

She was glad her mind still possessed enough power to stop the words from leaving her lips because it was crazy. It was way too soon. Dani had done things to her body that had her mind reeling, and she was obviously disoriented from coming too hard.

"Perfect," Dani mumbled.

Alex shook her head. "You don't know the half of it."

Chapter Eleven

caffè mocha

Alex had no idea where the time had gone. How had they blown through two weeks already? Two weeks of pouring herself into her journal between Dani's shifts at Brave, then picking her up after to go for walks, watch sunsets or movies before falling asleep on the sectional in Alex's living room. Dinners, concerts, and art shows, then stumbling into the penthouse after midnight with their hands and lips all over each other. Nothing but skin and heat, and Alex failing at trying not to fall for Dani any more than she already had. Mornings where Alex would roll over, robed in nothing but the sheets of her California king, and reach for Dani only to find her already awake, just staring. One morning in particular, where Dani had been hovered at a careful distance, snapping pictures of Alex.

Alex was probably the most camera-shy person to walk this earth, so of course she'd tried to bury herself deeper under the covers and pile every pillow in reach on top of herself. Somewhere between a laugh and a whine, Dani had tugged at the sheets, begging, "Baby, please, two more." Alex had rolled her eyes, huffing as she peeked out from beneath her fort. Her hair fell in unruly waves from having Dani's hands in it for hours last night, and she'd just woken like five seconds ago, so she probably had drool on her chin too, but Dani had used the magic word and well, it was Dani. So, now, there were pictures—semi-naked, draw-me-like-one-of-your-French-girls pictures—of Alex on Dani's camera. Just when she didn't think this thing between them could get any more absurdly romantic.

Two weeks gone, two days until Dani was, and Alex was terrified again. She couldn't stop any of it.

Stop the fear.

Stop falling.

Stop time.

Sitting up in her bed, she glanced down at Dani. Her eyes raked over Dani's dark hair, wild against her face, lips parted in gentle breaths, nothing but soft tawny skin from her shoulders to the arch of her back where the sheets covered the rest of her body. She wanted to lean in and kiss her, but Dani would open her eyes, and as much as she couldn't get enough of them, this was as close as it got to stopping time. A single moment of stillness and silent admiration.

She dragged her gaze away and made her way into the en suite. Pausing at the sink, she brushed her teeth, ignoring the sight of her reflection in the mirror—the fading mark on her shoulder, faint signs of scratches on her back, and a memory pulsing at the forefront of her mind. She turned off the faucet to the sink and stepped into the shower. Warm water gushed against her skin as she closed her eyes and raked her wet hair back, welcoming the invigoration of a long morning shower. Maybe she'd step out less brood and more someone capable of living in the moment, of making the best of the next two days, instead of getting stuck on how much she hated that Dani had to go. Minutes passed, Alex working shampoo into her hair before lathering her skin in vanilla body wash and not bothering to lift a hand to get the soap off. Then, she felt a draft. Cool hands landed on her hips, and lips pressed against her right shoulder blade. Her chest ached, and she squeezed her eyes shut tighter.

The water still poured, and Dani stepped closer, chest pressed against Alex's back. Alex swore their hearts were beating in sync, but time didn't stop.

She breathed in, placed her hands over Dani's, and held them around her waist. She didn't want to turn around because she didn't want to pretend she was fine, but she didn't want Dani to see she was bothered by something either, so she stood with the water falling against them for as long as possible.

With a slight nudge on her hips, Dani willed Alex to turn toward her. There was no avoiding it anymore. She faced Dani, immediately met with the lime-specked honey of her eyes, somehow bright as the morning and dark with something else all at once. She glanced down at Alex's lips before shifting to her gaze again, and they both leaned in, lips delicate and minty in the slowest of kisses.

Falling was too delicate. What Alex felt was too fast, violent on her guards—a racing car, with no airbag and no brakes.

Not falling.

Crashing.

She broke the kiss and pressed her forehead against Dani's. "You haven't been home in four days."

"I know." Dani shifted a hand to the back of Alex's neck.

Alex swallowed. "Maybe you should..."

"What's wrong?"

"Nothing's wrong."

Dani touched Alex's cheek, lifting her head. "Look at me."

"Dani."

"Alex, open your eyes and look at me. Please."

Alex licked her lips, dragging in a slow breath before doing what Dani had asked, though not completely. She clenched her jaw and shifted her gaze along every inch of the shower but the few Dani currently occupied.

"Baby."

Alex's eyes fell shut again, and the beat of her heart faltered. She took a step back as Dani caressed her face with both hands. "I"—she shook her head—"it's nothing. I just—" This was so pointless. What was she even upset about? Everything was great. She opened and shut her mouth, reaching for the glass door. "I can't do this right now."

"Do what, Alex?" Dani grabbed her free hand, and Alex sighed, allowing her hand to be held for a moment.

"Finish your shower. Please." She turned, gaze still evasive as she pressed her lips against Dani's forehead. Quick and tender. With a mumbled "Later," she left the shower, silently grateful she wasn't followed.

Skin barely dry, hair dripping a trail along her bedroom floor, she entered her closet and quickly got dressed—a gray underwear set, black sweatshirt, and shorts. She grabbed some socks and pair of low-tops from her sneakers rack, and then she made for the stairs. An image of Dani, not at all focused on getting clean but rather forcing herself to not go chasing Alex for an explanation, entered her mind. She hadn't even given Dani a chance, but it was just like Alex Van Kirk to get trapped in her head and push people away.

She grabbed her car key from the coffee table in the living room and made for the door.

So much had changed since the night of the open mic, even more since she and Dani had watched their first sunset in Central Park. Still, things were so plainly the same. Dani was still fearless, and Alex was still a coward, and this was what cowards did.

They ran.

*

Trinity Preparatory hadn't changed a bit since Alex had last been there three years ago. She didn't want to give that speech, but it was sort of an informal obligation. Outgoing valedictorians always talked to the newbies at orientation.

Four years stuck inside its old, almost castle-like structure, inhaling its traditions and cold air, reminding herself to not be too much of whatever went against everything it was supposed to represent.

Sanctity.

Purity.

Honor.

No one ever cared if she was really any of those things as long as it wasn't obvious that she wasn't. She made it easy for them. Perfect GPA, high levels of cocurricular involvement. Made it easier for herself too. It's not like she wanted anyone to look at her too long or too hard. But the air in the hallways and classrooms was dense, and the crossover tie around her neck always felt too tight, and this... A hundred by sixty-yard stretch of lush green lawn was the only place in this overpriced, underpopulated school where she could ever *breathe*, the only place she didn't feel suffocated by her own emotions. Maybe it was even the first place she'd confessed them, if only to herself. Not that she ever had to tell...

"Frankie..." Alex sighed. "Seriously, we don't have to do this."

Francesca adjusted the pair of gloves on her hands—blonde hair pulled back in a messy ponytail, tan skin glistening in the beams of the evening sun. For a second, her lips gave away something akin to a smirk, almost as if she knew Alex was staring. She probably did. Alex had never been any good at not staring at Frankie. Once satisfied with the fit of her gloves, her gaze flicked up to Alex's—oceans of greenish-blue crashing into Alex with the force a million rogue waves—and she beamed, crossing the lawn until they were standing too close. "You're one of the best strikers in the league, Alex, but you heard Coach. Your spot kicks need work."

"I know, but practice is over, and..." Alex tried to ignore the violent race of her heart as Frankie's gaze shifted lower and her smile broadened.

"And what?" She met Alex's eyes again.

Alex's lips parted. A few slow breaths passed between them. "And everyone already left."

Frankie brought one hand to Alex's abs and took her jersey in a playful grip. "I thought you liked being alone with me."

Alex swallowed.

She did. She *did* like being alone with Frankie, no matter how frightened and excited and guilty it made her feel all at once. She wanted to say it too. She'd wanted to say it that night when they'd all gone to Frankie's house for their first team bonding session, and Frankie—a year older and way more daring—pressed her against a wall, with more than a dozen other girls downstairs, and kissed her like it was the one thing she'd wanted all night. Grip tight on her hips, lips smooth, cherry-flavored, like that one Katy Perry song.

"It's okay." Frankie held Alex's gaze, taking backward steps toward the goal. "I like being alone with you too."

Years later, looking at the same goal, standing over the ball the caretaker had let her borrow—smiling as he yelled, "Say hello to your mother for me"—Alex's memories of the number thirteen and Calvano printed across the back of Frankie's jersey were as vivid as ever. She remembered being at Frankie's, not solely for team sessions but mostly to be alone with her. She remembered Frankie pushing her against the plush comforter of her canopy bed and straddling her—pinning Alex down with the intensity of her gaze, emptying Alex's mind of its entire vocabulary even though her phone was pressed to her ear and Dom was on the line. The way when her breath audibly got less steady, Dom asked, "VK, you good?"

Alex had shaken her head, lips parted in awe at the girl on top of her as she hoped it was somehow both a dream and reality.

Frankie had taken her phone, brought it to her own ear and told Dom, "Don't worry. I've got her," before throwing it across the bed and kissing Alex again and again. The same night Alex had been the one to initiate their kiss goodbye.

She remembered feeling something in her veins on her way home—something like adrenaline with ten times the rush—and she remembered the crash as she got to her room, wanting to be alone when the guilt and self-disenchantment set in.

It always set in.

An hour. Two hours. A day later.

It *always* set in.

She remembered not knowing what to do, how to stop wanting Frankie, or stop giving in at least, and she remembered the first time she dragged a blade across the skin of her thigh and tried to bleed herself free of whatever the fuck was wrong with her. And she bled, and bled, and bled, but she never felt any differently. So, she adapted to the cycle of laughs and kisses with Francesca Calvano and punishing herself for it later. Francesca graduated and moved across the country for USC, and Alex had another year at Trinity. No more cycle. Just sanctity, purity, and honor...and blood.

Four years of bad non-relationships, voices in her head, and trying to learn acceptance. Today, she woke up thinking she finally had. She didn't feel any guilt in being with Dani. She didn't hate herself for it. What they had felt real and good. But what would happen once Dani left in two days? Maybe real and good was merely an incredibly deceptive beginning to a whole new cycle. Maybe all she'd done these past two weeks was unknowingly put herself in a place to hemorrhage when this girl left too, especially now that her mom knew everything.

*

Alex showed up to Ryan's at almost two in the afternoon. Only then, needing to text Ryan that she was downstairs, did she even realize she'd left her phone at home. She forced the realization away. She didn't want to think about how that wasn't the only thing she'd left behind that morning, and she did it the old fashion way. An elevator ride, three knocks, and staring at her feet until Ryan answered the door—jet black hair a mess, dressed in a tank top and lounge shorts like she'd just gotten out of bed.

Their gazes met, and Ryan creased her forehead. "What happened?"

Alex parted her lips. She willed the words to come out, willed herself to tell Ryan everything, but she also didn't want to talk about it. Wasn't that part of the reason she'd shown up there to begin with? Dom knew too much—he knew everything—and it would probably take him two guesses before he got to Frankie. Alex dragged her fingers through her hair, trying to look somehow less bothered or broken. "I'm starving. Can we order from that place with the bad coffee?"

Ryan studied Alex for a moment longer, but then she simply rolled her eyes and stepped aside to let Alex into her loft. Maybe she understood that even if Alex wasn't capable of talking about it—yet or ever—this was Alex trying to do what she'd promised two weeks ago in the Hamptons. To let Ryan try to be there for the hard stuff. So, she sat on the couch, flicking through the channels on the TV while Ryan ordered sandwiches and caffè mochas, and they talked about anything but what was wrong.

Forty minutes later when the food arrived, and Ryan had pretty much just hopped into the shower, Alex paid and took the order back to the living room. Sandwich only a quarter eaten, three sips into still-too-bitter coffee despite all the whipped cream melting over it, Alex found herself reaching for the closest pen and getting lost in scribbles on every inch of the brown napkins. Except, nothing she'd written made sense once her tears had soaked through it all.

Ryan reemerged in the living room and paused at the entrance before taking careful steps forward. "Alex?"

Alex failed to stop crying, but facing Ryan was just as difficult, so she closed her eyes, breathing as she tried for the hundredth time to get her shit together. She was upset about something that hadn't even happened yet, and who the fuck did that anyway?

The sofa dipped as Ryan sat, wrapped her arm around Alex and pulled her closer. Alex didn't know what else to do, so she laid there—head on Ryan's lap, tears streaking her face until she was too exhausted to keep her eyes open.

When she woke, Ryan still close by, embarrassment set in at the way she'd broken down. But Ryan took her hand, gray eyes more piercing and somber than Alex had ever seen them when she spoke. "You were right. We are the same."

"Ry—"

"No." Ryan shook her head. "I can't watch you cry like that and not even attempt to get you to talk about it, so tell me what's going on, Lex."

Alex pursed her lips, glancing at the ceiling. "She's leaving."

"Who?" Ryan creased her forehead. "Dani?"

Alex nodded.

"Okay. So, she's moving? Going to school? What?"

"RISD."

Ryan shifted on the couch to face Alex completely. "Alex, that's like three hours away. One, if you fly."

Alex shook her head, dragging her fingers through her hair as she stood and took a few steps across the room. "It's not about the fucking travel time, Ry!" She closed her eyes and sighed. This wasn't fair either. Getting mad at Ryan for not understanding something she had never even attempted to explain. "I'm sorry. Maybe I should—I shouldn't be here like this. I'm going to go."

Ryan scoffed. "It's so push and pull with you. I guess it's kind of the way it's always been with us. I pull, you push. You pull, I push. But I'm still here, Alex. And you can cry, or you can yell at me, but you're my best friend. No matter what. And I know you have to do things on your own time, so I won't try to stop you from going, but maybe—maybe if you'd stop running just for a second, you'd see that whatever's chasing you isn't so scary."

*

Alex paused at the front the desk in the lobby of he Van Kirk. She rubbed her eyes, barely even acknowledging the woman behind it as she muttered, "I need a key to my suite."

"Of course, Miss Van Kirk."

The woman hastily disappeared into the adjoining room as Alex's mind wandered. Despite all her internal struggle, she'd wound up giving Ryan a synopsis of what was going on inside her head, which translated to a lot of rambling, unfinished sentences, and trying to help Ryan make sense of thoughts that never did if not written. It made it worse that she tended to do almost anything to suppress them. But she told Ryan anyway. She told her about Frankie and how it was torture to have *wrong* feelings and not know how to make them go away. She told her though she only sees her mother once a month now, at least twice a week she would randomly text Alex. Something like, *Alexandria, I saw a lovely purse in Bergdorf. You probably won't wear it, but I bought it for you anyway.* Sometimes, no more than a link to some news article like "Improving Education in STEM Programs for Girls." Except, there hadn't been a single text in the last two weeks. Not since Edward Chung recognized her on her date with Dani at The Modern.

It had taken hours for Alex to get the words out, hours before she stopped diverting their conversation to casual topics only for it to come back to her mom, Frankie, and Dani. Hours before Ryan made sure they were looking straight at each other when she said, "You're not responsible for the way your mom reacts to this. I know two weeks is a lot, but don't torture yourself for a reaction you haven't even gotten yet. Give her the chance to have the right one, and if she doesn't, we can talk lessons in having one shitty parent and one awesome one. I have a little experience in that department." She smiled. "As for this thing with Dani leaving and you being afraid of how you'll handle it, you're not eighteen anymore, Lex. That girl you used to be...You're so much stronger than her."

"Your key, Miss Van Kirk."

Alex's head snapped up. "Thank you." She accepted the keycard, and started off, only to stop after two steps. She faced the woman, making an effort to look at her this time. "Did Daniela uhm...Did she—" Alex shook her head. "Never mind. Thank you."

She turned and started toward the elevator. Dani wouldn't have left her key at the front desk. It was probably still lying on the coffee table in the penthouse. The empty penthouse. Alex entered the elevator and pushed the button to her floor. She had no right to feel sad about returning to an empty apartment. She did this. She told Dani to go home as if pushing her away now would somehow make her leaving hurt less. It didn't. Alex's head and heart and limbs—everything hurt anyway. Like corporeal manifestations of a loss. A dull ache. Enough of a constant reminder. Today was the worst she'd had in a while.

She slid her key into the lock and pushed the door open. The dark of her entryway hit first, signaling no one was home. Dani hated the dark.

Alex closed the door behind her and took her shoes off. Her stomach rumbled, forcing her mind back to the half-eaten sandwich she'd left at Ry's. She made her way toward the stairs anyway. Later she'd have the kitchen send her something. Right now, she wanted to get out of these clothes and into her bed. Falling asleep wouldn't be easy—not with all the memories of her and Dani—but she'd welcome the torture of it anyway. Maybe it would get her to pick up her damn phone and apologize for the millionth time. She attained a slower, more careful pace as she got to the top of the stairs and started toward the master bedroom, lights slightly brighter than dim, just like Dani preferred whenever they would lie in bed at night.

Alex froze in the doorway of her bedroom, eyes locked on the girl sitting at the edge of her bed with her head hung as she picked at her nails.

Alex blinked. "Dani?"

Dani's breath caught, tears streaking her face as she stood and started across the room.

"Dani, I'm so sorr—"

Dani's hand landed on the back of Alex's neck, and then Dani's lips were on hers. Alex raised her hands, half in an effort to dry Dani's cheeks, half to cradle her face with a mildness that was the complete opposite of Dani's grip on her. She didn't care about the tiny crescent marks that would probably take more days than they had left together to fade, or that their lips were pressed so firmly together she could barely breathe. She didn't care that this kiss, like their first, tasted like tears and drama. They all hit her the same anyway. Scary. Intense. A little like crashing.

Dani's grip on her neck loosened, and she broke the kiss, still holding Alex close.

Eyes closed, Alex took a few seconds to breathe her in before pulling away. She swept a few curly strands of hair behind Dani's ears and dried her face with her thumbs. "I told you to go home."

Dani shut her eyes tighter. "You did."

"But you stayed?"

"Of course I stayed." She shook her head, stepping out of reach as she opened her eyes. "What you did today—" She bit her bottom lip, a fresh stream of tears running down her face.

Alex was sure she was crying too, but she wished Dani would stop. "I'm sorry."

"No." Dani put a hand up. "It was selfish."

"I know."

"It was so fucking selfish, Alex. Because last I checked, we were fine. We were better than fine, and I get that you probably woke up with some things on your mind, but what happened to talking to me? You can always talk to me."

"I know."

"Then why not tell me what's going on? Why run away?"

"Because I'm scared, Dani!"

"Of me?"

"No!" Alex closed her eyes, dragging her fingers through her hair. "Of everything else. And"—she scoffed—"as of this morning, losing you tops that list."

"God, you really don't get it, do you?"

Alex sighed. "What am I not getting?"

Dani dragged in a deep breath, eyes locked on Alex's for a few silent moments. Then, she nodded and turned toward the night table left of Alex's bed. She picked up the Nikon camera Alex only then noticed was still there and powered it on.

Alex narrowed her gaze, watching Dani carefully. She didn't understand the relevance of Dani's photography now in the middle of their fight. Not that Alex wanted to be fighting in the first place. But she understood it was her fault, so she was willing to let it run its course.

Dani started across the room to pick up her camera. When she was standing in front of Alex again, she handed it to her. "This."

Alex's forehead creased, and she hesitantly pulled her gaze away from Dani's to focus on the picture being displayed on the screen. Central Park, the burnt orange and pink, imminent dark of the sky, and a girl—legs pulled up to her chest, book on her lap, fingers of one hand caught in her hair. The pounding against Alex's ribs picked up, and she gawked at Dani again. "Wh—"

Dani parted her lips, hesitance flickering in her eyes. "I believe that a person can be so taken by someone else's beauty, or demeanor, or just their very existence at precisely the moment they first lay eyes on them, that they feel drawn to the other person in a way that's entirely inexplicable."

Alex remembered the first time Dani had said those words to her at the open mic when they were talking about Dani's parents and love at first sight. She swallowed, shaking her head.

"You weren't the focus of the shot, I swear. I just saw you sitting there. Alone. Maybe a little sad. And I wondered why? Why you were by yourself, what you were thinking, and I—" She broke off, glancing at her feet. "I had the most bizarre urge to walk up to you and say anything to make you smile. But that would be weird. Of course that would be weird. So, I turned off my camera and I caught my subway home with that image of you stuck in my head. I told myself it didn't matter, because I'd probably never see you again anyway. The next morning, I was behind the counter at Brave, my first shift, with Brendan chewing my ear off about inventory and shortages even though I had plenty of experience as a barista. I was so glad when the first customer walked in and ordered because then he would finally shut up. I turned around to grab the cup, and I caught a glimpse of you."

And she dropped it.

The memory of porcelain shattering came to Alex more vividly than it had in months. Dani's hair caught in a messy bun, her beige Brave sweatshirt and blue jeans, the look on her face—eyes bright honey, lips slightly parted—before she bent to clean up the shattered pieces. And the way Brendan clenched his jaw before saying, "Sorry. She's new."

"You paid for your coffee, and before you walked away, you paused, and looked straight at me." Dani sighed. "Do you remember what you said?"

Alex's creased her forehead. "I just told you be careful not to hurt yourself."

"Yeah," Dani muttered, eyes shining with tenderness. "It still warms me up just thinking about it." She brought her hand to Alex's cheek. "But I'm looking at you almost three months later, and I know you still don't get how ridiculously in love with you I am."

Alex's eyes fell shut, and her chest rose and fell in an attempt at controlled breaths.

"I know I grew up with parents who believe in love at first sight, and I know to most people that's either terrifying or crazy. I'm not saying that's what this is either." She breathed against Alex's lips, and Alex tightened her hold on the camera to not drop it. "I'm saying...I'm saying this feels pretty damn close."

"Dani."

She cupped Alex's face. "Please look at me."

Alex complied.

"I don't need you to say it back. Not until you're ready. I just need you to believe me when I say I'm in this. I'm in it for all the brooding and selfish walk-outs that leave me wondering where you've been all day, and scared that"—she shifted her hand to the back of Alex's neck and tightened her grip—"maybe when you said I should go, you meant it."

Alex shook her head. "Baby, I didn't. I didn't mean it. But you're leaving and—"

"You're going to have to push a lot harder for me to not come back to you."

There weren't enough words. There weren't enough words for Alex to tell Dani how sorry she was for making her cry, and being such a coward, and not believing in this, in them. She shifted the Nikon to one hand and intertwined the free one with Dani's, guiding her toward the bed. Carefully placing the camera back where Dani had it earlier, Alex kept their gazes locked, and she gently pushed Dani onto the bed. "I'm guarded." She leaned in and brushed her lips against Dani's forehead.

"You are."

Alex stepped closer to stand between her legs. "And I never say enough when I should."

"Also true."

"With the distance"—she raked her hair back as she hovered over Dani, resting on one elbow—"it'll be worse. Sometimes, I won't even want to talk at all."

"I fell for your silence a lot sooner than your words."

She brought one hand to Dani's cheek, breathing the words into her. "I'm going to miss you so much, it already hurts."

"Then I guess we'll have to visit often." Dani's fingers trailed across Alex's lower back. "If you're trying to talk me out of this while being this close to me, it's never going to work."

Alex licked her own lips, forehead against Dani's. "I'm not. I'm just telling you what kind of girlfriend you're in for."

"Girlfriend?"

Alex nodded. "If you want me."

"I do," Dani whispered, tangling one hand in Alex's hair and pulling her closer. "Want you."

"Sure?"

She pressed her lips against Alex's. "So sure."

There were things Alex wanted in a relationship that she couldn't imagine sharing with anyone but Dani.

Slow kisses that burned right through her veins.

Long talks.

Sunsets shared in silence.

Her heart in all its fire and ice.

She eased out of the kiss, lightening the pressure with gentle pecks before opening her eyes to meet Dani's. Maybe liquid courage didn't always taste like vodka, or tequila, or any alcohol. Maybe sometimes, all it took was coffee with a number to measure her mood, from a girl who was every kind of beautiful, and a café that never failed to remind her of the importance of being brave.

"Just so you know, I'm ridiculously in love with you too."

Part Two

sanctity, purity, honor, blood

Chapter Twelve

prosecco

Alex leaned against a panel at the back of the ballroom, eyes roaming over the older crowd seated at round tables for the night. As if on cue, a chorus of laughter broke out, champagne and wine glasses set aside, utensils still against the gold tablecloth if only for a moment. She'd missed the joke, but the amusement on the face of the woman on stage told her there had been one.

Events like these made her the worst kind of anxious. Always had. Maybe for a second, following her parents' separation, she'd hoped she wouldn't have to endure them anymore. Wishful thinking. Even with both her parents dead—God forbid—she'd never be fully rid of these things. Of the practiced smiles and cheek kissing, and the failed attempts at clandestine visual exchanges to her mom or dad whenever someone asked, "what are you studying again," and she'd answer that she's a creative writing and film double major. She'd yet to decide if that was better or worse than them hopping to the assumption she was in med school like four people already had tonight. Unsurprising though. Her last name hadn't been hyphenated, but it may as well have been. There was no flying under the radar for Alexandria Laurent Van Kirk at a New York Memorial banquet thrown by The Laurent Foundation in a hotel owned by her father. It was her nature to try anyway.

She scanned the table at the front of the room, occupied by her parents and grandparents, the two empty chairs being hers and Dom's. Sitting there would mean ignoring so many things. Primarily, the fact that for nearly the last two months, there had been no dinner between her and her mom. No silence and seething over fine cuisine at Gabriel. No disapproval of her choices in general. They hadn't even been under the same roof since Edward Chung had seen Alex at The Modern with Dani. No attempts had been made on Alex's part, and every time her father broached the topic, her mom claimed to be busy. Not much of an excuse, except when coming from Annalise Van Kirk. Was there a time when she wasn't?

Alex's phone vibrated. She reached into the only pocket of the black, Yves Saint Laurent blazer she'd settled on for the night. The clear rhinestones adorning the edges of both sleeves wouldn't land any approval from her mother when they inevitably spoke. Neither would the plunging neckline nor the fact that slim fit trousers accompanied her heels instead of a dress, but her mom's appreciation of her sense of style was the least of her worries lately. She unlocked her phone to view the message she'd received.

Ryan: Still sane?

Alex: Assuming I ever was to begin with. Should've taken you as my date instead. Ten minutes in the door and Dom ran into some girl he knew, so now I'm lurking in a corner, while he's probably off making out on a balcony.

Ryan: LOL. Being your date would definitely be more interesting than being out with this guy, but we both know how much Annalise would love that.

Alex: That bad, huh?

Ryan: Yup. He said I'm pretty for an IT major, so I punched him in the face and excused myself from dinner.

Alex: Ry, what did we say about punching people in the face?

Ryan: Fine. I didn't actually punch him, but I am in the bathroom strongly suppressing the urge to.

Alex: Good, because I'm not making any more late-night trips to police stations to come get you.

Ryan: That guy was a dick and you know it.

Alex: That guy was your boyfriend.

Ryan: Your point? That's what he gets for calling me a bitch.

Alex grinned, typing back: *You are a bitch.*

Ryan: And you're the only one who gets to say it.

"Miss Van Kirk?"

Alex's head snapped up at the mention of her name, and her gaze landed on a man, probably her age, dressed in a crisp white shirt and black bow tie as he held an empty serving tray by his side.

"Sorry." He cleared his throat, turning to point toward the front of the room. "Your mother and father would like to see you."

Alex locked eyes with her mother's the second she followed the waiter's direction. Even with half the room between them, the displeasure in her mother's blue eyes was jarring. The break talking to Ryan had given her was over. Back to shallow breaths and apprehension and something remotely satisfying at having her mother look at her at all. Her mother broke eye contact, and Alex glanced at the waiter again. She nodded to release him of whatever obligation had kept him glued there. "Thank you."

Clearly, no corner of the ballroom was dark enough, so she raked her fingers through her hair, and started in slow steps toward the table. She typed out a quick message to Ry about talking later, and another to Dom that he better get his ass back to the ballroom because he was officially on standby for emergency extraction. But mostly, she kept her attention on making it to her family without doing something embarrassing like tripping over nothing or crashing into a champagne waiter. There were maybe ten feet left to cover when her dad and her grandparents noticed her.

She closed the distance to her grandmother—seventy years old, looking no older than fifty in a designer dress and diamond neckpiece—and leveled a light kiss on her cheek. "Hi, Grandma." She turned to her grandfather and repeated the gesture before slipping into the chair next to her father's. "Sorry I'm late."

"You would think that might be avoided considering you live in the building."

"Annalise," Grandpa Liam put in. "She did mention she would be delayed."

"And why is that, Alexandria?"

Alex sighed. "I was working on a paper." Not a complete lie. She had been working on a paper. She'd just finished it early.

Her father wiped his lips, finishing the bite in his mouth before asking, "How's it going?"

"Everyone just needs to stop interrogating my granddaughter. She's only barely sat down," Grandma Charlotte spoke up, eyes as blue as her daughter's, but somehow less cold. "How are you, sweetheart?"

"I'm great, Grandma. A little busy with school." Alex sounded like her mother, but right now she didn't care enough to make an effort to do otherwise. Besides, school did take up a lot of her time. It's just that she was also balancing her friendships and having a girlfriend who lived in another state too. The latter required quite the adjustment. It had occurred to Alex maybe two weeks after Dani had been back in Rhode Island that she had never had a *real* relationship before. At least, none that compared to what she had with Dani. Of course, there was no discussing that in present company. So, school it was.

"I'm sure you're handling it all perfectly well." Grandma Charlotte smiled. "Looking beautiful as ever too. Must be so much trouble trying to keep all those boys at Columbia away."

"Grandma." Alex breathed a laugh, glancing away. Coming from her grandmother, the comment was innocent, but she didn't miss the way her mother had shifted in her chair, and that was enough to make them both uncomfortable.

"You know, Xander," her granddad interjected. "It's you she got all this bashfulness from. Physically, she's her mother in almost every way, but Anna was all arrogance at this age."

"Confidence not arrogance," her dad corrected.

"See why I married him?"

Alex repressed the most dramatic of eye-rolls as her parents and grandparents laughed. She glanced around the room for a waiter. "I need some champagne."

"Have some of mine. I think I've had too many already," her grandmother offered. "The young man should be back any minute now. Until then, tell me more about what's been happening with you. School, and the writing, and all those final year film classes."

Despite the fact that her mother had always disagreed with what she'd decided to study, and knowing that was enough to make Alex even slightly unwillingly to talk about it at a table with her, Alex answered all her grandparents' questions anyway. It was strange—her mother constantly insisted how proud it would make her grandparents if she went to business or med school. But at no time had they expressed reservations about her or her studies. If they wanted her to study something, or be someone else, it had never shown. Maybe they were being polite by not pressuring her with their ideals—they did have plenty—or maybe they didn't give a fuck. She couldn't tell, and she wasn't willing to be any less complacent about it. She liked her relationship with her grandparents exactly as it was.

They talked about Thanksgiving being in a month and having a family dinner, and whether Alex would be spending Christmas Eve at the foundation to hand out gifts to the kids this year. She always did, except for last year when she'd flown to Jamaica with Dom to visit family and hadn't made it back in time because of bad weather. She promised she'd be there this year though, because it was the least she could do, and because there was something about Christmas that put her in a mood to want to make people, kids especially, smile.

The ceremony was three quarters of the way through—long service awards being currently presented—when the conversation shifted again and Grandma Charlotte asked, "Will you be taking anyone over for the holidays, sweetie?"

Alex parted her lips for a reply at the same time her father said, "She will."

The bite of Cajun pasta in her mouth flew down her throat and spurred her into fit of coughs. Her father's brown eyes narrowed to hers as a mix of realization and regret seemed to cross them. They still hadn't met in person, but he must have been thinking about one of the three video chats he'd had with Dani. Obviously, in all his excitement, he'd forgotten that the one thing she'd made him promise the day she'd come out to him.

"Yeah, no." She shook her head before turning to her grandparents as all other eyes around the table alternated from her to her father. "Maybe just Dom. Is tha"—she cleared her throat, taking a sip of her champagne—"is that who you meant, Dad?"

"Right. Dominic." He nodded, gaze shifting upward. "Speak of the devil."

"Good night, Mr. and Mrs. Laurent. Mrs. Van Kirk, Uncle Xander." Alex peered up at the familiar tenor of Dom's voice, thankful for his impeccable timing. He rested a hand on her shoulder. "May I steal her for a bit?"

She was out of her seat before approval had even been given, rolling her eyes at the way Dom prolonged the exchange instead of simply saying thank you and walking away when her grandmother mentioned how handsome he looked tonight. As if Dom needed anyone to tell him something he told himself at least half a dozen times a day.

Alex discreetly slipped her hand into his and squeezed. Still, another minute or so passed before he graciously stepped away from the table too. "Okay. I'll be sure to bring her right back."

"You may have well pulled up a fucking chair," Alex muttered as they weaved through the tables taking up most of the ballroom floor.

Dom laughed. "It's not easy being this charming."

"Is that where you've been all this time? Off being charming with that girl."

"Nah." He shook his head. "She was trying to smash, but I let her down easy."

Of course she was. This was why Dominic King thought he was one of God's gifts to women. Because he literally didn't have to try. He put on a designer suit and women were set to throw themselves at him. It didn't help his ego, but one of the things Alex had always loved about him was that Dom never let a girl get undressed for him, if he wasn't interested in more than that.

"Wish you would've let her down sooner, but thanks for the save anyway."

"Alexandria, Dominic," an unfamiliar voice called.

Alex glanced behind her to see a man with a camera dangling around his neck. The press pass on his vest told her who he was, but she was already annoyed by the request that hadn't even come yet.

"One for The Times?" he asked, brows raised pleadingly.

Before she'd even replied, Dom released her hand to wrap an arm around her waist and pull her closer, always so much better at the publicity than she was. They'd posed for so many of these photos together, half of New York probably thought he was her boyfriend. The camera flashed once then about three more times—it's never just one—and Alex walked off, pulling Dom along with her.

"Bar? There's literally a bottle of Dom waiting with my name on it."

Alex scoffed. "You're such a cheeseball."

"And you're a marshmallow, but let's not make a thing of it."

Her lips parted in attempt at a counter, but her phone vibrated in her pocket, stealing her focus instead. She reached for it and smiled as she took note of the caller ID before sliding her thumb across the screen. "Hey, baby."

"And that...is why you're a marshmallow."

Alex laughed, giving Dom the finger.

"What's so funny?" asked Dani.

"Nothing. Dom's being an ass, as usual."

"Whatever makes you laugh," Dani said with a smile in her voice. "How's it going? The banquet."

"Fine, I guess. Dad almost told everyone you're coming over for the holidays."

"Am I? Coming over for the holidays?"

Alex's brows drew together. "Is that something you want?"

"I was just asking, babe." Pause. "I'm guessing your mom hasn't said anything."

"She won't. Not here."

"Baby—"

"I know. I know I can't keep avoiding it. But it's the first time we've seen each other in weeks, and tonight's no good either way."

"Okay. Well, I was just calling to check on you. I'm going to hop in the shower. Talk later?"

"Yeah." Alex nodded. "I love you."

"I love you too."

The line went dead.

Alex stared at her phone, mulling over their conversation. Something was off. Probably due to the mention of topics that had always made her too tense. She made a mental note to bring it up again later, just to make sure Dani was okay. They were finally starting to get the hang of not seeing each other almost every day. The last thing they needed was another fight about how important communication was, now more than ever.

Alex lifted her head toward the bar, and her gaze landed on Dom before shifting at the sound of a laughing woman—sandy blonde hair well past her shoulders, tan skin left on display by backless dress. Alex narrowed her gaze, and the pace of her heart slowed.

"VK!"

Her head snapped in Dom's direction, thoughts failing to act with the same sense of urgency.

"Vodka soda?"

"Yeah." She nodded. "Yeah, that's fine."

She slid her phone back into the pocket of her blazer and started toward him, attempting to prevent her mind from slipping further into a segment of her past that was nothing but a persistent cycle of light and pitch-black dark. It was ridiculous anyway. What she'd been thinking.

"Everything good?" Dom asked, frowning slightly.

Alex chuckled as she joined him at the counter. "Yeah. I just thought I saw—" She turned, glancing back to where the woman had been standing, only to realize she was no longer there.

"Saw who, VK?"

"Glass of Prosecco, please."

Alex spun in the opposite direction almost the second the last word had fell on her ears—heart slowed to a stop before taking off, lips parting and closing—because a laugh, blonde hair and tan skin spotted across the room was one thing, but she didn't think she'd get that voice out of her head. Not ever. And she hated how small she suddenly felt, how her head was spinning like she'd been sucked into a whirlwind and spat out the tail-end. Sixteen and breathless, and guilty, every fucking time those blue-green eyes locked on her, and those lips—blush pink, but cherry-flavored—parted and said, "Hi, Alex."

"Frankie?"

Chapter Thirteen

chandon dom

The first time Alex saw Francesca Calvano she probably stared—blatantly, lost-in-this-girl's-existence stared—for a full five minutes.

Alex stood by her locker, Kason rambling along with the general chatter in the dimly lit hallways of Trinity Preparatory, just background noise as something impalpable slithered its way around her throat.

Freckled skin so golden, it wasn't of this dungeon of a school, or this end of the East Coast for that matter. Eyes so indistinctly blue and green, they immediately sent Alex back to memories of a summer spent off the shores of Naxos. Legs that went on forever in a skirt too short to meet Trinity's rules and regulations. And fuck. Her laugh. Alex firmly believed nothing could make the air in this school easier to breathe, but for a second—watching this girl's head tossed back as she laughed, surrounded by about six other amused juniors, despite the fact she was obviously new—the density of the air had shifted. Then, as if she had some sort of sixth sense for feeling uninvited eyes on her—brows knit in question, lips subtly curled in a lingering smile—she looked right at Alex.

And Alex choked.

Rolling over in her bed, Alex opened her eyes and ran one hand along her forehead and into her hair. She hadn't gotten much sleep, but the sense of fatigue coaxing her to stay put probably had more to do with her hangover, if the dryness in her throat and pounding headache was any indication. She threw the duvet back, realizing she'd been dressed in only a black bra and panties, though she lacked any memory of taking off her clothes last night. Or coming back to the penthouse. Her brain had suddenly decided to be unpleasantly vivid about memories from six years ago, and yet, there were holes in her recollection of the last few hours.

Go fucking figure.

She closed her eyes against the tilt of the room as she stood, allowing herself a second to let the dizziness pass. Following a brief and fruitless scan for her phone, she trekked into her en suite to pee and brush her teeth. It took longer than she'd intended since she'd fallen asleep in her makeup—one of the reasons she'd forgone anything but liner and mascara most times. But she always got a little more done up for family events.

When she finally made it downstairs, she had to use one hand as a shield against all the daylight filtering through the floor-to-ceiling windows of her living room. Must've been midday, at least, and the rays of sun beaming across the graying sky signaled nice fall weather. She was too groggy to appreciate it.

Coffee. She needed coffee.

"Slept at all?"

The beat of Alex's heart waned, and she closed her eyes briefly, releasing a heavy breath as a head of tousled jet-black hair and gray eyes became visible over the back of the chair. "Jesus, Ry."

Ryan rolled her eyes. "For someone so obsessed with horror movies, you sure scare easily."

"That's because usually in the movies if someone just pops up in your house, it's probably to stalk or kill you."

"Yeah, I lack the time for one of those and the stomach for the other, so just here to take care of my friend."

Alex frowned as she rounded the sectional to plop down in the first spot Ry's legs weren't stretched out. "What do you mean? What happened with your date?"

"Like I said, I wanted to punch him in the face a lot. I was already on my way home when Dom texted. He wanted to stay, but he spaced on his econometrics worksheet, and it's due by four."

"Yeah, but I wasn't even that drunk."

Ryan raised her brows, pointing to a bottle of Chandon Dom '85 lying on the coffee table. "You were clinging to that when I dragged you to the elevator."

"I don't even like Dom. Fuck, just saying that was annoying."

"Well, you did last night." Ryan laughed. "What happened? I think I know better than anyone how much you have to drink to get that smashed."

Alex did have a pretty good tolerance for someone her size, but her love for that champagne was practically nonexistent. It didn't have anything to do with the taste. She'd spent too many monthly dinners watching her mother sip it like she'd never tasted anything purer. How did she end up getting drunk off a bottle? She remembered Dominic ordering it for himself and a vodka soda for her, then seeing Frankie. She said hi, no more than hi—baring her stunned utterance of Frankie's name—and then she walked away with all the intimidation of the Alex Van Kirk her girlfriend claimed strutted into Brave most days. Realistically, she probably hadn't been daunting at all, because that wasn't their dynamic. Her and Frankie's. But she retreated to a panel like the one she'd been leaned against earlier, desperate for the minutes to speed by and the night to be over so she could finally go upstairs and cal—

"Shit. Have you seen my phone?"

Ryan slipped her hand under a nearby cushion and came up with the black iPhone. "Friends don't let friends drunk dial."

Alex released a chuckle at the phrase she'd said to Ry countless times in the past. "Thanks. I'll be right back." She hopped off the couch and started toward the stairs, ignoring Ryan's comment—something about room service—and unlocked her phone.

Four missed calls.

One unread: *Alex, is everything okay?*

Alex went straight to the Skype app she'd never found a need for until it occurred to her that FaceTime isn't very useful when the other person has an android, and she hit video call on Dani's contact. A few seconds later, Dani—reading glasses framing her face, messy twin bed and posters in the background—popped up on Alex's screen.

"Hey."

"I called you last night," said Dani. "Weren't we going to talk after the banquet?"

"I know, babe. I'm sorry." Alex pushed her bedroom door open and crossed the floor to sit on her bed. "I had too much to drink, and Ryan took my phone so I wouldn't do anything stupid."

"Ryan's there?"

"Yeah." Alex paused, incapable of ignoring the way Dani's expression grew bleaker by the second. "What?"

"She's there, Alex, and you're just...hanging out? Like that?"

"Like what?" Two seconds, a quick glance at her own image on screen, and it registered. "I just woke up and went downstairs. I thought I was alone, so I didn't bother getting dressed."

"You told me she was done letting herself into your apartment."

"She is. Dom asked her to stay because he didn't want to leave me alone."

"Why were you drinking so much anyway?"

"It was just a super stressful night." Alex sighed. "Are we fighting right now?"

Dani took off her glasses, rubbing her eyes. "No."

"Nothing happened. With Ryan. You know that, right?" Alex hated that she even had to ask, because that she did meant there was doubt. Maybe Dani didn't trust her as much as she thought, and how the fuck would they even work if that was a factor?

"I know." Dani shook her head, dropping her glasses in front her. "Of course, I know. I think I just...wish I was there with you right now."

"I wish you were here too. Are you sure there's nothing else going on?"

"Yeah."

Not entirely convinced, but not wanting to push Dani too hard, Alex bobbed her head toward the screen, recognizing Dani's position as being seated at the desk in her dorm. "What are you working on?"

"Cost and Management Accounts."

"I still don't know why you're doing a business minor. You hate the stuff."

"Your legacy is a hotel chain and an NPO. Mine's a bodega. Someday, my dad's going to be too old to keep up with the books, and I want to be able to help."

Literally the sweetest person in the world.

Alex smiled. "I like the way you say bo-de-ga. You never speak Spanish for me, except when I—"

"You don't speak Spanish yourself," Dani cut in before biting her bottom lip.

"Yeah, but my Italian helps me understand some of it."

"*Te amo.*"

Alex laughed. "Now you're insulting me."

Dani leaned forward and rested both elbows on her desk, her eyes glimmering. "By telling you I love you?"

"By being patronizing. But it's okay, because I love you too. So much." She wished she didn't have to rely on sometimes-spotty connectivity to be able to say that to Dani. It's the way it had to be. She didn't hate it any less.

*

Two hours after they'd hung up from their video call, Alex was on the helicopter to Rhode Island without saying a word of it to Dani. Dani would tell her not to come, especially if she believed Alex was only doing it because of their mini argument earlier. And Alex was going for Dani. Mostly, she was going for herself. Last night had her mind in all kinds of knots and doing things like getting blackout drunk on champagne she didn't even like wasn't the way she dealt. The last thing she needed was six years' worth of repressed emotions fighting free of the cage her ribs had served for them. She didn't need feelings she still hadn't processed, or her limbs seizing, heart racing for anyone but Dani. She stopped bleeding for Francesca Calvano a long time ago. A few hours with Dani would do plenty to reassert that.

She put her AirPods in and closed her eyes as she leaned back. Still no sleep—more of a wakeful doze—but she was glad the flight didn't feel any longer than usual. The time between Marcus handing her bag to the chauffeur outside the airport in Providence and Alex stepping out of the black sedan onto the curb of Dani's hill house at RISD felt even shorter.

Alex strode onto the sloped sidewalk and made her way up the entry stairs to the beige two-story house. As she rose her hand to knock on the door, it swung open and Dani's housemate, Asmee, stood beyond the threshold.

Asmee smirked, reaching up to pull her silky black hair off tawny shoulders and into a high ponytail. "It's like something whispered that now would be the perfect time for my run."

Alex scrunched up her face in embarrassment. "I won't be here long enough for that."

Asmee rolled her eyes and reached for the iPod stuck in the waistband of her shorts. "Sure." Then, she stepped past Alex. "She's in her room."

Offering a thank you over her shoulder, Alex entered the house and headed up the stairs. She'd seen enough of the tiny living room and its worn sofa, and the forever messy kitchen that drove her girlfriend nuts. It wasn't as if she'd ever been interested in a tour of anywhere but Dani's room. All one hundred and something square feet. She knocked on the door, patiently listening to the shuffles inside.

The door swung open to reveal Dani—dark hair naturally curly, eyes covered by her glasses, barefoot, dressed in one of Alex's Columbia shirts and raw-edged lounge shorts. Alex smirked, always a bit stuck between her love for seeing Dani in her clothes or getting Dani out of them. But she wasn't exactly there for either.

"What are you doing here?"

Alex shrugged. "I missed you."

Dani breathed a laugh, eyes wide with disbelief as she shook her head.

"You going to invite me in?"

Dani allowed Alex to enter her room. Alex closed the distance to the bed and dropped her bag on it as the door clicked shut behind her. She turned, glancing at the mess of books and papers on the small wooden desk in the corner as Dani took her glasses off and set it on top of the pile. "Still at it, huh?"

Dani took a few steps forward and gripped the collar of Alex's leather jacket. "Come here."

Alex let herself be led, more than willing to eliminate the space between their bodies. Dani wrapped both hands around Alex's neck, and Alex held Dani's hips. She went along with the glide of Dani's lips—slow, sensual—as the mint on her breath got acquainted with whatever Dani had been eating last. Sweet, tangy with the vaguest hint of grape. Dani's fingers threaded through the hair at the back of Alex's neck, and her lips parted, breaths heavier. Dani smiled as their tongues met.

Alex's grip on Dani's hips tightened and she pulled back, opening her eyes. "Babe—" Dani kissed her again and Alex laughed. "I told Asmee—mmm—I told her—we wouldn't do this."

"Why would you tell her that?" She dropped her hands from Alex's neck and replaced them with her lips as she pushed the jacket off Alex's shoulders.

Alex shut her eyes. "Because I didn't—" She swallowed, stumbling as Dani's tongue met her skin. "You have work to do."

"I do. Problem is..." Dani broke off, breath hot against Alex's skin. "My girlfriend showed up unannounced, and we haven't seen each other in weeks." She snapped the button of Alex's jeans open. "And she smells incredible."

Alex caught Dani's hands and took a step back. "I don't want to be a distraction."

"You clearly don't look in the mirror enough."

Dani grabbed Alex's shirt with her free hand, walking backward until she hit the door, their lips close enough to touch. She reached up to take Alex by the back of her neck again. Alex seized her hand and pinned it to the door. Dani's lips twitched with a smile. This was exactly her intention—herself in this position, provoking the fuck out of Alex's dominance. Against her better judgment, Alex leaned in and pressed their bodies closer. "Dani."

"Kiss me."

Strange, how having Dani trapped against a door was such turn on because it made Alex feel in control, and yet, the two words from Dani's mouth had filled her ears like a command. She took Dani's lips between hers, freeing both her hands to wrap them around Dani's waist beneath her shirt. Gentle, like they always started, like she had to make love to every inch of Dani's body before actually getting to it. She let her hands get reacquainted with Dani's body from her hips to the curves below her waist, and she squeezed.

Dani hummed into Alex's mouth, hands tugging impatiently at Alex's shirt. Alex caved and allowed her torso to be exposed down to the navy demi bra she didn't give Dani enough time to appreciate before reaching for Dani's top too.

Fuck.

No bra.

Alex brought her lips back to Dani's and both hands to her breasts. She rolled Dani's nipples, feeling them stiffen as she kissed her way along Dani's jaw to the lobe of her right ear and took it between her teeth.

Dani moaned.

"Are you sure—" Alex dragged her teeth down Dani's neck, and Dani's hand tightened in Alex's hair. "You don't want to—" She nipped at the flesh. "Work on your assignment?"

"Alex, I swear to God…"

"How much did you miss me?" Alex caught Dani's hand as it brushed by her stomach and trapped it against the door again, stressing each word when she repeated, "*How much*?"

They locked eyes, pupils blown, Dani resisting Alex's grip. "Let me show you."

Alex's brows twitched, and she loosened her hold and allowed her hand to be led by Dani's straight to the waistband of Dani's shorts. Alex's shorts. Fuck, it didn't even matter. Quicker breaths escaped her lips, the heat in the room baring down on her back as her fingers slipped into Dani's underwear, still being guided, past Dani's landing strip. Her eyes rolled back, and for a second her mind, every muscle in her body got stuck on how hot, and wet Dani was. She fought against the tingle in her fingers to start teasing circles on Dani's clit when the hand guiding hers disappeared, and she opened her eyes to find Dani's already trained on her. She increased the pressure of her fingers anyway. Just for the hell of it.

"*Alex.*"

Just to hear Dani whimper her name like *that*.

She pulled her hand out and tugged the shorts and underwear down Dani's legs. Dani kicked them off, and when their eyes locked again—Dani's so fucking impatient, breathing too unstable for a proper protest of Alex's pace—Alex slowly got down on both knees. She shifted her gaze to the apex of Dani's thighs, to the slight glisten of her skin before peering up to revel in the anticipation taking over her knitted brows and parted lips. Dani squirmed against the door as Alex leaned in and draped Dani's left leg over her shoulder. "I thought you wanted me to kiss you."

*

Dani snuggled closer to Alex, one hand wrapped around her waist as they cuddled in her twin bed. She was shorter—enough for it to be obvious. She always insisted on being big spoon anyway. It didn't matter. For the first time since last night, Alex could finally get some sleep. Maybe it was the comfort of being in Dani's arms, or both being multiple orgasms into a visit that was only meant to be Alex sitting silently with a book in her lap while Dani focused on finishing her assignment. Maybe it was both.

"I don't like it," Dani mumbled.

Alex slowly opened her eyes, shifting to look at Dani. "Like what?" She brushed the hair away from Dani's face.

"You walking around in nothing but your underwear with Ryan at your place."

"Babe—"

"I know what you said, and I'm probably being unevolved and insecure, and so not sexy right now, but she's seen you naked, Alex. She's had you. Like this. And I can't pretend that doesn't bother me."

"Hey. No one, not even Ryan has had me like this." She paused, waiting for the words to sink in. "But I get it. I have some proving to do."

Dani shook her head. "That's not what I meant. I don't want you to feel like you have to prove yourself to me."

"But I do, so let me. Let me show you that I'm yours. Heart and body."

Alex's phone chimed, and her gaze shifted in acknowledgment, only for a second.

"It's okay. You can get it."

"No."

Dani smiled, pressing her lips against Alex's in a quick kiss before rolling out of her arms and off the bed. "Get your phone. I'm going to go pee, and then we can finish our talk."

"Fine."

Dani stalked the floor for her shorts and top then slipped into them. After a quick smooth of her hair, she opened the door and closed it behind her. Alex laughed. If anyone had gotten home in the last hour or so, no amount of hair fixing would make her and Dani's actions any less obvious. The walls were way too thin, and Dani wasn't exactly quiet.

She reached over the edge of the bed and took her phone from the front pocket of her bag. A couple notifications from Tumblr and Instagram and a text from an unusual number. Forehead creased, she unlocked it and went straight to her messages.

The air slowly left her lungs, the way it always did.

555-810-5642: Hey, it's Frankie. You can totally say no to this, considering... But do you want to grab coffee sometime?

Chapter Fourteen

marocchino

Alex didn't say yes to Frankie's coffee invite, though maybe, somewhere deep inside, she wanted to. It was Frankie after all, and Alex didn't want to admit it, but Frankie had always affected her in ways that made her feel more out of control than anyone she'd ever known. There were plenty of things Frankie made her feel. So, she'd stared at the message and she let the words set in, and when Dani reentered her room, questioning whatever she'd seen on Alex's face, Alex hit delete and told her girlfriend everything was fine.

Everything *was* fine.

It didn't matter that sometimes Alex caught herself wondering why Frankie had even been at the banquet that night or how long she'd been home—if she was only back for a while, or forever.

"Marocchino." Brendan grinned, having completely butchered the pronunciation, but looking like he'd never been prouder all the same.

Alex accepted the cup and mumbled a quick thank you as she grabbed a few napkins from the nearby rack and started for the door.

Brave hadn't changed much. Still warm, comfy. The coffee and strudels were still great. Yet, something about hanging out in her favorite corner booth didn't feel quite the same. It was even kind of distracting now. No matter what, she'd find herself glancing up only to be disappointed by the fact that Dani wouldn't be working the floor, or counter, or even coming in for a shift anytime soon. She had a script to work on anyway.

With her free hand, she pulled up the collars of her jacket and braced herself for the recent drop in temperature. Fall. A precursor to the torture of a New York winter. Twenty-one years and she still wasn't used to the cold. Though it was her favorite time of year, she'd never acquired the taste for a white Christmas, never found it as romantic as people liked to think. The slick and smell of the snow, gathering all the grime and scum in the city only to leave it in the air for weeks.

She pushed the door open before briefly dropping her gaze as she dug into her pocket for her key fob. A hand wrapped around her forearm and pulled her back. Her head snapped up and she tightened her grip on the coffee cup. It was a bit delayed—it should've reacted to Alex being grabbed out of nowhere—but her heart didn't stop until her eyes locked with a pair of bluish-green. She blinked, swallowing. If this was fate, she hated the concept even more.

Frankie released her arm and took a step back. "I didn't mean to scare you, but you were about five seconds from crashing into a mini-suit and getting drenched in three different juice blends."

"Thanks." Alex scanned Frankie from her long, blonde hair to the pink dusk hoody, white shorts and sneakers she was wearing. Another blast from the past Alex didn't need. Frankie dressed for soccer practice, and Alex trying to keep the drool off her chin when she stared. A more advanced model, clearly still in love with the sport.

"So, it was me then," Frankie said.

Alex gaped. "What?"

"It's not that you didn't want to go have coffee. You just didn't want to have it with me."

Alex sighed. "Frankie..."

"Don't." Frankie shook her head, smiling a bit. "It's fine. Really."

Another thing Alex didn't want to admit—she knew Frankie too well to believe her lips when her eyes, her demeanor, said something else. A genuine smile from Francesca Calvano *always* reached her eyes. So much, she could light a whole room with her laugh. Alex's chest still had scars from the sparks, and the flames. "I'm sorry." She felt like she was apologizing for a lot more than an unanswered text from three weeks ago, but those two words would never be enough. Not even close.

"Alex." Frankie paused. Her lips parted then closed almost instantly, and Alex guessed she was thinking about more than the text too. Another fabricated smile. "See you around, okay?"

"Frankie, wait." Alex glanced down at where both their hands were now linked, and something remotely familiar ran through her, something like fire and ice. She released her grip on Frankie and raked a hand through her own hair, forcing down all the conflicting emotions wracking free of their cage. "Let me uh—Is it too late? To say yes, I mean."

For a moment, neither of them said anything, merely stood in the middle of a busy Manhattan curb with the buzz of the city around—honking horns and loud chatter, the slow thud of Alex's heart, oceans of bluish-green crashing into brown... And something Alex never had to do before. Wonder what Frankie was thinking. But this wasn't before. This wasn't Trinity. This was a few steps short of Brave and four years into the future. Things were different. Sort of.

"I don't know," Frankie answered. "Are you saying yes, Alex?"

Alex nodded. "I am."

*

Alex leaned against her parked car across the street from Brave, watching the door for Frankie to reemerge. She'd agreed to coffee, but she wasn't about to sit across a table in the café she'd grown even more sentimental about over the last few months with a girl she used to be *something* with. Dani would hate it. Dani would hate the idea of her spending time with Frankie period. But this was... Alex wasn't sure what it was. She just had to do it. Maybe it was guilt, or maybe she was curious about what Frankie had been up to all these years, and this was what old friends did. They grabbed coffee and they caught up, right?

The wooden-framed, glass door of the café opened, and Frankie emerged carrying a cup and paper bag. Once she'd gotten to the edge of the curb, she stopped—eyes locked on Alex for a second—before she checked up and down the busy street. It had always been difficult to cross there, but many a seasoned New Yorker timed it well enough to make a quick dash across. California born and bred, Frankie had only lived in Manhattan for two years. Still, she'd always been freakishly fast at adapting. When she made it across, she stopped in front of Alex—enough to not get hit by cars zooming by, but not enough to affect Alex's ability to think straight. Before, Frankie would always stand a little too close.

"So where are we going?" she asked.

Alex glanced at their surroundings. Early afternoon was too loud for a walk. "I didn't really think about it, to be honest."

"You know there's a perfectly good dining area inside the café."

"I know."

Frankie held her reply, watching Alex like she used to whenever there was more than Alex was saying but asking would get her nowhere. "Drive me home."

Alex narrowed her eyes.

"I take it this is your car." Frankie bobbed her head toward the black Maserati Alex still leaned against. "I live on the Upper West Side. West 60th."

The Van Kirk had always been West 53rd. There were few reasons for Alex say no. She tried the next best thing. "Didn't you drive here?"

"My teammate dropped me off. I was going to catch an Uber home."

"Teammate?"

"Let's talk about it in the car. I know how much you hate the temperature drops this time of year."

No point arguing. Alex did hate the cold, and she'd already mentally agreed to Frankie's suggestion. It wasn't standard for a coffee date—a twenty-minute drive—but it was probably best that was all the time they had. She pressed the unlock button on her key fob and they both got into her car. Alex started the engine and hit shuffle on her music app once her phone paired with the radio. She adjusted the volume to suit the ambience of ØRKA and silently observed until Frankie's seatbelt was secured across her chest, paper bag and marocchino tight in her grip. When Frankie's eyes met hers, Alex faced the street and drove out of the parking space.

Something awkward, tense, settled over them. Of all the things they'd been since the day they laid eyes on each other six years ago, neither awkward nor tense fit.

Intense.

Positively intense.

But never tense.

"I play for Sky Blue FC now," Frankie spoke. Maybe she sensed that Alex didn't know how to ease the tension. So, of course, she'd done it instead. Always wanting to make things easier than Alex deserved, only to make them more difficult in the end.

Alex glanced at her before looking back at the road. "What about LA?"

Frankie shrugged. "I missed my parents. I'd see my mom sometimes whenever she had layovers, but dad still thinks the restaurant here needs him more, so I'd hardly ever see him. And I never saw much of them to begin with, but I don't know. No matter how messy we were sometimes, home feels less like home without them, you know?"

Alex did know. It's why she'd travelled, but never left New York for good, no matter how much she hated the city sometimes. She couldn't imagine living somewhere that didn't have breakfast with her dad or problematic dinners with her mother. Acknowledging that would resurrect sentiments of kindred and vulnerability, even more than it had already, so she didn't say anything of it. "I always knew you'd go pro."

"You could've too," Frankie answered. "You were definitely good enough."

"You always thought I was better than I actually was."

"I just saw things in you that you refused to see in yourself."

The words hit Alex in a way that made her reach for her coffee and take a sip. She didn't know what to make of them, but no question they were laced with something unrelated to soccer. Before her mind went chasing answers, she carefully placed her cup back in the holder and asked, "How long have you been back?"

"Just this season. I finished my undergrad in PT first."

Again, Alex forced her mind not to wander. She was beginning to remember why she didn't want to do this, why she'd disappeared before Frankie had even properly greeted her at the banquet. Everything provoked a memory. And that was the last thing she needed right now. If she let Frankie back in, getting wasted on a bottle of Chandon Dom and waking up with a hangover would be the least of her worries.

"Maybe someday I'll pursue it further," Frankie went on. "Right now, I kind of just want to play soccer."

"I get that." Alex kept her gaze steady, ignoring Frankie's eyes on her. She figured it was partly in her head anyway. Francesca Calvano was too used to being looked at to do much looking herself. It was natural. She was gorgeous and the most confident person Alex had ever known without being arrogant. It made her too easy to like, to fall for. But that was everyone else's problem. She directed Alex to a spot on a block of reserved ones, and Alex parked but kept the engine running.

"That's me. When I'm not in Jersey anyway." Frankie angled her head to point up at an apartment on the other side of the street. Modern structure, large glass windows, most likely a doorman and lots of luxury amenities.

Alex nodded. "It's nice."

"Yeah."

Frankie unbuckled her seatbelt but lingered, outwardly battling with getting out or staying put. For the first time since they'd locked eyes at Brave, Alex didn't look away, no matter how much the invisible pressure on her chest weighed more by the second.

"Do you want to come up?"

The air got thicker. "I uh...I was headed home to finish a script. I should probably just do that."

Frankie nodded, again undoubtedly knowing there was more, but not pushing. "What's it about? Your script."

"A love story."

"Right." Frankie glanced up. Down. Back to Alex's eyes. "Do they end up together?"

Alex shook her head. "I don't know. I never really know."

"I hope you figure it out," answered Frankie. The mild crunch of paper drew Alex's attention as Frankie picked up her bag from Brave and grasped the handle of the door. One leg out, she glanced back at Alex. "See you, Van Kirk." Her lips didn't twitch quite the same when she said it, there was no edge to her voice, but as the door slammed shut behind her, Alex spiraled into a memory that had come too fast to fight.

It was Alex's birthday.

Her sweet sixteen.

The ballroom was filled with associates of her parents and half of Trinity's student population. Sure, she played soccer, but it was only JV, and she *was* the sophomore rep for the student body, so almost everyone knew her name. But she also happened to be best friends with the vice captain of the basketball team and dating an upperclassman.

It was Alex's sixteenth birthday.

So, there were more than a hundred over-dressed strangers in the ballroom of The Van Kirk, talking and dancing, eating and drinking, and probably wondering where the fuck the birthday girl was. Sitting on the edge the pool, ruining the least extravagant of the dozen dresses her mother had picked for her, fingers busy with the *4 Pics-1 Word* game on her phone.

"The party's inside, you know."

A current passed through Alex's chest to settle in her stomach and her fingers went still before she'd completed the word it had taken her the last five minutes to figure out was "overkill." She tuned in to the click of heels as a wave of chlorine and something sweet, like lavender, laced her next breath. The clicks paused. The moment dragged. Alex shifted just in time to see Francesca sit so close their shoulders were touching. It was ordinary. She and Francesca weren't exactly friends. They were both on the soccer team—JV and varsity, but same team nonetheless. Plenty of girls sat this close all the time. On the other hand, they'd played together all season and had barely even acknowledged each other, so it *was* strange. Actually, it was Francesca who'd never noticed Alex. Alex had noticed Francesca plenty. She hadn't been able to stop since that day in the hallway and having her this close was making all the conflicting feelings Alex had been having for the last eight months a million times worse.

"I mean"—Francesca moved her feet, making ripples in the water—"it is your birthday. You can totally cry if you want to. Although"—she studied Alex—"I would hate it if you did."

Alex's heartbeat slowed, and she parted her lips as a breath made its way out almost reluctantly. "I'm not going to cry."

"Sure?"

Alex nodded.

Francesca held her gaze a few moments longer, pinning her down, making it harder to breathe or think. And then she looked away. "Why aren't you inside?"

"I don't like talking to strangers."

"Does that mean I'm bothering you?"

No.

Francesca wasn't bothering her. At all. She wasn't sure why Francesca was sitting there, talking to her, why she was even at her birthday when they'd barely even spoken. Her head spun. Her heart kept racing and slowing down, and her stomach was in knots she didn't think would ever unravel. Maybe something in her did want to be left alone, especially by Francesca Calvano, but she wasn't being a bother.

"Alex?"

Alex found Francesca's greenish-blue eyes trained on her again, and for some reason, her mind got stuck on the way she said her name. All the soccer players kind of went by their last names. The only time Francesca had even spoken to Alex, in practice last fall, when the ball had rolled to a stop right at Alex's feet and Francesca asked her to pass it, she'd called her "Van Kirk." And plenty of people called her Alex, but somehow—sitting by the pool, isolated from a party full of people, the round bulbs nearby subtly lighting the night—coming from this girl, "Alex" felt strangely intimate.

"I don't know," Alex muttered.

Francesca smiled, the light glinting in her pupils. "You don't know if I'm bothering you?"

"I don't."

Francesca brushed a lock of hair behind Alex's right ear. Goose bumps rose on Alex's skin, and her body went still. Francesca parted her lips, holding her hand and gaze steady. "I think I'd rather you be sure. Happy birthday." She retracted her hand, and Alex's gaze followed as she stood and picked up her heels. "See you, Van Kirk."

As the memory faded, Alex closed her eyes, running her free hand through her hair, the other tightened around her steering wheel. No matter how much she wished she'd be able to, she was beginning to realize that this—the memories, emotional riot in her chest and veins—wasn't something she'd be able to avoid. Maybe that was supposed to happen when someone who used to be important to a person came back into their life. Not that a ride home meant Frankie was back in Alex's, but there was no rejecting that Frankie had been vital to Alex's happiness and pain once. If they were keeping score, Alex had hurt Frankie a lot more anyway. Maybe that's the reason, despite knowing how damaging revisiting her past could be to the present, this time when Alex's phone vibrated with texts, she read them through a new lens.

> *424-810-5642: It was nice seeing you and actually being able to talk. If you're up for it, I'd like to do it again. Maybe lunch since coffee worked out so great.*

Alex breathed a laugh, and her phone vibrated again.

> *424-810-5642: No pressure though. You don't even have to reply. Unless you're sure.*

Frankie had never pushed her, never made her do anything unless she was certain it was what she wanted. It made for a lot of visual exchanges and mental interrogations between them that almost always ended in *yes*. Alex glanced toward the loft to see the silhouette of a woman standing by a window upstairs. The view was somewhat obscure with the distance between them, but there was no question it was Frankie.

There were things that were different about her, less forward than the Frankie who used to sit too close without Alex's permission, knowing what it did to her. Strangely enough, there was something more vulnerable about her now too. Still confident, albeit less invincible. Alex wondered how much the way things had been and ended between them had to do with that. So, it was guilt that caused her fingers to move across the screen again, this time adding Frankie's contact instead of deleting it. This time replying: *Yes*.

It was guilt.

It was also something else.

Something that felt agonizingly close to holding on to someone she'd never let go in the first place.

Chapter Fifteen

iced coffee

Alex tried to remember exactly how it happened last time. Francesca Calvano came out of nowhere—new transfer from Los Angeles, showed up at Trinity for her junior year because her father was expanding his restaurant franchise—and locking eyes with her was all it had taken to contort Alex into shapes she still hadn't undone.

It had been months. Months of Alex stealing glances at the new girl in the hallways, cafeteria, and on the soccer field. She'd even found that out there, she had next to no restraint. Her eyes always found Frankie's legs during quad stretches, or the light freckles on the bridge of her nose whenever the beams of the sun hit just right, or after practice, especially after practice when she'd pull her jersey over her head before they'd even gotten to the locker room—beads of sweat rolling down her tan neck and abs, the middle of her chest, disappearing into her sports bra, sucking all the air from Alex's lungs—as Coach Matthews lectured her for the hundredth time about *modesty*. Frankie would laugh, unknowingly adding to Alex's asphyxia, because she went to Trinity Preparatory now but "Sanctity, Purity, Honor" *wasn't* her creed. She was still so Californian and free and achingly beautiful for absolutely all of it.

Alex wanted to think her birthday had changed everything, the moment by the pool, Francesca's eyes not so blue then—green, greener than Alex had ever seen them—when she replied, "I'd rather you be sure." But she'd been unable to stop thinking about Francesca for a while. She didn't know what she was meant to be sure about. She didn't know why Francesca would hate it if she cried, or why she liked it that Francesca had called her Alex instead of Van Kirk when they were alone. Well, she did know. She just *couldn't* know. Even when...

Alex leaned back in the pivot chair by the desk in her bedroom, books open and unattended as she barely registered Kason mumbling over his worksheet. She kept her gaze locked on her phone, more than a little distracted, but not having the will to do anything about it.

When Francesca had texted her the Monday after her birthday, the first thing she wondered was how Francesca had gotten her number, then why she'd even wanted it to begin with. After the fifth unanswered text in a twenty-minute span, when Francesca asked, *"Are you seriously going to leave me on read? Because I don't think my ego can take that,"* Alex caved, inevitably smiling as she answered with an extremely shy, *"Hi."* They'd been texting ever since. Early morning. Late at night when they were supposed to be sleeping. Sometimes between classes. They still hadn't spoken face-to-face, but Alex didn't mind. It was better this way.

> *Francesca: I know it's barely ended, but I already miss soccer season.*

> *Alex: You're obsessed.*

> *Francesca: Maybe a little. But there are other things I miss about it. Besides playing.*

> *Alex's heartbeat strengthened.*

> *Alex: Like what?*

> *Francesca: The other girls on the team, I guess. It's different during off-season.*

Alex released a breath. Relief. Disappointment. And then her phone vibrated again.

> *Francesca: Where do you disappear to after school these days anyway?*

It still wasn't the answer that would probably make her equally exhilarated and terrified. It wasn't Francesca saying Alex was what she missed about soccer season, but it also kind of, maybe just a little, feel like it was. She began typing again. How ridiculous. They'd barely even spoken. Of course Francesca didn't miss her.

Alex: Just other clubs and stuff.

Francesca: Stuff like hanging out with your boyfriend?

Kason put his hand on Alex's shoulder, and she immediately hit the power button to lock the screen of her phone. There was nothing to hide. Her talks with Francesca were just... private. She lifted her gaze to see Kason standing over her—his dark brows furrowed, hazel eyes shifting from her phone in clear suspicion. "Aren't we doing homework?"

"We are."

Kason glanced at the Chemistry worksheet on Alex's desk, the only response on it so far being her name.

"Okay." Alex set her phone on the glass surface as she visibly considered Kason. "I'm sorry. I'm a little distracted." She picked up her pen. "Try again?"

Kason regarded her—eyes roaming her face—and then he bent and pressed his lips against hers. Alex let him kiss her, even leaning into it as she brought one hand to the back of his head, his buzzcut hair soft in her palm now that it had lost the prickle of a fresh cut. His tongue slipped between her lips, and the chair steadied under the weight of both his hands on the arms. Too fast. Too wet. Always too fast and wet. It was okay though. Kason had never been the best kisser, but his athletic build and biracial features made him handsome in a way that was patent. He was focused. Driven. Pretentious. Her mom loved him.

He took her hands and pulled her up from the chair. Maybe if she took the lead, showed him how she wanted to be kissed, her body might catch up to the slight bulge between his legs pressing against her. But his body wasn't listening to hers. Not even a little bit.

Her phone vibrated. She pulled her lips away from his and spun toward her desk before her mind even had time to consent.

Kason huffed. "Seriously?"

"Just give me a second."

"Whatever."

Alex picked up her phone.

Francesca: Is that not something we talk about?

Alex tilted her head for a moment, and then she realized she'd probably taken too long to reply. Now Francesca thought she didn't want to talk about Kason. She didn't. Francesca was the last person she wanted to talk to about him. She replied anyway.

Alex: No. That's not it. I just have some homework I should be working on. Chem ☹

Francesca: I'm awesome at Chem.

Alex laughed, then another text appeared in the thread and her lips wired shut.

Francesca: Taking three AP sciences next year.

Alex: Wait. Seriously?

Francesca: Yeah. I can help. If you want me to.

Though Alex was completely capable of doing her worksheet alone, and she had Kason if she needed help, she wanted to say yes to Francesca anyway. All she'd been wanting was to say yes to this completely unanticipated... friendship? But there was something else too, something dark and enchanting, and there was no saying yes to one without accepting the other. So, instead, she brought her fingers back to the screen, and she typed: *Maybe next time.*

"Alex?"

Dani's voice snapped Alex out of her recollection, and she tuned in to now—not Trinity, not Frankie, not five years ago. This supermarket, her girlfriend, two days before Thanksgiving. She tightened her grip on the shopping cart as if to anchor herself to the present. "Sorry. I'm a little distracted."

Dani stepped away from the spices and dropped a bottle of nutmeg into the cart as she stopped next to Alex. "What's on your mind?"

"The past." True, though incredibly cryptic. The way Dani drew her brows together gave away as much. Alex neglected to elaborate anyway. Dani had only gotten back yesterday, and she'd been home to her parents' first. It was a few hours ago before Alex had even gotten a chance to see her, and now they were in a supermarket shopping for the Ramírez's Thanksgiving grocery list. It was so domesticated, especially for someone who didn't even know what it was like to buy her own groceries, but it also felt good. It felt good to have Dani back next to her, and Alex didn't want to ruin that by saying more. She leaned in and slowly brought her lips to Dani's. For a second, she held them there, letting the warmth fill her chest. "I love you."

Her declaration had never been more random. It was so fucking random because they'd been standing in the spices aisle for a while, thanks to Dani's insistence on having everything her and her mom would need to get the sweet potato pudding just right, and yes, Alex *was* distracted. She'd been distracted for weeks, but right now all she could think about was how in love with Dani she was.

Dani brought one hand to Alex's cheek, concerned eyes scanning her face. "Baby, is everything okay?"

Alex nodded. "Just remember that." The second the words left her lips, she hated how much they echoed like preemptive reassurance. Like an in case. She was with Dani and intended to keep it that way, but all this remembering how she used to feel about Frankie had her more twisted up than she wanted to admit even to herself. And it wasn't like she still felt all those things for Frankie, but now that she was back in New York, now that they'd started texting again, it was like danger in her veins, sniffing through her blood stream. Whenever it found her heart and dug its claws in, bleeding was inevitable.

*

"Are you going to talk to me about it?" Dani asked.

Alex peeped up, having spent the last few feet trailing the carpeted floors of The Van Kirk—through the lobby, the elevator, almost all the way to her penthouse—and locked eyes with Dani's. She'd been excessively quiet all afternoon, dragged her feet through their trip at the supermarket, focused on the road the whole drive back to Manhattan. Even Dani's parents noticed something was off. They'd revealed as much when they'd both wrapped her in a hug less than an hour ago, and Lucia offered a tender, "Feel better, mija."

Alex sighed, dragging the hand not holding Dani's through her hair. "It's nothing."

Dani nodded, the slight purse to her lips telling Alex that may not have been the answer she wanted, but maybe she was expecting it anyway. Alex wished she had another one. She wished she was able to come out and tell Dani everything about her past with Frankie, and how now that Frankie was back, all her buried emotions about the last three years of high school were revolting inside her. She wanted to tell Dani how they'd started talking again—nothing too deep, *how are you, how was your day, was practice good*—but in conjunction with what all those simple words used to mean for them, it was almost taxing to remind herself the distinction between then and now. Maybe that was precisely why she shouldn't have kept talking to Frankie, but—with the banquet, running into her outside of Brave, driving her home, the memories—

Alex had ripped the stitches out of wounds she'd sewn up ages ago, only to realize the damn the things had refused to heal. Not just hers. Frankie's too apparently. And Alex didn't know how to hurt her any more than she had before. So, she couldn't stop. If she was being honest, she didn't want to. It didn't mean she loved Dani any less. As if she could love Dani any less.

They got to the door of the penthouse, and Alex took out her key to offer it to Dani. It had become something of a habit since their date to MoMA and there was a part of Alex that wanted to hand that key to Dani, never having to claim it back. But it was too soon to even consider. No matter how many months Alex had spent in her denial before, they'd only been together for just about three.

Back against the door, Dani accepted the key. She lowered her gaze as she ran her fingers over it. "Tell me I have nothing to worry about."

Alex frowned as she brought her hand under Dani's chin and forced their eyes to meet. "What do you mean?"

"Something's wrong. I wasn't sure before." She shook her head. "Maybe I just missed you, or maybe you were just being Alex, but now that I'm back...I can feel it. And this? The not talking, the emotional distance, it's exactly how it happened w—"

Alex dropped her hand, closing her eyes. "You really think I'd cheat on you?"

"That's not what I'm saying."

"Then what are you saying, Dani?" Her eyes opened again. "Because I know I'm not all that but holding me to the standard of your cheating ex"—she scoffed—"kind of stings."

"That's not fair." As if Dani could sense Alex forcing away all the emotions she should be letting through—the ones she didn't know how to deal with—and giving way to an anger that was too close to the surface, Dani brought one hand to Alex's cheek. "I wasn't comparing you to her. Not intentionally. I just meant, the wondering, it makes me insecure, okay?" She took a step closer, shifting her hand to the back of Alex's neck—all honesty and patience—and a sense of calm settled over her, diffusing everything else. "Sometimes, it still feels like this isn't real yet," Dani said softly. "And we're still at Brave, me making coffee and you writing in your corner booth, and I'm still waiting for you."

Alex got it. In a way, it's how anyone she'd ever gotten close to felt about her. Like no matter how much things had changed between them, she'd always be too Alex to fully let anyone in. Always so set on going it alone. It didn't always feel that way, but when the emotional distance hit, she tended to drift so far, any semblance of closeness seemed practically illusory. She'd been through it with Dom, Ry, Frankie. Even her dad. Clearly, being with Dani hadn't made her any better in that regard.

"It's real." Even with how complex everything else seemed, saying that felt simple enough.

True. Pure. Brave. Just like her girl.

She pressed their lips together in a slow but brief kiss, keeping her eyes closed when she mumbled the words again. "It's real, Dani. And you're right. There is something, but I don't want it to affect us if I can deal with it alone. I just need to do that in a better way than I have been."

"Baby, you don't have to do anything alone. I want to help."

"But I don't think you can." Alex opened her eyes in time to catch the disappointment flash in Dani's. "I'll tell you about it. Everything. But I'm not ready." They weren't ready. "Is that okay?"

"Of course." Dani nodded. She closed her eyes and wrapped both hands around Alex's neck before joining their lips in another kiss. Longer, languid, both moving their lips against the other's like they hadn't just spent the last month apart. It was one of Alex's favorite things about their relationship. One minute they'd be so heated they were trying to rip each other's clothes off, next they were so content—even after an argument, sometimes especially after an argument—that they'd kiss like they had forever. Both made her fall more each time.

Dani eased out of the kiss, lips enclosing Alex's lower then top lip before she broke it completely. "I do iced coffee, you do the popcorn, and then we fight over the movie?"

By fight over the movie, she meant Alex would probably pick something scary, because anything too sweet and Dani would cry, which would lead to both of them crying, and then laughing about it, then making out, because Dani's dimples still made Alex weak. But Dani would pout, and whine "Babe, you know horror makes me weird about shadows at night," and they'd wind up doing all that anyway. It was okay though, because some of their best kisses tasted like tears, and the movies that made Alex cry always turned out to be amazing.

She brushed her nose against Dani's. "Sounds perfect."

Dani pecked her on the lips then turned to open the door.

Alex slipped out of her shoes and started on her jacket as she took a few steps through the entry way. "Should we take a shower first?"

"I'm never going to get you back down those stairs if we get into your shower together."

"Me?" Alex glanced back at Dani, chuckling. "Sure, babe." Halfway to the kitchen, she felt Dani's arms snake around her waist.

Dani's lips parted, breath hot against Alex's ear. "Fine. Me. You're just..." Dani slipped one hand under Alex's top and flattened her palm against her tensing stomach. "Kind of irresistible with your clothes off."

"Just with my clothes off?" Alex shifted to look at Dani over her shoulder.

Dani laughed, shaking her head. "All the time."

"Even when I'm all broody and broken."

"Especially then."

Alex brushed her lips against Dani's and placed her hands on her hips. Dani took Alex's bottom lip between hers.

Someone cleared their throat, and that particular action wasn't something Alex imagined to be distinct, but something about it rattled so Annalise Van Kirk, there were inches between Alex and Dani before she'd even considered stepping back. Her gaze snapped up and her forehead creased. It *was* her mother. Almost nine o'clock at night, here in the penthouse, in a pristine designer skirt-suit tailored especially for her. She held Alex in place with her icy blue eyes, pushing Alex's heart rate higher—not like Dani did, or even Frankie, nothing like that. Alex's head pounded from an instant headache.

Her mother knew. She'd known for months—something Alex had discerned from all her not-so-subtle changes in behavior. No more monthly dinners or random texts. Not even a call. The only time they'd even seen each other was at events they'd been required to attend as a family, and Annalise Van Kirk would die before addressing her daughter's non-heterosexual tendencies in public.

She glanced at Dani, her expression harder somehow. Dark hair framing her clenched jaw, lips thin as a line. "You must be the girl Alexandria has been flying off to see so often. Daniela, is it?"

Chapter Sixteen

vienna

The first time Alex's mom came home late, as always, and opened Alex's door without a single knock, as always, Kason was half on top of her, hands low on her hips, lips seconds away from making her his the only way he knew how. The look of genuine shock on her mom's face was priceless, but then she smiled—almost bashfully—apologized, and closed the door.

(Teens will be teens.)

The first time Frankie came to the penthouse...

Was the last.

Alex sneezed, pausing at the foot of the stairs to let the shiver pass through her body. Two days ago, when she'd first started sneezing at lunch in the courtyard, Dom had carefully pulled his turkey sandwich and Gatorade away and scrunched up his face as he glared at her. "I love you and everything, but you're definitely going to stay away from me with that."

Alex had rolled her eyes, silently wishing away the migraine she'd had all day. "I'm not sick."

"Right. I have a game on Friday, so I seriously can't afford to be *not sick* too, VK."

"You're not the only one with a game coming up. Mine's Saturday. But it doesn't matter. Neither of us will miss our games, because I'm not sick."

(Alex was definitely sick.)

She dragged her feet through the living room and across the open floor plan to the kitchen. Her grandparents' voices stirred in her mind, reverberating the importance of lots of fluids in her recovery, and since she was trying to fight off the flu in the next three days, it was no time to be stubborn. As she opened the fridge, the doorbell rang. She paused, huffing as she turned and started toward the entryway of the penthouse. She just wanted to drink her juice and crash. She didn't have the patience for whoever had decided it was a good time to casually drop in.

She pulled the door open, and all her internal rambling subsided as her eyes took in the person outside—blonde hair caught in a tight ponytail, eyes fixed with curiosity, royal blue Doves pinny to match her striped white shorts and slides. She always wore slides after practice. Except, it was barely three, so practice wasn't even close to being over.

"I would've brought you some stuff." Frankie frowned as she glanced down at the marked cup of Vienna in her grip. "For your cold, I mean. But I ran into Dom and he told me he already made you go to the pharmacy and get everything you need."

"He did." Alex shook her head. "Frankie, what are you doing here?"

"I wanted to make sure you're okay. I mean, you're not, but..." She let the rest hang in the silence.

Alex stared at her. "You never skip practice."

"You're never sick."

Was it that simple? Alex wasn't feeling well, so instead of picking up the phone and texting her, Frankie had shown up on Alex's doorstep? Plenty of the girls on the team had missed practice for no other reason but that they didn't feel like being present one day or another, but Frankie's dedication was unmatched.

She took a hesitant step closer—one was all she needed—and Alex's pulse picked up as Frankie's fingers brushed her face. "You look pale."

Alex's eyes shut. She dragged in a slow breath. "Frankie..."

"I won't. I want to—God, I really want to, Alex—but not if it means another two weeks of us not speaking."

Not talking didn't sound so great to Alex either, and as much as she wished Frankie was wrong, she wasn't sure shutting herself behind her castle-high walls wasn't exactly what she'd do this time too.

She sighed. "I'm contagious anyway."

It was a weak retort, but Frankie just laughed, forcing Alex's eyes open, because she couldn't not look at Frankie when she laughed—eyes bright, pink lips stretched with something so authentic, lighting, setting fire to all the darkest places inside Alex's chest.

"As if I'm here because I give a damn how contagious you are."

Frankie's hand still on Alex's cheek, their proximity, acknowledging that Frankie just blatantly confessed to wanting to kiss Alex again, smiling about it... filled Alex with something other than anxiety. She almost felt brave enough to lean in, give her mind newer, more recent memories of Frankie's kiss. Instead, she pulled her gaze from Frankie's lips—not missing the lump that slid down her throat—and met her eyes. "I'd invite you in, but I should get some rest if I want to play on Saturday."

Frankie nodded.

"Unless...you want to stay?" The words left Alex's mouth in the most passive way. All she could do was hear herself say them.

"Are you asking me to take a nap with you, Van Kirk?"

"Alex."

Frankie nipped her bottom lip, her eyes glinting. "Alex."

The edge to her voice sent something foreign through Alex's veins, spiraling her mind to over a month ago—her body hot and cold under Frankie's, back to a wall, faced with something, someone she was too afraid to want. Someone she *couldn't* want.

Almost as if she'd read Alex's mind, Frankie broke eye contact, not even brushing shoulders when she stepped past Alex, into the penthouse. "I'll stay until you fall asleep. Then I'll let myself out, okay?"

"Okay."

There were the things that were expected of a normal, straight Alexandria Van Kirk. This wasn't one of them.

When Alex woke up from her nap, it was—she checked her phone—9:17 p.m., and Frankie was still curled up in her bed, not an inch of her skin in contact with Alex's. A part of her wondered anyway, what it would be like if they could just...

She shifted her gaze away from the out-of-place strands of hair screaming that she sweep them back from Frankie's face, the way Frankie slept with her lips slightly parted, so now there were two puddles of drool on Alex's bed, instead of the usual one.

The second thing Alex noticed was that her door, which she'd always kept closed whether alone or not, was now open as far as its hinges would allow. So her mother was home. Her chest heaved in slow but shallow breaths, and she tried to remind herself that they were just sleeping. Girls did that all the time. Didn't they?

It didn't help. It didn't help the imaginary constrictor snaking its way around her neck feel any less palpable, or make her feel any less guilty, or wrong.

She dragged herself out of bed and toward the stairs. The only way she would stop her mind from dredging up all the worst possible assumptions her mother had made was to see her and prove to herself that she had no reason to freak out. The second she set foot in the living room, her mother stood from the couch, blue eyes sharp with disappointment, something familiar, but new when directed at Alex, in the shape of her lips. Something like disgust.

"Alexandria, have you lost your mind?"

Alex's eyes darted around the living room. In a second, everything from confusion to rage to shame was rioting inside her. "Mom, what are you talking about?"

"You know very well what I'm talking about."

"No, I don't." Alex clenched her jaw, nails digging into her palms, eyes stinging with the imminence of tears that would never fall. Not in front of her mother. Never in front of her mother. "If you have something to say, just say it."

"I've said what I needed to say. Now, ask the girl in your bed to leave, or I will," she demanded.

Annalise Van Kirk didn't have any other way of speaking. Not really. Her word was final. No rebuttals. Zero explanations. Black and white. Never grey. So, Alex did what she was meant to. She woke Frankie and masked everything beneath the surface when she asked her to leave. When she unwrapped a new razor less than ten minutes later and almost meticulously marked her skin, taking some obscure comfort in watching the red stain the side of her bathtub, she didn't cry. And then she washed the blood away, and all she could do was cry, until she couldn't breathe.

It wasn't the first panic attack she'd had, but it was the first time she'd called Dom and told him everything only a best friend would already know.

Alex's mind was reeling. Of all her memories of her feelings for Frankie and her mother's feelings toward things like this, the one thing she'd always been glad for was that the two had never come face-to-face. That night, her mom *had* seen Frankie in her bed, but with her sleeping and Alex asking her to leave, they'd never spoken. And for as long as Frankie never came to the penthouse again, they never would. Her mother didn't go to her soccer games, and the co-curriculars she did bother to support weren't ones Frankie did too. So maybe, there had been points where her mother's proclivity to work, work, work had been convenient.

A physical meeting of her feelings for a girl she cared about in more than platonic ways, that girl and her mother was possibly Alex's worst nightmare. She swallowed the lump in her throat, stepping forward the second Dani's lips parted to say, "You must be Alex's mom."

"Dani." Alex grabbed Dani's hand and tugged so they faced each other. She parted then closed her lips, struggling against the urge to cradle Dani's face and look even remotely okay at the same time.

"Alexandria."

"I need you to go," Alex pleaded.

Dani shook her head. "I'm staying."

Alex bit down on her bottom lip, closing her eyes against the daggers her mother was staring into the side of her head. "Dani, *please.*"

"Let me do this with you."

"Alexandria, I'm losing my patience with this display, and at this rate, my dinner will be next. You have five minutes to put an end to this. I'll be in the living room."

Alex turned in her mother's direction, a scoff escaping her lips. She was ready. She was so ready to ask Dani to leave then sit and take her scolding like a big girl, listen to her mother tell her all the things that were wrong with her *lifestyle*. It would hurt, but at least they would finally acknowledge it, and her mother could stop making herself feel better by pretending not to know. Yet, something about her words, her commanding tone, reverberated differently. Maybe it was because it had been more than three years since Alex had made the penthouse her home and her mom had moved back to Staten Island. Three years of the literal and figurative distance and Alex attempting to get better at not hating herself. "You really think I'm still a kid, don't you?"

Her mother faced her, then shook her head. "No, Alexandria. Which is exactly what makes this juvenile show of rebelliousness everything but endearing."

"Rebelliousness?" Alex raised her brows. "Is that what we're calling it?"

"We're not having this conversation with your friend as an audience." She turned to leave, and Alex didn't consent, but her legs were faster, moving until she'd stopped directly in front of her mother.

"No. We *should* talk about it. What? Are you too afraid you might have to acknowledge your daughter's homosexuality in front of another person?" Her throat tightened, something prickling the corners of her eyes as she shrugged. "Unfortunately for you, my friend is even gayer than me, and I can assure you we've been pretty gay togeth—"

Her mother's palm connected with her cheek and her head snapped from the impact. A low ring echoed in her left ear, punctuated by the gasp she was sure had come from Dani. Her eyes opened and tears hit her face, and brown—brown and too much like her father's—met the blues of the only other person who was *supposed* to love her. Strangers she'd met in the most unfriendly city had been kinder.

She breathed out then nipped her top lip to stop the tremor, and she nodded. "Nice talk, Mom. I'd show you the way out, but I'm not feeling very hospitable at the moment."

She still cried for hours after, curled up in her bed—Dani stroking her hair, pressing kisses to her forehead every so often.

No blood.

No choking on conjecture.

Catharsis.

Chapter Seventeen

bicerin

Alex had lost track of how long it had been since she'd rolled out of bed and adjusted the covers over Dani before crossing her room to the en suite. Maybe ten minutes from when she'd brushed her teeth and showered then combed through the knots in her wet hair.

Tomorrow was Thanksgiving.

It was the morning after the argument with her mother over her relationship with a woman, and tomorrow was Thanksgiving. She was a shit storm of emotions too busy battling with each other for one feeling to make its way to the surface.

On one hand, she was sort of relieved to have it in the open—all her anxiety about what would happen if her mother were to find out replaced by... just something else. No more speculation on either part or feeling compelled to prolong a delusion. No more, "I used to be so worried, Alexandria. I don't know what your father and I would do if you turned out to be one of them."

Alex was one of *them*, and she knew exactly what her parents would do.

Her face still tingled where her mother's palm hit. The resulting tinge was gone now, but she'd spent long enough staring at it after Dani had finally fallen asleep last night for an imprint to be left in her mind. It wasn't watching herself bleed as she dragged a blade across her thigh. Her blood didn't run warm to cold, snaking a stream to nowhere, staining the tips of her fingers. No faint hint of metal lingered in the air.

It wasn't the same.

But it was.

Staring at her red, tear-stained face felt a lot like cutting; a lot like wanting something she shouldn't, like becoming—*being*—something her mother would never accept.

Like torture and purging.

And bleeding.

Without perceptible scars.

*

Dom crossed the living room of the penthouse, taking a few gulps of the Muscle Milk protein shake in his grip as he plopped down on the opposite end of Alex's sectional. Satisfied, he twisted the screw top back on and leaned forward to put the bottle on the coffee table. Alex rolled her eyes, lifted the bottle, then used the sleeve of her sweatshirt to wipe away the water droplets on the glass surface. She wasn't always this anal about her furniture, but being a broody, aspiring novelist wasn't the only cliché of which she'd been guilty. She had to be a stress cleaner too. Making sure the penthouse was pristine, though housekeeping already had, helped somewhat. It wouldn't kill Dom to use fucking coaster either way. As she leaned into the sofa, she stared up at the high ceiling and focused on the faint sparkles littering the white paint, instead of the way Dom was watching her every move.

"So, Dani left?" he asked carefully.

"Yeah. Over an hour ago. There're all these relatives coming over for Thanksgiving, so they have airport runs and cooking, and...Yeah."

"She coming back later?"

"Probably not. It's Thanksgiving, D. She should be with her family, and so should you. So don't even think about hanging around here all day. Your aunt is literally flying from Jamaica with that escovitched snapper you're so obsessed with, and you better be at your dad's to eat it tomorrow."

Dom sighed. "At least tell me you're still going to take them up on their invite."

Alex pursed her lips.

"Your grandparents then?"

"That one you know the answer to."

"VK."

She pulled her gaze from the ceiling to face him. "Are you really going to try to talk me into that, knowing my mother will be there?"

"It's not about her. What about your dad, your gr—"

"Of course it's about her, Dom! Have you ever known it not to be?"

"Exactly! But she knows now. It's out there. So why are you still hiding?"

"I'm not hiding," Alex muttered indignantly.

"Yeah, that was real convincing, VK."

"Whatever." Alex shook her head and stood. "I don't want to fight with you. I should be getting ready anyway."

Dom narrowed his eyes at her. "Ready for what?"

"I told you. I'm meeting Frankie for lunch."

Alex had told him. A week ago, seated outside the Columbia Business School as they waited for Ry to finish her last twenty minutes of calculus, Alex's phone had vibrated for the third time since they'd sat, and Dom murmured, "Tell Dani hi for me."

"It's not Dani." Alex bit into her granny smith apple.

Dom creased his forehead as he scrutinized Alex expectantly. She rolled her eyes. "It's Frankie. We've been catching up. Sort of. I don't know. She just wanted to make sure Calvano's is okay for lunch next week."

"You guys are having lunch together?"

"Mhm."

In the corner of her gaze, fingers busy with her response, she'd noticed Dom's brows knit even closer, and he still eyed her, but his only response was, "Okay."

Standing in her living room nearly seven days later, under his watchful stare, Alex felt stuck in that moment all over again. Stuck in Dom's skepticism and something in his deep brown eyes resembling concern. This time, he didn't leave it unstated. This time his lips parted in a steady, cautious, "VK..." For a second, they regarded each other, and he hesitated, but this was Dom. There wasn't anything he couldn't say to Alex. Almost two decades of friendship. Blood couldn't make them any closer. "You sure you know what you're doing here? With Frankie?"

"I love her, Dom. Dani. I'm so in love with her."

"I know, but that wasn't what I asked, VK."

"I don't have any other answer." Alex shook her head. "You're worried about me. I know you are, because—" She breathed a humorless laugh, dragging one hand through her hair. "It's Frankie. But that's exactly why I have to do this. Because *it's Frankie*. I can't pretend she doesn't exist. I was never any good at it."

"Fine." He got to his feet and closed the distance between them. "Just don't forget what's at stake, okay?"

Alex shook her head. "Come on, D. You know I was never any good at that either."

*

The eight minutes of searching for parking close by had left Alex late by just about fifteen. Usually, she'd try to show up early, or at least on time, hating any occasion where she'd left her friends or family waiting. She'd done so today too, but even with all the thoughts of Thanksgiving on her mind, she'd underestimated the traffic to make it over to the East side on the eve of a celebration. Still, she had to stop for another minute to appreciate the restaurant she'd avoided for years—built on a corner she'd driven by countless times, only sparring a glance at its dark, walnut doors and red bistro-style awning, its narrow, curb-side dining, always at full capacity. The best Italian she'd had since the passing of her father's mom, and she hadn't brought herself to set foot inside the place in years.

Until today.

She raised one hand and pulled the door open before stepping into the warmth. Her eyes scanned wall to wall, raking over the people seated at the small, wooden tables, waiters milling around busily, smiling as they took orders, made conversation, or returned from the kitchen with dishes imbuing the air with spices and cheese.

Alex met Frankie's eyes—bright as always, despite the dim-lit atmosphere—and something inside her shifted. The steadiness of her pulse, direction of her thoughts, clarity of her conscience.

Sixteen and guilty.

Going on twenty-two, restless with remorse.

She went further into the restaurant, past the row of tables lining the center, and toward the back-corner booth where Frankie stood.

"Hey." Frankie beamed, eyes sparkling even after they'd exchanged the most awkward hug—both going left, then right, faces too close for Alex's nerves, hands high on each other's backs. It's what was appropriate, but it only made the exchange even more inelegant and overthought, and the last thing Alex needed was to think more. "I wasn't sure you'd come."

Momentarily, Alex got stuck looking at Frankie. Wavy blonde hair a tad shorter than years ago, still messily groomed in a way that told the world she wasn't the type of girl to spend hours in the mirror every day, brows perfectly arched though, eyes like the ocean, freckles not suffocated by layers of makeup. God knows she didn't need it. Californian girl, sat in a New York bistro midfall, wearing nothing but a thin hoody barely made up for by blue jeans and ankle-high boots. And Alex was the one with the chill in her bones. "I'd tell you before," she replied, "if I changed my mind."

"I'm glad you didn't."

Francesca Calvano. Seventeen and invincible.

Twenty-two. Everything she used to be, and something Alex was dying to put her finger on.

"Yeah, well this is one of the only places I can have authentic bicerin *and* pollo parmigiano in one sitting," Alex teased, making a conscious effort to lighten the mood.

She remembered one of the only times she'd had the drink at the Calvano's home—how Frankie's dad had gifted them with the perfect mix of espresso, chocolate and milk in the shot-sized glasses because they'd been huddled up in Frankie's bedroom for hours already, actually studying, and neither felt confident enough to take on their next-day final. The memory didn't shake Alex. She was even counting on it. What she hadn't been counting on was Frankie's laugh—full-bodied and light— or the weight of her accent when she spoke again.

"*Tu sei qui solo per il cibo allora.*"

Alex bit down on a grin. "*Cos'altro?*"

"*Mi?*"

Of course, I'm here for you. Luckily, the words only resonated in her head. She didn't mean them the way they'd come out. She did. But she didn't. Before her mind began to over-analyze, she reached for the menu set in front of her and redirected their conversation with a playful, "Order up, Calvano. After all, I *am* just here for the food."

*

Lunch had been going great, better even, and not only because of Alex's perfectly tender chicken breast, or al dente penne, or the extra mozzarella she'd insisted on. The conversation too. No awkwardness. They just ate and talked. Alex mentioned how in love with writing she was, though studying it got too technical sometimes. "I mean, my mom hates it. Wants me to be a doctor or a power suit..." She broke off, gaze fallen. "Although, she probably doesn't want me to be anything anymore." A silence dragged out, Alex allowing herself to dwell in her mother's disappointment—what would she do without it anyway—and Frankie listening and waiting, never pushing. But Alex didn't want to talk about it, so she finished with a simple, "It keeps me sane though."

Something in Frankie's eyes suggested she wanted to ask, but instead they moved on to her reliving her undergrad in physical therapy and how much she loved it too. One time, during practicals, she had to work with a sophomore who had a torn ACL. She started off with how glad she was that it wasn't career-ending because he was "so, so talented, Alex, and way too young to never play again," and how he was sweet, for an athlete with "the most annoying entourage," but then one day, after a half hour session, "he got a boner, and it was just really awkward. I mean, I knew it was possible, but it never happened to me, you know?"

The realization hit them both at the same time. Frankie clenched her teeth, a silent *fuck* trapped between them, and Alex's gaze shifted to the bar across the room. It did nothing to stop the prickle at the back of her neck or the way her heart went racing after her mind, both too fast to stop.

Strangely enough, the argument between Alex and her mom didn't change much of anything. Not immediately anyway. If anything, it was the starting point to changes in Alex that would only leave them further at odds as she grew to realize that the view that girls being attracted to girls, or boys other boys, was unacceptable, wouldn't make it any less of a reality. Her reality.

She still wanted Frankie, and she still hated herself for it. So, she tried to keep their relationship as platonic as Frankie's disinclination to suppress her periodical confessions would allow. As time went by, they got easier to hear anyway. Maybe it even made Alex feel good whenever Frankie would casually admit how much she loved when it was just the two of them, how soccer wasn't the same without Alex and that's why she missed it so much during off-season. Because then, she'd never see Alex enough, and it would make her so jealous, thinking Alex was with Kason.

Sometimes—after Alex had said something that made Frankie laugh particularly hard—Frankie's eyes would seem greener, not so blue, and she would look at Alex long, crushing, yearning, and Alex would just stop breathing until the intensity in Frankie's gaze let up. Sometimes, she'd look at Alex that way for no reason at all. Like three questions ago when Alex let out a frustrated groan at realizing she still had a whole page of her chemistry worksheet left to go through, and she'd already been at it for an hour. She dragged the fingers of her hand through her hair, catching sight of Frankie—seated on her bed, books also open in front of her, but eyes fixed in Alex's direction. It lasted the most grueling ten seconds since Alex had stepped into the Calvano's home that evening, then Frankie said, "Come here."

Alex shook her head. "I'm not done."

"You would be, if you'd just let me help."

"Yeah, but you have your own homework, and I don't see how you voluntarily decided to take only AP sciences this year."

It would probably be Alex's fate her senior year too, considering her mother insisted it would be good for premed, but Alex didn't want to think about it.

Frankie smiled. "Alex, *come here*. Please?"

Alex stayed put, still not used to the intonation of her name from Frankie's mouth, but also slightly hesitant about getting on her bed. There was a reason she'd claimed the sofa in the corner almost the second they'd gotten to Frankie's bedroom. But then, with a sigh, she released her pen and shifted the book and paper off her lap to stand. As if she was going to say no.

She took slow steps across the room and stopped directly next to Frankie when she got to the bed.

Frankie swept a strand of hair from her own line of vision then used same hand to make a twirling motion. "Sit."

Alex swallowed, cautiously doing as she'd been told. "Frankie, what are we—" Frankie placed her hands on Alex's shoulders, and Alex's body tensed, which clearly wasn't the intended effect considering Frankie seemed set to give her a massage.

"You're too tense." Frankie shuffled closer. "You keep rubbing your shoulders and rolling your neck.

Mostly during practice, but once or twice since you've gotten here too."

Alex took a conscious breath, trying not to focus on the pressure of Frankie's fingers on her muscles. "I don't know. I don't know if this is a good idea."

"I won't cross any lines. You know I won't. Besides, if I get in, I'll be going to USC for physical therapy next fall, which will mean a lot of this in my future."

"This is different."

Frankie stilled her hands. "Do you trust me, Alex? Do you believe me when I say I'd never push you to do anything you don't want to?"

Frankie had been true to her word. It had been months since the kiss, but she'd never done anything remotely close to what happened at her house the night of the team bonding session—the night of their first kiss. Alex was happy for that. Not always. But it was better this way.

"Of course I do."

"Then just relax, okay? Only a massage. Nothing else."

Alex had had massages before. None of them made her feel like *this*. Maybe it was because in all the other cases, it'd been a stranger's hands working out the knots in her body. Maybe it was because she understood there was nothing to it—they were doing their job. Maybe it was because neither of them had taken her lips in an unforgettable kiss.

Maybe...

None of them had been Francesca Calvano.

As Frankie continued working her way down Alex's back—the weight of her body bearing down on Alex from where she was seated on Alex's butt—Alex tried to remind herself that this was supposed to be equally clinical. A solution to the tension in her muscles. Something to help her relax. Except, she couldn't. Not with her mind fixed on the way Frankie's fingers were now pressed against her skin, kneading and rubbing, and sending all the tension somewhere else instead of getting rid of it entirely. Alex should've stopped it the second Frankie's hands had slipped under her top, but the skin to skin contact felt so much better, and it was something she'd never allowed herself to have with Frankie. Now that she had, she didn't want it to stop. She didn't know how to stop.

Frankie lightened the pressure of her hands and gently trailed the edge of Alex's sports bra. Goose bumps rose on Alex's skin. She parted her lips, steadying her breaths as a silent battle raged in her mind over immediately putting an end to this or letting it happen.

Frankie cleared her throat and gently pulled Alex's shirt down to her waist. "Was that okay?"

"Ye—" Alex cleared her throat too. "Yeah. Thank you."

"Anytime."

The weight on Alex lifted as Frankie reverted to her spot on the bed, and Alex rolled over—slowly, as if getting up too fast would leave her head spinning. Ridiculous. Frankie left her dizzy every time they were together anyway. When she finally sat up too, Frankie's eyes were already fixed on her. These days, it didn't feel so much like choking whenever they looked at each other. Nothing so forceful. Alex figured it was because her will to fight the intensity of Frankie's pull was waning. Or maybe she was just weak. Everything from the green in Frankie's eyes to the glow of her skin and hair, the way she treated the fact that she was genuinely brilliant—honor roll, future pro women's soccer brilliant—like it didn't even matter, like she wasn't the closest thing to perfect Alex had ever seen, made Alex weak.

"I'm going to—to uhm..." Frankie trailed off.

Had Alex ever heard her stutter before?

"Yeah. Water." Frankie stood. Alex caught her hand and tugged gently. She shifted her gaze skyward instead of looking at Alex.

Heart racing, breaths shaky, Alex's got to her feet. It left her too close—her chest grazing Frankie's back despite the two-inch height difference—but she didn't know how to stop herself from reaching up with her free hand and wrapping it around Frankie's neck, making Frankie face her.

Frankie squeezed her eyes shut.

"Why won't you look at me?"

"You know why."

Alex did know why. And she didn't want to say this time would be different because she didn't know that. She didn't know much of anything anymore.

She brought her lips to Frankie's. Feather light. It would almost be like it hadn't even happened but for the way Alex's ribs were pretty much rattling, how the room felt warmer, how Frankie now had a tight grip on Alex's hip. Alex leaned in and trapped Frankie's bottom lip between hers for the most blissful second.

Frankie stepped back, pitch black pupils swallowing the green in her eyes. "Alex, what are you doing?"

"I don't know." Alex shook her head. "I just..."

"You just what?"

It was nothing Alex could explain. So instead of trying to, she closed the gap between them and pressed her lips against Frankie's. Zero hesitance. Pure want. Frankie dropped her hands to Alex's hips and for a second, it seemed she was going to push Alex away, but then her lips parted—breath hot against Alex's as she deepened the kiss—and she stumbled forward. The momentum sent Alex toppling onto the bed and Frankie right on top of her.

A dam broke. Weeks of pent up tension, of suppressing the urge to do this spilling out as nothing but lips and tongue and teeth, crumpling paper and hardcovers hitting hardwood. Fast and wet, but nothing like kissing Kason King.

Frankie slipped her hands under Alex's top and lightly dragged her blunt nails down Alex's side. The shiver that ran through Alex's body and the fact that she was literally shaking left her so confused. She squeezed her eyes shut, toes curling as she tried to stop the noise fighting to escape the back of her throat.

She failed.

"Alex."

She couldn't even process that she'd moaned for the first time ever. Before, she'd never understood why people had to, always questioned whether it actually felt that good. But it did. Everything about Frankie felt unbearably good. She tugged at the hair tie holding Frankie's ponytail. Inches and inches of blonde waves flowed free, and Alex buried one hand in them. A second of reveling in how soft Frankie's hair was, and then a leg slipped between Alex's thighs. Her grip tightened, her gasp and Frankie's whimper muffled between their lips. Alex didn't know if it was on purpose, but Frankie rocked forward, and she had to break the kiss. She couldn't breathe if she didn't. She couldn't breathe either way.

"Alex."

The second time Frankie said her name hit Alex right in the lower abdomen. She could feel the buildup of something as foreign as the heat between her thighs. Frankie brought her mouth to Alex's neck and dragged her teeth against Alex's skin. She pushed one hand further up Alex's shirt, treacherously close to her bra, leg still moving between hers. When she lifted her head again, breathing Alex's name against her lips, it took a while for Alex to realize she was waiting for a response.

Alex opened her eyes, gaze glossy, chest heaving as she tried to stop her body from quivering, and her hands from gripping Frankie's hair and lower back any tighter, tried to stop period. And then Frankie—parted lips swollen and red, hair a tangled sexy mess—slipped her fingers beneath Alex's bra and squeezed.

Something snapped.

Alex threw her head back against the bed—tremors in her legs and mumbles from her lips and everything in her screaming for more but knowing she couldn't possibly handle another ounce of whatever she was feeling.

When her muscles finally loosened again, her mind felt suspended in a state of euphoria. She tuned in to the weight of Frankie's body still on top of her, and her eyes opened at the realization of what had happened. She'd never had one. Now that she had, there was no mistaking it.

Frankie's jaw went slack. "Did you just..."

"I should go." Alex rolled Frankie off her and ignored the way her legs felt slightly less capable of functioning the way they should as she crossed the room and started stuffing her books and paper into her bag.

"Alex." Frankie touched Alex's forearm.

Alex faced her, but she couldn't look her in the eyes. Not after they, not after she...

"I'm sorry." Frankie reached up to stroke Alex's cheek, but pulled back midway. "Just...Don't go. Please."

Alex's heart clenched. Frankie had nothing to be sorry about. Alex was the one who... She swallowed and made herself look up. "I just need some air. It's getting late anyway." She combed back a strand of Frankie's hair. "I'll text you later."

There was something in Frankie's eyes when Alex said her last words. Almost as if she knew Alex was lying.

"Sorry." Frankie shook her head, lips parting and closing, only to repeat the cycle. "I didn't mean to—Fuck, Alex, I know you don't like talking about that stuff."

"Frankie." Alex was surprised by the steadiness of her own voice. "It's okay. Really. We're not seventeen anymore. Well, I'm not. You were always a few years ahead."

The breath Frankie released made Alex wonder exactly how long she'd been holding it. "Still, I'm sorry. The last thing I want is to make things awkward between us, especially now that you aren't actively trying to avoid me anymore."

"I wasn't avoiding you."

Frankie laughed, shooting Alex a look. "Come on. You couldn't get away from me fast enough that night at the banquet, and then you screened my texts for weeks."

"I didn—Okay. Can you blame me though?" Alex countered, happy they'd managed to get past the memory and recover the initial mood of their lunch—light, fun, a little like old friends catching up. "It was like seeing a ghost. What were you even doing there?"

It was something she'd been wondering since the night in question. Francesca Calvano at a Laurent Foundation hospital banquet, being held at The Van Kirk. There was one explanation, but Alex preferred to leave the lines of that conclusion to be drawn by someone else.

"My dad and your dad have been in conversation about opening a Calvano's in The Van Kirk. He catered that night as a kind of test run, and since it went pretty well, it may work out."

Alex narrowed her eyes. Her father *had* been scouting options to fill a new opening at the hotel, but she didn't know Calvano's was one of them. Then again, she didn't know any of the prospects.

"From the look on your face, I'm guessing your dad didn't mention it. Mine didn't either. But he was here the other day. Yours, I mean. He kind of recognized me so—"

"Wait, what do you mean he recognized you?"

"I met him, while we were going to Trinity."

Alex's mind blanked. She'd purposely made sure her parents and Frankie had never come to face-to-face, and though there had been a close call with her mother, she had no memory of that had being the case with her dad. "What do you mean you met him?"

"The day I skipped practice. You had the flu and I wanted to check on you. So, I came over and we talked, and then you—"

"Asked you to stay." Alex nodded. There was a looming reminder of how the night had ended—how she'd been reliving it last night—that made her want to shut down, switch topics, but she had to know what any of that had to do with Frankie meeting her father.

"After you fell asleep, I was going to leave like we planned. Then your dad came up, and it was the weirdest thing. I was sitting next to you on your bed, stroking your hair...and he kind of caught me. But he just asked my name and said I must be a friend of yours. He felt your forehead. I remember thinking it was so cute because he was head to toe in designer, and I heard his phone vibrating, so I knew he was probably too busy to be trying to gauge your temperature instead of having someone look after you. Then he made me promise to stay with you and tell you he'd be home late."

Frankie frowned and shook her head.

"But then you woke up, and I don't know if you were mad at me for overstaying or what, so when you asked me to go, I left. And I forgot to tell you he was ever even there."

"Frankie, I—" Alex raked a hand through her hair, still trying to process the whole thing. "I wasn't mad at you. Not even a little. It was just that my mom came home and I—You met my dad? While we were at Trinity? And he walked in on you, stroking my hair?"

Frankie released a bashful laugh. "Yeah, probably should've left that bit out."

"No." Alex couldn't help but laugh too. "No. It's fine. I think I would've liked that if I'd been awake." For the Alex she was now, it was easy to look Frankie in the eyes and admit that. Most things were easier now.

Maybe the girl she'd been then was too scared to let it happen, to let herself want Frankie as much as she did. Not only in a way that made her shiver and burn. In ways that could piece her heart together and break it too. In ways that did break it. Being who she was had become so much easier once she'd told her dad. She was still hiding—Dom was right—but it hurt less. She bled less. Finding out that it all might've happened sooner, that maybe her dad's only response had been "Okay," when she'd come out to him because it was no surprise, she couldn't help but look at Frankie and wonder where they'd be now, if she'd become this person before she ruined it all.

Chapter Eighteen

caffè americano

Alex rolled onto her back, tugging the duvet closer to her chest as she contemplated the hour-long drive to her grandparents' compound in Staten Island. She didn't want to go, but she also had a stubborn tendency to want to do—be—whatever was expected. She'd been getting better at it over the years, but it wasn't enough to completely erase the longing for her mother's validation. Even after their argument the night before last, Alex still didn't know how to face her. Their Thanksgiving had always been intimate, and with the way her mother had reacted, she wasn't sure what would happen once they were forced to sit through a meal with her father and grandparents as company. For the most part, her mother's views stemmed from her own upbringing. Alex wouldn't know how to process her grandparents' disappointment either, and she didn't want to lose them. She took comfort in the idea that her dad wasn't going anywhere. If anything, her talk with Frankie yesterday, hearing her father had probably known about her sexuality long before she'd told him, made her even surer. He loved Thanksgiving. If she were to miss it, he'd still be the last person to pressure her about why.

And then there was Dani.

The Ramírezes would be so disappointed if Alex didn't show up. They were as adorable as families got, and they'd invited her weeks ago when she and Dani were still barely even official. But Alex wasn't good company right now, and the last thing she wanted to do was taint what promised to be the perfectly extravagant, homey Latino-American Thanksgiving. And maybe it was selfish. Surely she could do this one thing for her girlfriend who'd never ask for anything. Yet, she still wasn't up to the task. She didn't want Dani to have to juggle getting reacquainted with aunts, uncles, and cousins, and her shitty mood at the same time. So wasn't it better to stay home?

She mentally combed through all the ways to let Dani down.

Text?

Call?

Hop in her car and drive to Brooklyn to do it in person?

Her phone chimed. She aimlessly moved her right hand beneath the ruffled, charcoal duvet in search of it. When she finally felt the smooth surface, she gripped and brought it into view.

Text message Francesca Calvano.

Alex creased her forehead as she opened her messages app. Her eyes shifted to the time. 8 a.m. Normal for Alex and Frankie back at Trinity. Hell, six was normal. For them now, still amid a debatably dangerous catch-up phase, this was unorthodox. But who was Frankie, if not a little lawless?

Frankie: Hey ☺ You up?

Alex: Unfortunately.

Frankie: Perfect. Meet me outside in fifteen.

Alex drew her brows closer, fingers already moving across the screen of her phone again.

Alex: You do realize April Fools is in... Well, April.

Frankie: LOL. Yes, smarty. Which is why I'm not kidding. I'd wave, but I'm pretty sure I look like an indistinguishable speck from the top floor of that castle of yours.

Alex: Wait You're actually serious?

Frankie: Yes! Now get your ass out of bed, Van Kirk. When's the last time you had a good fall a.m. workout?

Alex pulled her bottom lip between her teeth, staring at the message in consideration. Going with

Frankie probably wasn't a good idea, seeing as early, late, workouts period was a huge part of what they'd had. At the same time, there was a reason they'd loved and needed it so much. Fall workouts were therapy for every unspoken musing. About each other. About everything else. Alex really needed some therapy.

Alex: Fuck fifteen. Be down in ten.

*

Alex stepped through the rotating glass doors of the Van Kirk as the doorman offered an airy, "Happy Thanksgiving, Miss Van Kirk" that she paused to answer with an amiability so atypical for her this early on a cold, autumn morning. She directed her gaze to where Frankie leaned against a silver Audi, parked by the curb—hair caught in a messy bun, red tinge to her cheeks and nose, brightest grin when she extended an arm to offer Alex the coffee in her hand.

Alex grinned as she accepted the offering. "You think you can just show up on my doorstep, bribing me with nostalgia and"—she took a sip of the warm beverage—"Americanos?"

Frankie laughed as she turned to open the driver's side door of the car. "The coffee was my mom's idea." She glanced over her shoulder, and for a second, it was like she hadn't aged one bit. "Good to know you're nostalgic though."

Alex breathed a laugh, shaking her head as she rounded the car to hop in. She *was* nostalgic. There was no point denying it. Besides, if there was one thing being with Frankie all those years ago had taught her, fighting the pull would only make everything unnecessarily difficult. This wasn't their second chance, not romantically, but it was. Maybe getting the friendship right, even without the romance, would help Alex finally put it all behind her so she could be everything she wasn't to Frankie for Dani.

*

The second they pulled up in front of Trinity was too much on Alex's memory already. Frankie had been clear—they were going for a workout—but somehow Alex didn't think it had meant going back to the site of the crash. She should have known though. Being let into Trinity by the caretaker during closed hours or days was as authentic as their fall a.m. workouts got. Pre- and post-practice practices, quad stretches and laps that left their lungs on fire, despite the cool weather. Moments of staring that stretched a bit too long with Frankie as ad hoc goalkeeper, and Alex over the ball, waiting for her pulse to slow and her focus to return, only to realize it never would. Frankie's whispers in the wind when she'd stand too close, Alex's jersey in her grip purely for the sake of it. Today, it was a little like that—a little like being sixteen, seventeen, scared, guilty, silently suffocating on the weight of her own thoughts. Really, it was a lot more like being twenty-one and not so scared, yet not as invincible as she wished she was, breathing easier, still brooding on all the ways she was too much of a disappointment to everyone she loved.

For the next hour or so, she managed to force it down—never far enough—and after a few too many laps and passing the ball in silence, realizing how much she'd missed playing, she and Frankie collapsed on the field, breathless, familiar. Too sentimental. Enough lawn spread between them for their bodies not to touch, and on Alex's part, it was conscious. For the first time, she kind of realized that she'd been doing this for weeks already, ever since she ran into Frankie outside of Brave. She'd been trying to maintain a distance between them that felt respectable because God knows, despite whatever they were doing, she'd never cheat on Dani, and she didn't want Frankie to think otherwise.

"Do you remember the first time we did this?" Frankie's voice pulled her out of her thoughts, her breathing finally back to some semblance of normal. She kept her gaze locked on the gray sky. "Not the workout. Just lying here."

"Yeah," Alex murmured, her mind already drifting off. "Of course."

Alex lay in bed, the last few hours fresh in her mind—preseason bonding session at the Calvano's, the way she'd been distracted all night, the way she'd never think straight ever again. Her phone vibrated and she stared at the incoming message.

> *Francesca: Are we going to talk about what happened tonight?*

Alex: No.

Francesca: Alex, I kissed you.

Alex: I know.

Francesca: You kissed me.

Alex: I know.

Francesca: Then why can't we talk about it?

Alex: I just can't, Frankie.

Francesca: Fine.

It worked. In fact, if Frankie was even the slightest bit affected by Alex's rejection, it hadn't shown. She was still so entirely herself—light on and off the field, nothing but golden hair, tan skin and ocean eyes, and carefree laughter that haunted Alex in and out of her dreams. This wasn't how these things went. Alex had turned down her fair share of guys in her two years of Trinity. She was used to the downward pull or purse of their lips when she told them she wasn't interested. It's how it's supposed to happen. Except, when it came to Francesca Calvano.

Somehow, Frankie had escaped that night completely unscathed, and Alex was the one unable smile without effort or focus long enough on anything but her. Every time she closed her eyes, she felt Frankie's hands and lips, the thud in her own chest, chill down her spine. And nothing she'd done had made it stop.

Not tears.

Not blood.

But it was different now.

Alex had been developing an inexplicable attachment to Frankie since the second she'd texted her back the first time. Sure, it was physical—more now than ever—but it also wasn't. She'd breathe shallow breaths all day if it meant being able to just *talk* to Frankie. And it was strange because it wasn't as if they had the deepest conversations. It was almost always superficial. But there was an undercurrent to what they had that didn't necessarily need more. Something in them just knew. Even if they never said it. Even if Alex never said it.

She stood by the edge of the field, watching as Frankie explained for the third time that Coach Matthews had to cancel practice because his wife was in labor and the assistant happened to be out for the day. The gym bag slung across Alex's chest bore down on the knots in her shoulders—she'd been nothing but tense lately—and the constant tapping of her foot made the cuts on her thigh prickle with a reminder that they were still fresh.

This was a terrible idea.

She adjusted the strap of her bag, turning to leave.

Frankie locked eyes with Alex, gluing Alex in place. She furrowed her brows ever so slightly, glanced back at the girls she'd been talking to and smiled as their conversation came to an end. When she turned toward Alex again, she kept her gaze on her own bag and pulled back the zip before stuffing a pink water bottle inside. "What's up, Van Kirk?"

There was zero venom in it. Still, it hurt—the way she wasn't looking at Alex when she spoke, the way she called her what every other girl on the team did. And she was supposed to, but they were alone now, and alone it had always been, "Alex."

Frankie stilled her hands on her bag. The moment dragged. She zipped her bag closed and pulled it over one shoulder, sighing as she faced Alex again. "What's going on, Alex? Are you okay?"

No. She was so far from okay she didn't think she'd ever be okay again.

"Are *you*?" Alex asked. There was a part of her that didn't want Frankie to be, that wanted to know Frankie was as much of a mess, that wished her eyes burned from thirteen nights of fragmented sleep, and her body ached from too many hours of running only to realize there was no escaping her thoughts. And that her insides were sick with conflicting feelings she couldn't begin to process.

Again, Frankie knit her brows, the motion disappearing almost before Alex had caught a glimpse of it. Then, she licked her lips—kicking the beat of Alex's heart to another gear, ruining her a little more, even though it was clearly unintentional. "I've been better."

Three words appeared in Alex's head. They'd been there for days. Amid everything else she'd been feeling and thinking, one thing felt constant.

I miss you.

She couldn't say it.

Frankie looked Alex dead in the eyes, like she used to—before the kiss—and she held her there. Alex didn't hate it so much that Frankie had this power over her. Maybe it wasn't even a power at all. Maybe it was Alex's subconscious allowing her to be honest the only way she was capable right now. Even if what she felt wasn't sanctified, pure or honorable, even if it meant she'd never stop bleeding.

"Do you want to just—"

Alex took a step closer. "Just what?"

"I don't know. Stay here for a bit." Frankie shook her head. "We can lie on opposite ends of the field and text like—" She sighed, glancing at her feet. "I just want to talk to you, Alex. Is that okay?"

Alex took it back. She didn't want Frankie to feel anything remotely close to the torment she herself was in. She didn't want anything but to see Frankie laugh, shooting sparks that burned right through her chest.

"Frankie..." The words lodged themselves in the back of her throat, and since she couldn't force them out, she swallowed them back. "Okay."

"Okay?"

Alex nodded. "Yeah. We can stay."

"I think it's the first time I realized you were never going to talk to me," Frankie murmured, drawing Alex back from the memory. "Not about anything real anyway. You weren't okay, and I could feel it. I could see it too. But you refused to let me in."

Alex sighed. "Frankie."

"Don't. Don't do that thing where I try to talk to you, and you say my name and suffer in silence. What you said yesterday, you were right. We're not seventeen anymore, Alex. I'm not the girl you used to kiss in secret, and you're not the one who used to—"

Alex opened her eyes, her mind stuck on it. She's not the one who used to what?

Frankie released a heavy breath. "It's not the same. We're not...them, but I still know when you're not okay, so...If you won't talk to me, I hope you're talking to someone, instead of dealing the way you used to."

Alex mulled over the apprehension in Frankie's tone, trying to read it for what it was. On one hand, it seemed completely out of nowhere. It also felt like she wasn't the only one trying to work through her suppressed emotions, like everything Frankie had said was years overdue.

"I don't—" Alex shook her head. "I don't do that anymore, Frankie."

Frankie met her gaze. "You don't?"

"No."

"Okay."

Alex parted her lips then closed them again, and before she'd made sense of the sudden desire to explain she muttered, "It was my mom."

Frankie narrowed her eyes.

"The reason I was so scared all the time." Alex swallowed. "I mean, it was me too. I wasn't…" She licked her lips, shrugging. "I don't know. Brave? You deserved brave, Frankie, but I kept thinking how much she'd hate me if she found out, so every time we got cl—"

"Alex—"

"No." Alex heard the *it's okay* before it had even come out, but it wasn't Frankie's job to make everything easy for her anymore. It had never been in the first place. "You deserved so much better than me. And I'm not saying that to sound self-depreciative. I'm saying it because it's true, and because I'm supposed to be different, stronger. Not seventeen, not scared, but she knows now, and instead of sucking it up and being what Dani needs, I'm still running away."

Something shifted. The weight on Alex's chest from saying everything that had been bothering her, Frankie's eyes, Alex's chasing them.

"Dani is…" Frankie trailed off.

"My girlfriend." The words left Alex's lips softer than intended, as if she'd been too honest today already and those were better left confessed another time. She couldn't explain it. It just felt that way. So, to make it more concrete, to show her relationship the respect it deserved, she added, "Two months officially."

Frankie nodded. "Do you love her?"

"I do."

The moment dragged—chill fall air and Manhattan in the backdrop, buzzing all around them.

"I came out to my parents an hour before our quarterfinal against Convent of Mercy."

It was the last thing Alex expected Frankie to say, and yet, it immediately got her attention. It had taken her months to stop wondering about that day, to stop wondering why Frankie had been so off during the game. So upset.

"It was awful." Frankie released a humorless laugh. "My mom yelled, then she cried, then my dad yelled at me for making my mom cry and I—" She shook her head. "And I didn't even know why I told them at that moment. I mean, I would've. Eventually. But it was so random. My mom was getting ready to leave again. Long flight to Prague. Dad was having a special catering at the restaurant, and I was still waiting for you to finally text me back after what was...day nine, I think."

It *was* day nine. Nine days since Alex had crumbled—shaking and shivering beneath Frankie—her first orgasm, their first real make out, Alex ashamed to look Frankie in the eyes once she'd left the Calvano's that night.

"And even though you weren't talking to me, I knew if we won, you'd be coming to the restaurant for the celebration dinner. For some reason, I had this image in my mind of being in the back by the kitchen and kind of secretly pointing you out to my dad, telling him...*that's her*."

Alex swallowed, her chest aching.

"You weren't ready, but I couldn't help feeling like someday you would be. And when it happened, I wanted to be too. Even if it meant coming out to my very Italian parents, who had rifled through all of Manhattan for the most catholic school they could find before we moved."

"Frankie..."

Frankie waved off Alex's unstated apology. "We're fine now. They're over it. Besides, even though I played like shit that day, moments like the one in the locker room and later that night..." She laughed. "They were so worth it."

Alex could map the lines of Frankie's laugh in her sleep. Everything from the stretch of Frankie's lips and scrunch of her nose, to the creases by her eyes, the way they glimmered greener than blue. And this version— whatever it was—was a complete rip-off.

"What I'm saying is, Alex...She's worth it. Dani. If you love her, then she's so fucking worth it."

Alex heard the words, trusted, appreciated them. But there was an undercurrent to Frankie's story and the point she was trying to make that Alex's conscious mind couldn't afford to tread. Because then...

She was sure to drown.

Chapter Nineteen

pinot noir

Alex had finally made her way through the ridiculous deadlock of traffic from Manhattan to Brooklyn, half regretting not calling a driver instead of driving herself. Her dad had only ever kept one driver on-call for the holidays, though. Disrupting the festivities of food and football with their family to avoid navigating traffic she'd have to sit through anyway didn't seem right.

She shifted into park, staring out the window at the Ramírezes' quaint, old Victorian—the fading blue paint on the outside, small but well-kept garden. It was easily the most vibrant home Alex had ever set foot in. Today would be no different. She could already see the shadows moving by the windows. The last time she'd been this nervous about being here was the night Lucia had noticed her car and all but insisted she come inside to meet Javier. Today, she and Dani weren't fighting, and she'd seen enough of the Ramírezes to know they loved her, but meeting Dani's whole extended family was another thing. Besides, if Alex got too wrapped up in being there, she'd change her mind about the one thing she'd been thinking the whole drive back to The Van Kirk when she told Frankie goodbye, showered, then hopped into her own car and made her way here.

The door opened and Dani stepped into the cold, rubbing her hands together as she made a dash to the small metal gate. Alex reached across the center console and pushed the passenger side door open, shaking her head in wonder at why her girlfriend wasn't wearing a jacket in this weather, smiling because she was so goddamn adorable.

Dani hopped in and slammed the door shut as she turned to Alex, breath visible through her parted lips, grin wide as a happy kid's on Christmas. "You're here."

Alex laughed, pulling Dani's hands between her own to warm them up. "Baby, where the hell is your coat?"

"My little cousin said there was a cool car outside, and I figured it had to be you. Didn't stop for a jacket."

Alex shook her head. "And now you're freezing."

"Warm me up then." Dani freed one hand and tugged on the collar of Alex's jacket before kissing her.

Alex brought one hand to Dani's cheek, parting her lips to take Dani's between hers, heads tilting in sync as Dani's hold shifted from Alex's collar to gently brush the hairs at the back of her neck. An all too familiar shiver went straight to Alex's toes and she smiled against Dani's lips as she pulled away. "Don't want to get too warm."

Dani laughed, "Speak for yourself," leaning to kiss Alex again. With a lingering touch of their lips, she opened her eyes and stroked Alex's face. "How are you?"

Alex understood why she needed to ask. Two nights ago, she'd been there to see Alex's mom finally react to knowing Alex wasn't straight, and it had been anything but pleasant. There was the fact that Alex had cried, no words uttered, for hours after. Besides their brief goodbye the next morning—Dani arguing to stay longer and Alex insisting she doesn't—they hadn't seen each other. It felt like yesterday since the whole thing and ages ago all at once. "I'm okay."

"Baby."

Alex shook her head. "I am. I just…" She breathed out, bracing herself for the words, for what it would mean if Dani agreed. "Will you do something for me?"

"Anything."

"Come to Staten Island."

Dani creased her forehead. "Your mom and grandparents live in Staten Island."

"They do."

"Alex, what are you saying?"

"Thanksgiving. I want you to come. If you want to."

"Alex—"

"My dad is dying to meet you in person. It would make his day. And I don't know what my grandparents will say." She swallowed. "I mean, they did raise my mom, but they're also like, so supportive of me. I don't know. Maybe they'll finally set it in stone that I'm a disgrace to the Laurent name, or maybe they'll love you as much as I do. Either way, I'm sick of being scared, Dani. I'm sick of not being braver for you, and never being brave enough for—" She shook her head and dragged a hand through her hair. "I know half your family's inside, and it's exactly where you should be. Just...Let me be brave. Just this once."

For a while, Dani stared at Alex, thumb steadily stroking her cheek. And then she leaned forward and pressed a soft kiss to Alex's lips. "I think I might need that jacket now."

*

They'd wound up staying at Dani's a few more hours. Dani had explained how she'd already told everyone Alex would be coming over, and while half her family were still super traditional—not exactly understanding the concept of women being attracted to other women—they didn't seem completely revolted by the idea. Alex hoped her family would be even half as accommodating. They didn't have to love Dani so much they'd want her at every family event, or egg them on about living together, marriage, kids, the way it always happened in those movies Dani loved so much. Only one of those didn't completely terrify Alex right now anyway. She only needed to know the way they saw her, loved her, wasn't primarily based on the sex of the person she happened to fall for.

So, she didn't make anything of Dani's grandmother's insistence on calling her "Daniela's friend," because the woman still welcomed her with a hug and the warmest of Ramírez smiles, and three of five of Dani's aunts still affectionately shoved food in Alex's direction every chance they got. A younger uncle had shot Dani a pair of thumbs up. What for, Alex wasn't sure. Then, there was Dani's youngest cousin, Natalia, who was fascinated by everything from Alex's car to her leather jacket and boots, and the fact that "You live in a hotel?"

Before they left, Alex promised Natalia that for Christmas she'd have her own leather jacket, even if Alex had to hand-deliver it to Natalia's home in the Dom Rep herself.

She slid into the driver's seat of her car, Dani closing the passenger's door on the other side. Starting the engine, she took another couple of seconds to stare back at the house and let it set in that she'd just met half of her girlfriend's family and it wasn't a complete disaster. She silently plead for her own family to be even half as receptive. Just thinking about it set her on edge. Maybe this was all a terrible idea. Maybe she'd made too much of her talk with Frankie earlier. She wasn't brave or strong, and they should really just go back inside.

"Hey." Dani reached across the console to touch Alex's face, willing Alex to look at her. "You were great. You were perfect." She swept a few strands of hair behind Alex's left ear. "Now it's my turn. Whatever happens next, I can handle it. *We* can handle it. Okay?"

Alex shook her head. "How can you be so sure?"

"If they hate me, if they hate that we're together..." She took a breath. "Will you walk away?"

"No." If after everything that had happened between Alex and her mother the last couple weeks, she was still here with Dani then today wouldn't change anything. She loved her grandparents. Their opinion was important to her, but she couldn't change the way she felt about Dani. She didn't want to. And she couldn't force them to love her for or in spite of it. A love that had to be forced wasn't love anyway. "I couldn't if I wanted to."

Dani held Alex's face in both hands, leaning in to press their lips together. Slow. Gentle. Burning through all of Alex's doubts. She pulled away, her hands still in place. "That's how."

*

It was close to two hours before they'd turned onto the stone driveway of the Laurent home in Staten Island. They hadn't made a single stop, Haux streaming from the speakers amidst a silence made comfortable by Dani holding Alex's hand. They talked a little—Dani asked about what Dom and Ryan would be up to today and Alex answered that they'd both be seeing their families too. She'd also commented on Alex's weird taste in music, at which point Alex had to remind Dani that the first time she'd heard her sing, it was a song by Ryn Weaver, so Dani had little room to judge.

Alex loved that they both would listen to almost anything, regardless of genre or origin. It made her wonder why she'd never tried harder to get Dani to sing for her. She'd always been content to listen whenever she'd caught Dani harmonizing to whatever was playing from her earphones. Maybe later they'd change that.

Dani stared out the window, occupied with taking in her new environment—the three-story main house with its stained glass and gabled roof, verdant lawns, and perfectly tended rose bushes. To someone who'd never been there, it probably struck as elaborate. Alex had never seen it any other way. She'd always found all eight thousand square feet of the property beautiful, from the exquisite interior to the private beach access. Once or twice, she'd caught herself wishing she'd grown up here, amid the sort of isolation she sometimes craved being raised in the city. Would today change her memories of it forever?

She squeezed Dani's hand. "Ready?"

Dani dragged in a deep breath and nodded as she glanced back at the house then turned to Alex again. "Yeah. Totally."

Nerves emanated from them both. Now that they were at the house with Alex's mom, dad and grandparents inside, it had started to feel more real. Maybe it was because she'd spent nearly the whole drive imaging all the possible outcomes. Or maybe a huge part of her was already expecting the worst and Dani, being Dani, most likely had her heart set on some outcome where all she had to do was be herself and it would all be okay. If it went bad in there, she would be the last person to blame.

"The second you feel like leaving, all you have to do is say the word," Alex reassured.

"Babe, it's going to be okay."

"No." Alex shook her head. "Things get too uncomfortable, you tell me. Okay?"

"Okay." Dani nodded, gaze dropping to Alex's lips before shifting back to her eyes. "Can I kiss you?"

Alex laughed. "Since when do you need to ask?"

"Since we're sitting in the driveway of this extremely intimidating house with your family inside, and I'm not sure if you'd be okay with me ki—"

Alex pressed her lips against Dani's and cradled her face with one hand, holding until she breathed a relaxed sigh. "Better?"

Dani hummed against Alex's mouth, bobbing her head slightly as she drew out the kiss. "Better." She rested her forehead against Alex's. "So, we're actually doing this?"

"Yeah." Alex pulled back for a look at her. "Unless you don't want to anymore."

"No. No, I do. I just..." She glanced down and took Alex's free hand in hers. "I need to know whatever changed your mind about this you're not just doing it for me. Nothing's more important than you being okay at the end of this, and I'd hate it if you were doing it all before you were ready because you think it's what I want."

Alex wasn't doing it *because* of Dani. She was doing it *for* her. She was also doing it for herself, because Dom was right. Hiding no longer made sense. Maybe her talk with Frankie this morning was the extra push she'd needed.

Earlier, before they'd left the Ramírezes, Dani was so sure they'd be able to get through it no matter what. The roles had somehow been reversed along the way, but that was okay. Alex would happily take turns being strong or sure every day for however long this thing between them lasted. Instead of saying the words, she slipped her hand from Dani's and opened the door to get out. She rounded the hood of the car to Dani's side and reached for the handle, already wanting to get inside the house so long as it meant not hanging out in the cold. "Come on."

Dani took her hand and shut the door behind them as they started around the lawn and up the short flight of stairs leading to the front of the house. She tightened her grip on Alex's hand, and Alex gave hers a squeeze, ignoring the uptick in her own pulse as she rang the doorbell. Ten slow seconds passed—long enough for Alex to press a reassuring kiss to Dani's forehead, unsure of whether she'd done it for her girlfriend or herself.

One side of the double doors swung open to reveal her dad, garbed in a gray dress shirt and dark pants, holding a glass of wine to his lips with one hand. He lowered the glass, grinning. "Daniela?"

Alex laughed, shaking her head. It was as if the universe knew how badly she needed her dad to be her and Dani's first point of contact today. Anyone else and she didn't know what to expect.

"Mr. Van Kirk, hi." Dani released Alex's hand and stepped forward to wrap him in a hug.

His eyes widened, and he steadied the glass in his grip, glancing at Alex. She may have forgotten to mention she didn't come from a family of huggers. Her father closed one hand around Dani's back anyway, mumbling something about it being so nice to finally meet her in person.

While the sight warmed Alex in the best way, she found herself narrowing her gaze at him. "Should I be offended you greeted a stranger before your only daughter?"

He chuckled and turned to her as Dani stepped back, laughing too. "Well, if your decision to bring her here is any indication, she might be my daughter too. Someday."

Alex rolled her eyes, forcing her mind to not dwell on the implication. "Jesus, Dad. She's not even in the door yet."

"You're right. Where are my manners?" He stepped back, permanent grin set on his face as he waved them in. This was why he wanted to meet Dani so badly. So he could embarrass the hell out of Alex with all his stupid charm and enthusiasm, and God, she couldn't possibly love him anymore for making this the easiest intro ever.

As she and Dani went inside, her eyes roamed the foyer anyway, shifting everywhere from the winged staircase to the archways leading into the great room. She turned toward her dad, who'd apparently said something Dani found too hilarious. "Is Mom here already?"

He stared at Alex, his amusement fading. "She's in the great room with your grandmother. Grandpa's in the rec. Football," he added with a shrug.

Alex nodded, willing the beat of her heart steady.

Her dad rested a hand on her shoulder. "I know today's a big day for you." He briefly shifted his eyes to Dani. "Both of you. But I've known your—"

"Xander, honey, who's at the door?"

It took about five seconds for Alex's mind to catch up—for her to process the tone of her mother's voice and turn to where her mom and grandmother had crossed into the foyer. She dawdled between the image of her mother glaring at her, completely taken aback by her having the audacity to show up here with *a woman*, and on the echo of her mother calling her father *honey*. The last time she'd heard it was a distant memory, and something about its sudden reemergence made the moment all the more daunting.

Grandma Char came closer, smiling. "Alex, who's your friend?"

Alex swallowed the lump in her throat and forced her gaze from the crippling blue of her mother's to her grandmother's much kinder shade. Always so much kinder. "Grandma Char, this is uhm..." She glanced at Dani and latched on to her calm, her faith. "This is Daniela." She locked eyes with her grandmother again. "My girlfriend."

"Alexandria," her mother gritted out. "The great room. *Now.*"

Grandma Char held up a hand. "Annalise, I'm sure whatever it is can wait until Alex is through introducing her guest." She looked at Alex. Sharp. Sure. "So I understand, girlfriend like you are with Ryan or—"

Her father choked on his wine, coughing an, "Excuse me. Wrong pipe."

Alex was going to kill him.

She shifted her attention to Dani though, just to make sure she was okay, so she understood the implication was entirely innocent. Unlike her dad, Grandma Charlotte wasn't privy to Alex's past... adventures. Dani nodded a silent *it's okay*, so Alex redirected her attention to her grandmother. "No, Grandma. Not like with Ryan. Dani and I—It's—" She took a breath. "It's not platonic. I mean, it is. Just not..." She swallowed. "Not *just* platonic."

Alex wasn't sure how long it had been—probably seconds with the effects of an hour—that the air grew denser, her throat tightening from the silence and pierce of her mother's gaze.

Grandma Charlotte stepped forward—gray hair and blue eyes and soft, wrinkled features more lucid than ever—and she took one of Dani's hands between both her own. "Well, Daniela"—she smiled—"it's lovely to meet you."

Alex closed her eyes and released a breath that left her so light she could just float away. She didn't even know how much she needed this. She couldn't remember feeling anything but weighed down by her own feelings and all the expectations she hadn't met. Somedays, she'd all but buried herself beneath it all. No wonder breathing had always been so fucking hard.

"Come." Her grandmother took her hand, still holding Dani's too. "Dinner's still going, and I want to hear all about this not just platonic relationship of yours."

*

They'd been at it for at least an hour, talking and laughing as if they'd known Dani forever and Alex was the in-law. Somehow, Dani and Grandma Char had managed to find common ground over art of all things, going on about abstract expressionism and surrealism, and topics Alex hadn't even begun to imagine held her grandmother's interest. Had it not been for today, she probably would've never found out that Grandma Char had wanted to be an artist once. A painter. From the mild shift in Alex's mother's expression—a lapse from the scowls and glares she'd been wearing for almost as long as they'd arrived—she hadn't known either.

When she asked why her grandma hadn't pursued it, the woman waved it off, smiling. "It was a less impractical time. Besides, I was just as in love with being a surgeon, so it's not like I threw my dream away."

Like the discontent fixed on her mother's face, Alex tried to ignore the way her father had surpassed all the other empty chairs in the great room to sit on the arm of the one her mother was in. She tried to ignore the way their hands brushed sometimes, or the way her father's gaze would shift to her mom whenever someone had made a joke, almost as if he were waiting for her to laugh too.

Her mother was neither happy nor amused with Dani's presence. All she had were questions about Dani's *breeding*. "Where did you say you were from...Were you born in the Dominican Republic too...What do your parents do? RISD is a good school. For the arts anyway. You must be swimming in student loans."

"Actually," Alex interjected, holding one of Dani's hands, "Dani has a full-scholarship."

"Which is an indication of how good you are," her father commented.

"Xander, it's photography. I'm sure anyone has the capacity to do it. Right, Daniela?"

"Annalise."

"No." Dani shook her head. "She's right. Anyone does, but I like to think I'm a bit better than just anyone."

"Well, you'll have to bring that portfolio of yours the next time you come by."

Dani glanced at Alex, eyes questioning—*will there be a next time*—but no words left her lips. Instead, she redirected her gaze to Grandma Charlotte and offered a closed-lipped smile that gave away all her uncertainty. "Of course."

Ten minutes later, they went down to the rec room to introduce Dani to Grandpa Liam—an introduction that had gone over even easier than the first two. All it had taken was Dani commenting on how, "Forty-four is small for a defensive lineman, but he's pretty fast," and Liam was already making room for her on the sofa.

Alex's eyes widened. Her knowledge of the NFL was minimal at best, but Dani's comment echoed her own comprehension.

Dani shrugged. "My dad."

She hadn't realized she'd been staring, even after Dani was no longer looking back, until her grandmother inched closer. "She's beautiful, isn't she?"

Alex leaned into the frame of the doorway and glanced at her feet. "Yeah."

"Sweetheart." Her grandmother touched her hand. Alex avoided her eyes. "I know your mother isn't happy about all this."

Alex sighed. She didn't want to get into this today. Or ever. "Grandma."

"Let me finish. She loves you, Alex. I don't think there's anyone in this world she loves more than you."

Alex swallowed, shifting her gaze skyward as she tried not to focus on the words, the way they hit right in her chest, the way they kept hitting. She wasn't sure if it was because they resonated like the cruelest lie, or because somewhere in the back of her mind, in a warped sense, she found them to be true. The memory of Edward Chung seeing her with Dani at The Modern that night, how he'd mentioned the picture her mother kept on her desk at work, surfaced again. She tried to push it away, tried to push away this constant conflict about her mother's hate and love, disappointment and approval. The latter always there. Never quite in reach.

"She worries about you," her grandmother went on. "What kind of life you'll have."

Maybe that was true. Maybe her mother hated the idea of seeing her fail at writing, and that's the reason she'd always pushed the business and medicine angles so hard. Still…

"It's *my* life, Grandma."

"Yes." Her grandmother nodded. "And I'm so proud of the woman you're becoming. I know you'll land on your feet no matter what. So, I'll tell you something I should've told Anna years ago." She ran her thumb over the back of Alex's hand and made sure Alex was looking at her directly. "Live by your heart, Alex. It is the very thing that keeps you alive."

*

It came out of nowhere.

Postdinner, Alex and her dad prewashing dishes before loading them into the dishwasher, sleeves of his shirt rolled up to the elbows, hands sudsy and wet. One of their more mundane bonding rituals—volunteering to do the dishes on Thanksgiving and Christmas because there'd be next to no staff, and neither of them could cook for shit. Their contribution, and an excuse to get tipsy on more pinot while Alex's mom and grandparents talked about the foundation. The holidays were a busy season for the Laurents. And while Alex was as much a Laurent as a Van Kirk, where both sides of her family's business affairs were concerned, she'd always been pretty content to show up where she was needed when the time arose.

She'd spent the last ten minutes thinking over how to broach the topic of her parents' renewed closeness when her father spoke up first.

"So…" Back leaned against the counter, he dried his hands in a towel before dropping it and picking up his wine glass for another sip. "What changed your mind about bringing Dani?"

Alex mimicked his actions, hardly thinking about it when she reached for her glass too. "A lot of things, I guess. But an old friend told me something this morning and it kind of resonated."

"Would that old friend happen to be Francesca?"

Alex narrowed her eyes at him, half wondering how the hell he guessed on the first try, half thinking he was way too looped in to be her dad.

"I ran into her at the restaurant a while back," he explained. "I figured it would only be a matter of time before you found out she was back in town too."

Alex nodded, but now that they were on the topic, unanswered questions of how much he'd learned about Frankie had begun flooding her mind. "Dad..." She stared at the glass in her hands as she turned the spine between her fingers. "Why didn't you tell me? That you met her back when we were going to Trinity."

Her father shrugged. "You never mentioned her. I didn't think you wanted me to know. Besides, we'd only met once, and it wasn't until the quarterfinal against Mercy that I guessed how important she was to you."

Alex tilted her head slightly as she looked at him again. "What do you mean?"

"Well, don't you remember that day?"

Right. She gazed down at the wine in her glass again, almost if remnants of her memories swirled in the red, and her mind drifted off. "Don't think I'll ever forget."

It took a while for Alex to allow herself to be alone with Frankie again. They both expected it. The way Frankie sat back and let the days drag by suggested as much. It was like their first kiss all over again. Worse. Frankie so alive—nothing but glow and laughter and fire—in the hallways at Trinity, and after school during practices. A phantom—soft lips parted, strands of blonde hair splayed across her freckled face—fast asleep in Alex's bed, haunting her dreams. Cherry and lavender Alex had failed over and over to bleed from her veins.

She never cried anymore, never really had to begin with. A natural penchant for razors over tears, torture on her body rather than her mind. Maybe it's the reason she strived in situations like this—forty-three minutes into a quarterfinal that felt like it'd been going for two hours at least. Contrary to their name, Convent of Mercy showed none—racing like stallions, tackling as if somewhere around the twenty-minute mark they'd forgotten this wasn't the fucking NFL. Didn't matter. For the most part, the ref had found nothing wrong with their tossed elbows and smashing of cleats into ankles.

The Doves were getting their asses kicked.

Alex clenched her teeth, swallowing as she doubled over to rest her hands on her knees for a few seconds. Only a few. She didn't have much more with the Gazelles set to take their fifth corner of the half, but her gaze strayed anyway and locked in Frankie's direction instead of where it should've been, where the opposition's number nine was set to launch the ball into the box.

One hand pushing back locks of hair clinging to her damp forehead, Frankie used the other to maintain contact with her mark, set on not letting the other girl get free enough for another header that would put Trinity three down. She was off, Frankie, probably still kicking herself for the miss-pass that had resulted in a goal barely five minutes ago. She was off, and whenever their captain was, the rest of the team didn't gel as well as they had all season. But the quarterfinals weren't the place to ruin their unbeaten streak.

The whistle pierced through Alex's thoughts. She snapped upright as the Gazelles' number nine whipped the ball into the Doves' eighteen-yard box. Their goalkeeper, Greenfield, dared forward through grappling bodies to catch the ball mid-air. Acting on the momentum, she swung her arm back and threw the ball toward Tanaka on the right wing, and Alex redirected forward.

The Doves were recovering fast, set to catch the Gazelles on the counter and get one back before half time. The stands roared with support. Alex lifted her head, kicking her sprint into another gear, waiting for the pass as Tanaka kept moving the ball up the field. Tan peered up—a quick visual exchange between her and Alex—as she whipped the ball through the air and Alex brought it down with the inside of her left foot. The pair of defenders on her tail were gaining on her, but she was quick, especially under pressure. She set her sights on goal, ready to drive the ball past the keeper and into the back of the net. No time for finesse with her team two down.

A stinging force cannoned into her feet, knocking them right out from under her. She crashed to the pitch, screaming through the uproar and grabbed her right ankle with both hands. The blare of the whistle barely registered as she squeezed her eyes shut tighter, rolling onto her side. Her mind locked in on the pounding of her foot, and her first instinct was to flex it, make sure she'd be able to continue the game. She was relieved to find that despite the ache, she could.

Somehow, through the roar and chatter, her ears tuned into a, "What the hell was that?" yelled in a voice distinguishable among any, and she forced her eyes open. The three or four teammates hovered over her shimmered, their faces distorted. She blinked for clarity.

"Calvano, take a step back!" the referee ordered.

"Are you not going to card her?"

"Frankie, come on."

"No, Tan! This is bullshit!"

Alex shifted upright, set to get on her feet when she felt an arm on her shoulder. She heard the coaching assistant mumble, "Let me take a look," but she fixed her gaze where Tanaka had one arm wrapped around Frankie's in an attempt to pull her away. A failed attempt.

The referee reached into her pocket and came up with a yellow card. She quickly scribbled something onto it then showed it in Frankie's direction.

"Frankie," Alex tried. More of a groan with the assistant twisting her foot in any possible direction.

She didn't hear it, not over all the noise, but she discerned Frankie's scoff. "Is that a joke? You're giving *me* a card, while *they're*"—she pointed a finger at the pair of smug-looking Gazelles nearby—"out here playing a freaking rugby match!"

Alex pulled her foot out of the assistant's grip. "I'm fine." She stumbled upright and pushed through the ache and feeling of having the wind knocked out of her to put herself directly between Frankie and the referee's last warning.

For a second, Frankie stepped forward anyway, forcing Alex to level both hands on her shoulders and push back. "Hey."

Frankie's chest heaved as she stared back at Alex, and a visible gulp slid down her throat. But it was almost as if Alex could feel the calm take over, like their breathing was one, heartbeats slowing in sync. And then the intimacy of it set in—the memory that this was the first time they'd even been this close since the massage, since Alex...

She took a step back, pulling her hands away from Frankie's shoulders. "You okay?"

Frankie nodded. "How's your leg?"

"Fine."

The rest of the team started moving into position for the free kick they'd been awarded, forcing Alex and Frankie to cut their exchange short and move too.

"Aren't Doves supposed to fly?" mumbled one of the Gazelles' defenders.

"Guess Van Kirk missed the memo."

Before Alex managed to stop her, make her let it go, Frankie started toward the two players and shoved the defender back a few steps. "What did you just say?"

The whistle pierced through the chatter again—third time in too short a time span—and the referee took out her yellow card as she moved in quick steps toward the scuffle. Alex barely had time to process Frankie's name and number being taken again, and the card being pulled back out of sight.

Second yellow.

"Ref, come on," Tanaka pleaded, crowding the official as half the team followed.

But Frankie was already headed off the field—the captain's armband ripped off along the way—past Coach Matthews toward the locker room without a second glance back.

It all happened too fast. Even after both the Doves and the Gazelles had been forced to settle down and play the last few minutes of the first half, Alex still hadn't processed the moment Frankie had been sent off. If she'd been scolding herself for having a bad game before, she would never forgive herself now. Soccer was everything to her, and if anyone deserved to have a say in every second of the season, it was Frankie. First in, last out of practices, all skill and dedication, and a temper Alex didn't know she possessed.

Halftime flew over her head almost as quickly. Coach Matthews paced the locker room, screaming, "What are you guys doing out there?" and "You"—he pointed his finger at Frankie, her eyes glued to the floor, head hung as he shook his—"you're their captain!"

Didn't he think she understood that? Did he seriously think ripping into her after she'd already been sent off would help the rest of the team go out there and play better?

"And I know," his tone softened. "I know that referee is making some pretty terrible decisions."

"Understatement of the damn year."

"Language, Tanaka."

Alex rolled her eyes. *Catholic school.*

"We can't afford to lose our heads," Matthews went on. "That's not how we win this."

"Coach, we're two down with ten players."

"So, what? We just give up? No..."

It wasn't on purpose that Alex had tuned him out. She just wasn't in the mood for a scolding turned pep talk at the moment. It didn't feel like the thing that would light a fire in her chest and under her feet, make her go out there and play the match of her life. She was too worried about Frankie anyway. She wouldn't be able to stop worrying without knowing Frankie was okay—as okay as she could be, having to sit out the rest of the game. So, when it was time to head back to the field, Alex let the rest of her teammates leave and reassured Coach Matthews she'd be right there.

"Thirty seconds, Van Kirk. We still have to finish this game without her, and I'd rather not have to do it without you too." He closed the door behind him.

Alex turned in time to see Frankie drive her left cleat through a nearby water bottle, and send it smashing into a row of lockers. She hung back a few feet away, absorbing the scream that came next, then Frankie ripped her own jersey over her head before opening her assigned locker to stuff the crumpled fabric inside. When Frankie bit into her own bottom lip, closing her eyes against the stream of tears on her face, Alex's body shifted to autopilot.

She stopped directly behind Frankie, whispering her name with an instinctive tenderness. A muffled sob punctuated the silence and Alex put one hand on Frankie's hips—bare and slick and heated beneath her fingertips—willing Frankie to face her. She didn't care that they were standing too close, or that the last time her hands were on Frankie's body had sent her own into a shockwave of something she'd never felt, that made her tense and loose, high then so low. She didn't care that they were alone again or that she was too concerned.

It was Frankie.

For the first time since they'd met, nothing else mattered.

She adjusted her hold on Frankie's hip—firmer, surer—and moved her free hand to wipe away the tears on Frankie's face, and then she joined their lips. Slow, tender, laced with *I'm sorry* and *It's okay*, because maybe she didn't know how to say the words, but more and more, they were learning how to do this. Communicate want and longing and everything that mattered with touches of their hands and lips.

Frankie brought her hands to Alex's abs and left them there before taking handfuls of her jersey and holding on, pulling Alex's body into hers as their kiss got deeper, but no less languid. After a few more seconds, she pulled back with a brush of her lips against Alex's, grip tight as if to keep Alex in place, as if to keep Alex from running. She opened her eyes—the darkest blue Alex had ever seen them, still glossy from the tears. "How long do we stop talking this time?"

"Frankie—"

"You lied to me. And I knew you weren't going to text me that night. I guess I just hoped I was wrong." She glanced down. "But every time we get a little bit closer, you push me away again. And I get that this is scary, Alex. I do. But I miss you every single time. So just tell me. How long?"

Alex parted her lips as she brought their foreheads together. "Frankie." She hated that the only thing that readily left her mouth in moments like this—moments where Frankie didn't seem so invincible, so cool and unbothered—was Frankie's name. There was so much more she wanted to say. Every day she felt more for her, and she didn't know what to do, but she hated this part. She hated coming back almost as much as leaving. It was the only time she could see the cracks in Frankie's armor, succumb to the fractures in her own.

"You should go." Frankie loosened her grip on Alex's shirt. "They're going to start any second now."

"I know."

"You're still here."

"I know."

"Alex—"

"Tell me again how I'm one of the best strikers in the league. Tell me my spot kicks need work, but I'm one of the best, and if I believed that, I'd be unstoppable. Tell me that..." Alex paused, breathing Frankie in—blood, sweat, tears, lavender. "And I'll go out there, and I'll show them Doves *do* fly. We'll win. For our captain. For *you*. And I'll be right here, in this spot after."

Frankie knit her brows, confusion reflecting in her eyes.

The door swung open and Alex's hands fell from Frankie's hip and cheek. For whatever reason, her legs hadn't followed the same reflex, but she was okay with that.

She was okay.

Even temporarily.

Tanaka glanced from Frankie to Alex—her eyes brown and alight with energy and a complete lack of suspicion or surprise. "VK, it's time." Alex turned to Frankie again. Tanaka crossed the room and took Alex by the arm. "Come on. She'll be here later."

She knew. There wasn't a lot to her words, but they'd told Alex as much. Tanaka knew.

"Alex..." Frankie called.

Alex paused at the door, and Tan huffed impatiently. She met Frankie's gaze anyway, comforted by the lack of tears streaking her face, warmed by the fire alive in her eyes again, reinvigorated by the confidence in her voice when the next words left her lips.

"Crush 'em."

"When you came running onto the field," her dad picked up. "There was something different in you. You played the game of your life, Alex. And I don't think that was unrelated to Francesca being kicked out or you being late for the second half kickoff."

"So, you knew...for like, over a year, that I was..."

"I knew there was a girl who was special to you." He laughed before taking another sip of his wine. "Every night you were out late, I had Ren park down the street from her house so when you were ready to go, it wouldn't take too long to pick you up. Those got more frequent after the quarterfinal, and as much as I didn't want to think about what that meant, at least I didn't have to worry about becoming a young grandfather."

Alex winced. "Dad..."

"I never liked Kason anyway. He was arrogant, especially for his age." Her dad grinned. "Maybe that's the reason he and your mother got along so well."

Alex laughed, shaking her head. It was the perfect opportunity. She locked eyes with her father again, question on the tip of her tongue. "What's with you guys any—"

"Babe, we should get going if you still plan on—" Dani broke off, gaze shifting between Alex and her father, expression all kinds of bashful. "Sorry. Mrs. Van Kirk mentioned she was coming to see if you guys were finished with the dishes. Something she needed to talk to you about. That was ten minutes ago, so I figured you were with her, and Alex was alone."

Alex's dad waved away the explanation. "No apology necessary. I'll go see what she wanted." He turned and lowered his glass to the counter before facing Alex again. "Remember we're still on for breakfast on Sunday."

Alex nodded. "Yeah."

He crossed the hardwood floors to Dani. "You're welcome to come too."

Dani smiled. "That's really nice of you, Mr. Van Kirk. We'll see."

He exchanged a final look with them both and exited the room, Dani looking after him. Alex closed the gap between them and pulled Dani's attention to her when she intertwined their fingers. "You okay?"

"I should be the one asking that question. You did just come out to your entire family by introducing them to your girlfriend, on Thanksgiving."

Alex took a moment to think about it then leaned closer to brush her lips against Dani's. "When you put it like that, it sounds like a lot."

"That's because it is a lot, babe."

"I'm fine."

"Sure?"

"Mhm."

Dani freed one hand and reached up to stroke Alex's cheek. "And what about us? Are we fine?"

"Of course."

Dani held her gaze for bit—something indiscernible behind her eyes—and then she joined their lips in a soft, but brief kiss. She took a step back, one hand still in Alex's as she turned in the direction she'd come. "Let's go say goodbye to your grandparents."

Chapter Twenty

cappuccino

The drive back to Manhattan felt longer somehow. Alex attributed it to Dani not being quite as talkative as she'd anticipated. Dani always talked more whenever she was happy or excited, and Alex loved hearing the thoughts that occupied her mind, no matter how random. So, she'd sort of been expecting all kinds of hand gestures as Dani delved into how well their afternoon had gone—Alex's family even inviting Dani back to the house for Christmas. Instead, she surprised Alex with well-composed statements about how, "It's kind of crazy that your grandma wanted to be an artist too. I mean, you want to be a writer, but painting's just as expressive. Maybe art's in your blood, no matter how much your mom hates it."

It *was* surprising that Grandma Char wanted to become a painter once upon a time. The revelation forced Alex to wonder how much she'd yet to learn about the woman, outside of the prim, proper, prestige of surgeon the rest of the country knew her to be. She realized having

Charlotte Laurent as her grandmother and Annalise Van Kirk as her mother didn't make them feel any less like spectacles. Then again, maybe Alex was so afraid of her own emotions, it had created an unnecessary distance between her and her family. Of course, with her mother's resistance to Dani being in her life, she didn't see things changing anytime soon.

As they pulled into The Van Kirk's underground parking structure, she made a conscious effort to not think about it anymore. Dani hadn't uttered another word since around fifteen minutes ago when her own mom had called to ask how everything had gone and whether she'd be coming home tonight. The plan was to take Dani back to her parents' house, but to her surprise, Dani had answered, "No. I think I'm going to stay at Alex's."

Alex glanced over at Dani as she finished the call. "*Te quiero también, Mami.*"

Alex hadn't asked why the change of plans. They could always do with more time together, especially seeing as Dani would be headed back to Rhode Island the coming weekend. They could talk about whatever was on Dani's mind once they were settled in the penthouse.

"I hope it's okay that I decided to stay over. I probably should have talked to you about it first."

Alex shook her head, stepping closer until she stood directly in front of Dani. "You can always stay here. No questions asked." She narrowed her gaze to Dani's and stroked her cheek. "You were really quiet on the drive back though. What's wrong?"

"I'm just worried. I know you said you're fine, we're fine, but with today and everything you've been dealing with lately...I don't want to make it any more overwhelming than it already is. So, when we talk about everything, I want to make sure we're both ready."

Of course. When wasn't Dani thinking about Alex's well-being?

Alex smiled, leaning in to place a chaste kiss on Dani's lips. "You're too good for me, you know that?"

Dani frowned as Alex pulled away. "I still hate it when you say that."

"Doesn't mean it's not true."

"It's not."

Alex laughed, turning to make her way through the living room and up the stairs. "It's been a long day, and if we're going to have a running debate, I'd prefer to do it cuddling."

"It's not a debate though!"

Alex slipped out of her jacket, smiling as she threw it on the back of the antique armchair in her bedroom. She disappeared into her closet and pulled the plain crewneck over her head, only to reemerge with a pair of fleece lounge shorts and a fresh shirt in hand. She locked eyes with Dani before Dani shifted her gaze lower, clearly distracted by a now shirtless Alex, sheer bra on full display. Alex bit her lip. "I'm going to go brush my teeth."

"Yeah, okay." Dani nodded and glanced up at Alex again. "I'll just...grab some clothes to sleep in."

Alex was halfway through brushing her teeth—eyes locked on her own reflection, remnants of toothpaste escaping the corners of her mouth—when she noticed Dani come in and lean against the doorframe, still dressed in the jeans and ruffled cami she'd worn to dinner. Alex paused, waiting for Dani to say or do something other than stand there watching, eyes dark with something familiar but so out of place this moment. Sure, Alex was half-dressed, but she was also literally foaming at the mouth and last she checked, her girlfriend didn't have any weird kinks.

She finished up, shook her toothbrush and dropped it in the nearby holder. "You just going to stare at me all night?"

As if finally having an invitation, Dani crossed the few tiles between them and trailed one hand along the nape of Alex's neck. She pinned Alex against the counter, and Alex gripped the edge as Dani leaned in, her breath hot against Alex's lips. "I miss you."

Alex's brows twitched as she tried to process the words, her pulse instantly reacting to the shift in energy.

"I really"—Dani raised her other hand to the left strap of Alex's bra, along the cup to circle her nipple over the sheer material—"really miss you."

Alex's grip on the counter tightened. She hadn't realized how long it had been since the last time they'd done this. Just over a month, when she visited Dani at RISD, the longest they'd gone since making things official. And it wasn't that she didn't still want Dani in ways that made her heart race and her lower abdomen ache every time their kisses got a little too intense. But lately, the timing had been off.

Dani pressed a kiss to Alex's neck, her jawline then nipped the lobe of her ear as she brought one hand to the button of Alex's jeans. "Tell me what you want."

Alex breathed a laugh. "That's my line."

"Tonight, it's mine."

Dani planted both hands on Alex's hips and led her a few inches right. She snapped the button of Alex's jeans open before slowly pushing them down her legs. Alex swallowed as Dani got to her knees to take the pants off. For a moment, she stayed there, eyes trained up at Alex, daring her to lace her fingers through Dani's perfect curls and guide her mouth right where she needed it. But Dani hadn't made any moves to get Alex out of her underwear, clearly intent on taking it slow, and Alex was so close to dragging her back into the bedroom and leveling the playing field.

She got to her feet and Alex reached for the hem of her shirt to pull it over her head. The second Alex went in to unbutton her jeans, Dani grabbed Alex by the hips and pushed her up onto the counter. Alex's breath caught as Dani parted her legs and stepped between them. Complete reversal of roles. Dani could be dominant, but Alex had never experienced it to this degree. Now that she was, she felt stuck between challenging Dani—showing Dani why she was better at this—or being good for her.

Dani's hand drifted between Alex's thighs and teasingly rubbed over her sheer panties.

"Dani."

Dani brushed their lips together. "You're not telling me what you want."

Alex grabbed her by the back of her neck and kissed her hard. She tilted her head, slipping her tongue into Dani's mouth, unintentionally opening her legs wider, moaning embarrassingly loud when Dani's fingers pressed harder on her clit. Her chest heaved, brows drawn close as she nestled her face against Dani's neck, reveling in the sweet smell of her skin.

Dani shook her head, pulling back, breaths short. "No." She used her free hand to push Alex's chin up. "I want to hear you." She slid her fingers beneath the underside of Alex's underwear and glided through her arousal, making Alex whimper. Dani hummed. "You feel so good."

"Dani."

"Yes, baby?"

Alex wrapped both hands around Dani's neck and brought their lips back together, breathing the words into her mouth, her veins. "Fuck me."

"What took you so long?"

Dani held Alex's gaze, one hand laced through her hair as she slipped two fingers of the other inside her, knuckle-deep, lips parted as if to mimic the groan stuck in the back of Alex's throat. For a moment, she kept them there. Steady, deep, taunting Alex's hips to an impatient jerk. Heat bore down on her back, between her legs, leaving the counter slick beneath her. There was something strangely erotic about it all—about being taken like this, not in a bed, Dani almost completely dressed, Alex little less than naked—that had Alex so turned on she was aching for it, ready to say please like a good little bottom if Dani demanded it.

Dani started a slow pace, fingers thrusting in and out, pushing Alex closer to the edge with every curl. She leaned in and whispered an "I love you" against Alex's ear before pressing her lips against her neck and biting, licking, leaving her mark all over Alex's skin.

"Babe..." Alex dragged in a breath, tightening her grip on the edge of the counter as Dani increased her pace and added another finger. Her abs tensed, her entire body taut with the buildup, and she tried to make it last a bit longer. "Fuck—Dani, I'm—Dani!" She grabbed Dani's face and kissed her—wet, fast, messy—moaning into her mouth as her toes curled and her orgasm slammed into her.

Dani slid her fingers out and dragged them over Alex's clit as the aftershock passed, tremors and quakes at every touch, and breaths with never enough oxygen. She pressed her lips to Alex's and held them there for a while, other hand stroking her cheek with nothing but tenderness. Then, she stepped back, eyes almost pitch black as she pulled Alex off the counter and turned her around to bend over it. "Stay right there."

*

Alex had barely opened her eyes before replays of last night started looping in her head. She wasn't sure what had gotten into Dani—what had led her to be so dominant, borderline relentless, barely letting Alex breathe between orgasms—but she hoped it wouldn't be the last time. If they didn't have at least one more marathon like that before Dani had to go, Alex would be on a plane no more than a day later.

"Morning."

Alex glanced over to see Dani snuggled against a pillow—strands of curly dark hair messy against caramel skin, eyes honey and lime. "Have I mentioned how ridiculously beautiful you are?"

Dani beamed, dimples on full display. "You always get so soft after sex."

Realistically, Alex was soft 90 percent of the time. She just happened to be shit at hiding it after someone had literally been inside her, after her mind had lost control of her body, and left her nothing but a mess of shivers and whimpers of their name. *Soft* was perfectly descriptive for Alex's post-sex mood, especially when she'd been with Dani. "Is that a bad thing?"

"Never." Dani shook her head. "I love vulnerable Alex. I don't think I get to see her enough."

In that regard, Dani was probably speaking on behalf of everyone else in Alex's life. Alex was working on it though. She reached across the empty space between them. "Why are you all the way over there?"

Dani glanced down and laced their fingers together as she shuffled closer. "I didn't want to wake you. But now that you are..." She propped up on one elbow, brushing a few strands of hair behind Alex's ear as she leaned in.

Alex winced in anticipation. "Mornin—Mmm—Babe, morning breath."

"I told you." Dani shook her head, breath minty against Alex's. "I don't care."

Despite herself, Alex mumbled, "You taste good."

Dani grinned, "Those words are vaguely familiar," pushing Alex's chin up with the bridge of her nose to press a kiss to her neck.

"If we're going to go another"—Alex glanced skyward, mind chasing an accurate number to describe last night's events, only for her realize she couldn't come up with one—"I don't know." A gulp slid down her throat as Dani's hands slipped under the sheets and squeezed her bare hips. "Ten rounds? I'm going to need recovery therapy. A shower, maybe a cappuccino. Nothing too exotic."

"Now you know how I feel every time..." She brushed her lips against Alex's chest. "You go..." Kissed her right breast. "All alpha." Dani grazed her nipples with her teeth then Dani sucked one into her mouth, making Alex's eyes roll back.

Alex pressed both hands to Dani's shoulders and wrapped one leg around her in a flip that left her on top of Dani. They locked eyes. Honey and brown, pupils blown.

Dani tightened her grip on Alex's thighs, drawing Alex's attention downward.

Alex narrowed her eyes to the sweatshirt Dani definitely hadn't been wearing when they'd gone to bed last night. The beat of her heart slowed as she processed the sky-blue color, the number thirteen, the crucifix at the center of Trinity's crest.

Sanctum.

Pudicitiam.

Honoris.

Dani sat upright, creasing her forehead. "What is it?"

Alex parted her lips, words she hadn't decided on stuck on her tongue. She shifted from Dani's lap and dragged the sheet around her as she stood. "Take it off."

"What?"

"The hoodie. Take it off. Please."

"Baby." Dani got to her feet too. "What's wrong?"

"Just take it off, Dani!" Alex closed her eyes, raking a hand through her hair as she reopened them. "I'm sorry. Just…" She dragged in a breath, catching a glance of the Calvano printed in all caps on the back as Dani pulled the hoodie off and dropped it on the bed.

Dani kept her eyes trained on her feet, long enough for Alex to step forward and apologize again.

Dani lifted her head, lips pursed. "I'm guessing it's hers then."

Alex knit her brows.

"Francesca."

"How do you—" She took a step back. "What are you talking about?"

Dani opened her mouth and glanced skyward, something like reluctance in her demeanor before she focused on Alex again. "I overheard you and your dad talking about her. Yesterday."

"You mean you were eavesdropping?"

"No." Dani shook her head. "I mean, yes, Alex. Because you've been off for weeks, and you wouldn't talk to me, and I was scared, okay? I *am* scared, so when I heard your dad ask why you changed your mind about wanting to take me to Thanksgiving, I stood there longer than I was supposed to."

"Okay. Okay, fine." Alex nodded. "You heard my dad bring up a girl from my past, so you come home and put her clothes on?"

"I didn't know it was hers! Not until you freaked out just now."

"Is that what last night was about? The way you..."

"No." Dani took a step forward, eyes glossier. "I meant what I said. I missed you. I missed being with you that way."

"And I always get so soft after sex, right?"

"Don't do that. Don't make it sound like I used us being together as some sort of manipulation. I just wanted to be close to you. All I've ever wanted is to feel close to you, but you don't make it very easy, Alex!"

"Yeah, well you knew that when we started this, didn't you?"

"This isn't the same thing! This isn't you being guarded. This is—" She swallowed, clenching her jaw. "This is someone you clearly used to be in love with."

"I didn't." Alex shook her head. "I wasn't..."

"I got that from less than five minutes of hearing your dad talk about how you were with her, and if you're about to tell me that you weren't in love with her, you're either lying to me, or you're lying to yourself."

Alex refused to process the words. She would reach in and pluck them straight out of her head if she could. "Dani."

"It's fine. Someone like you..." She breathed a humorless laugh. "I'd be more surprised if you didn't have at least one really intense romance in your closet. Because that's how you love, Alex. Intense. Deep. Scary, passionate love. I may be the one who believes in love at first sight, but you're the ultimate romantic. You put yourself all in even while trying to fight it. And that's exactly how I know if we don't deal with this...I'm going to lose you."

"You're not going to lose me."

"Well, someone will," she muttered, and for the first time, Alex saw Dani's fear. "You can't be everything for everyone. So, whatever this is with Francesca, figure out what you are to her. Or we don't stand a chance."

*

It was like déjà vu.

Dani leaving.

Their arguing about Alex's feelings for someone else.

Alex tried to explain that sure, she had been spending some time with Frankie lately, and yes, she was off, because Frankie represented fragments of her past she hadn't dealt with yet, and her coming back hadn't given Alex much of a choice but to face even some of it. But that's all it was. Alex hadn't laid a finger on Frankie, hadn't even considered it. She wasn't anything to Frankie anymore. Not really. A phantom. Someone she used to know. Frankie was the reason Alex had even brought Dani to Staten Island to begin with. Didn't that count for anything?

Guess not.

Dani still left with tears in her eyes and an "I love you" pressed to Alex's lips that tasted a lot like goodbye.

"Cappuccino."

Alex glanced up from her corner booth in Brave as the barista—a curvy redhead with a distinctly southern accent—placed her coffee, cradled on top of a porcelain saucer, on the wooden table. She eyed the generic swirls in the cup, no number to measure her shitty mood, and she frowned. Expected. Disappointing all the same.

"Can I get you anything else?" The redhead beamed. "All our pastries are fresh-baked."

Alex forced a smile and shook her head. "I'm good. Thanks."

"Al'righty then. Just holler if you change your mind."

She reeked of newness. New to Brave. New to the city. One New York winter would eclipse every ray of sunshine spilling out of her. Then again, Dani had lived here all her life, and she was still the sweetest person Alex had ever met.

She sighed, redirecting her attention to her open laptop. Her postworkshop analysis wasn't going to write itself. But she'd never enjoyed getting too critical of someone else's art, and too many thoughts occupied her mind for her to remember her train of thought with the two sentences she'd managed to get down.

What did she expect?

Torturing herself by coming to Brave the second Dani had left the penthouse—insistent on taking the fucking subway instead of just letting Alex drive her home—was the epitome of counter-productive. As if she could dissect the effectiveness of foreshadowing and alliterative sentence structures when all she could think about was Dani and Frankie. She caught sight of a familiar face as the door opened and her forehead creased.

Tanaka?

Same silky black hair and high cheekbones, dark eyes both playful and lethal in ways that had nothing to do with the fact that she'd been forced to start learning a martial art at three years old. She glanced over her shoulder in anticipation of someone following, and when he did, laughing as he helped her out of her coat, Alex almost thought she was seeing things. Because this guy— well over six feet tall, arms and shoulders products of years in gyms and on basketball courts, skin like the deepest shade of umber—looked a lot like her best friend, a lot like Dom, but Dom would tell her if he'd been hanging out with someone as important to Frankie as he was to Alex. Wouldn't he? As if he sensed her presence, he lifted his head in the direction of her booth and their eyes locked. He pursed his lips, and Tanaka followed his gaze. They could have been friends. Alex and Tan. They could've been friends if not for...

Their first team event. Preseason bonding session like they always had. Except, it had never been at the Calvanos'. For a second, Alex wondered what they all had been thinking—voting Frankie captain of the team. She'd just started Trinity. Still, there were no questions about her talent, experience or ability to lead. The only reason Alex had even made varsity was because Frankie had pushed her to it. Two weeks of insisting Alex was too good for JV. Another of them both putting in extra workouts so Alex wouldn't bomb her tryouts. Maybe that's the reason being at Frankie's place made her so uneasy. Because team event or not, Alex didn't want to be sat on the stairs of the Calvanos' home with Frankie on the other side of the room, and fifteen other girls between them.

"What about you, Van Kirk?"

Alex's eyes shifted right of Frankie to find Tanaka—starting right-winger and Frankie's closest friend—watching her expectantly. She blinked, briefly attempting to recall what they'd been talking about, only to come up with nothing. "I'm sorry, what?"

"Which of the King Brothers do you think is hotter?"

Alex scrunched up her face. She didn't know why, but she'd never liked the way everyone referred to Dom and Kason as the King Brothers, apart from the fact that they weren't related by blood. Just friends who happened to have the same last name. Maybe it was because she'd known Dom almost all sixteen years of her life, and he and Kason weren't anything alike. Most days, she didn't even know why they hung out. Before Kason cheated on her and Dom stopped speaking to him.

"Isn't it obvious?" Greenfield piped in. "She was with Kase for over a year."

"That doesn't necessarily mean anything. Lots of people are secretly into their best friend."

Alex shook her head. "Yeah. Not me."

Sure, Dom was attractive. Alex wasn't blind. But it wasn't like that between them. They were more like the siblings neither of them had.

"Come on," Tanaka pressed. "You seriously don't think he's hot? He's literally six feet of chocolate. How does anyone resist that?"

"Tan," Frankie entered, pulling Alex's eyes back to hers. "Question asked and answered. Besides..." She paused, drowning Alex in the pull of her gaze. "She's clearly out of both their leagues. Right, Van Kirk?"

"Right." Alex stood, swallowing the lump in her throat. She took a hopefully casual glance around. "Bathroom?"

"Upstairs," Frankie offered. "Second door on the left."

"Thanks."

Alex started up the flight without a glance back, heart thudding, mind racing. Almost a year since she'd first laid eyes on Frankie, four months since they'd been texting, spending time together face-to-face of late, and Alex still wasn't used to it. She wasn't used to the sentiment that she couldn't breathe when Frankie looked at her all spellbinding and intimidating and everything that made Alex sure she would never look at Francesca

Calvano the way girls were meant to look at other girls. The possibility just didn't exist.

She got to the landing of the stairs and started down a short hallway with two doors on each side. She passed the first one, vaguely remembering the word second leaving Frankie's lips, and twisted the knob of the foremost door on the opposite side, only to be met by near complete darkness. Light filtered through a window set in one wall. Enough to make out the four posts of a canopy bed and what appeared to be three shelves of trophies.

Definitely not the bathroom.

Her hand raised to take the knob in her grip again when someone caught it and spun her toward them. A tousle of wavy blonde hair and teal irises flashed before her eyes, and then lips were on hers. The breath in her lungs caught, and her heart called it quits—completely stopped beating—for the longest second before her back hit something hard.

Frankie's lips felt exactly like Alex imagined. Soft didn't even come close to being sufficiently descriptive. And how the fuck did she taste like actual cherries after Alex had seen her down half a bowl of popcorn?

Frankie pulled away, breathing against Alex's lips, leaving goose bumps on every inch of her skin. "I'm sorry."

Alex opened her eyes slowly, her chest heaving.

"I told myself I wouldn't do that. Not until you..." Frankie dragged in a breath. "I just—"

Alex reached up with one hand and touched Frankie's lips. She grazed the lush, pink layer with her index and middle finger as if to assure herself she'd just been kissed by them.

"Alex..."

Frankie opened her eyes too, and Alex froze as she got stuck on just looking, overcome by a sudden need to memorize everything from the pattern of freckles on Frankie's nose to the angle of her cheekbones, teasing flare of her lips. Alex locked eyes with Frankie again. Frankie held her gaze, question in her darkened eyes as she brushed a few strands of hair behind Alex's right ear, just like the night of her party, and cupped her cheek.

This time, it started with her body—hips and chest pressing Alex further against the wall, and Alex giving up on any hope that her heart would ever beat normally with Frankie this close. Frankie waited, silently asking for permission, but Alex couldn't make herself say yes, and it seemed equally impossible to say no, so for a while, that was all it was. Just breathing and wanting and dying. And then, Frankie gently took Alex's bottom lip between hers, and Alex completely melted into gestures of *yes*. Taking a fist full of the jersey Frankie wore and pulling her closer. Breathing Frankie straight into her veins. Tilting her head to kiss Frankie deeper, slower, longer. And thinking...

This was how she wanted to be kissed.

She pulled away and took a second to fail at catching her breath before she reopened her eyes. She swallowed everything she felt, and she made the words leave her lips with all the conviction she possessed. "Don't ever do that again."

She made for the stairs, through the living room and out the door.

Alex didn't know when Frankie had told Tanaka about them—that night, right after their first kiss, or weeks later. They'd never talked about it. Just like they hadn't talked about Alex telling Dom. Tanaka and Alex had never been much more than teammates anyway, even when Tan was so mad, she could take Alex's head off with a well-aimed ball. She'd tried at least once. Alex didn't blame her.

Tanaka started toward Alex.

Dom sighed as he followed. "Kaida, come on."

First name basis. Definitely sleeping together.

Tanaka weaved her way through the tables at the center of the café and slid right into the booth across from Alex, never one to be delicate. "You just couldn't help it, could you?"

Alex drew her brows closer and glanced up as Dom stopped next to the table. "Kaida, stop. You have no idea what happened."

Alex shook her head. "What happened with what? Apart from the fact that you two are clearly more than *friendly*."

"I was going to tell you."

Tanaka scoffed. "You don't owe her any explanations, Dom."

"Okay, I get that you just want to protect your best friend, but don't forget Alex is still mine."

"Will one of you tell me what the fuck is going on here?" Alex put in. "Because last I checked, I was literally here just minding my own business."

"Yeah, well, that's the problem, isn't it, VK?" Tanaka answered. "Always too into your own shit to give a shit about anyone else."

"Kaida!"

"No." Alex raised a hand before Dom could say another word, eyes locked on the girl seated across from her. "What are you talking about?"

Tanaka tilted her head a bit, look on her face anything but impressed.

Alex's gaze wavered, all the sting gone from her tone when she answered. "What did I do?"

"Nothing." Tanaka shrugged. "At least that's what she's saying. You didn't do anything. But I know what she's like after Hurricane Alex blows through, and right now she's pretty damn close."

What did that even mean? What she's like.

It didn't matter. Apparently, all Alex did was hurt Frankie. Past and present.

"What does she need? I mean..." Alex swallowed, glancing down at her hands before looking at Tanaka again. "Just...I don't know what to do, Tan."

For a while, Tanaka examined Alex, searching for something Alex wasn't sure she'd found. "You know, I didn't always hate you for her. I even forgave you almost as many times as she did. Helped her rationalize your indecision and damage. I mean, she knew the day she laid eyes on you in that hallway, but she's Frankie." Tan breathed a laugh. "We all know she's fucking fearless. She didn't have to come to terms with her feelings for the first time after being stuck in that school for two years already, and while she had a boyfriend? I get that it was hard. I defended you, Alex. And just when I thought I was right, you—" She shook her head.

Alex's chest ached, her head pounding as she absorbed the words. Tanaka didn't have to finish her statement. No matter how much she hated Alex for what she was about to say, no question, Alex hated herself more.

"It wasn't that you were a coward that I hated. It wasn't even how you'd take her to the top of the world then leave her all alone. It's that you knew exactly how she felt about you. You just couldn't admit it, no matter how much it was killing you both."

Chapter Twenty-One

chardonnay

The quarterfinal against Convent of Mercy changed everything.

Alex wasn't sure if it was the fact that she'd confessed too much—even if the words hadn't left her lips—alone with Frankie in that locker room, or the realization that she'd never run that fast, struck with such precision, been as determined to demolish the defense with every bit of natural and learned skill she possessed. Until it was for *her*. She had played for the team, done her best because she owed them that much every time they took the field together.

She also hadn't.

Every ounce of blood, sweat, and tears she'd shed that second half was as much for Francesca Calvano as she'd been spilling in the dark of her room for months already.

She couldn't admit it, but...

The quarterfinal against Convent of Mercy changed everything.

She knew it when the Doves returned to the locker room—loud, rowdier than a group of Catholic, private school girls were supposed to be, with Alex all but smushed in the middle of her teammates' praises for a hat trick which had come out of nowhere.

She knew it when she met Frankie's eyes—brown and blue and too honest—and Frankie's apprehension shifted into pure, unrestrained joy at the realization that they'd done it, Tanaka on top of her voice when she screamed in Frankie's direction, "You should've seen her out there!"

Alex still had no idea what to do with the knowledge that Tanaka clearly knew there was something more than friendly between her and Frankie, so she just let them cheer her on and pretended the look in Frankie's eyes wasn't putting her at threat of combustion right where she stood. She even managed to sound half casual when she shrugged and mumbled, "Team effort."

When the first set of girls disappeared into the showers, Alex's mind wandered three cubes down where she'd seen Frankie go in seconds before tossing the towel over the door. Her breath caught, and her lower abdomen ached from something so unrelated to the grueling match she wasn't even an hour free of... and she knew.

Later that night, it was impossible to not know. The setting sun barely casting a glow over Frankie's golden hair and tan skin, blue and green of her eyes sparkling in a way that made her look downright fucking ethereal. Too close when she breathed Alex's name. Always too close. Worried if they kissed again, Alex would run. Through the racking of her heart against her ribs, Alex took a handful of Frankie's sweatshirt—tight yet trembling, scared but surer than she'd ever been—and she pressed her lips to Frankie's.

It was how it happened the last time too—Alex's surrender being the thing to shatter Frankie's control, give her permission to act on the confidence to push Alex onto her bed and straddle her. Forceful enough to kick the beat of Alex's heart higher but make her want Frankie that much more. Eyes locked, forever wanting Alex's consent. Breath hot against Alex's lips, all cherry Blistex and postmatch gourmet pizza from Calvano's.

And it hit Alex, her eyes closed as Frankie burned a trail down her neck with her lips, their hands desperate, clutching and clawing.

This is how she says yes.

With every kiss, and touch, and too-long stare.

Yes, yes, yes.

They lay in the dark after. Not wrapped up in each other's arms, but close enough. Shoulders brushing. Not naked, but too vulnerable all the same with the way the buildup had become too much for Alex again. The way her body had succumbed to what felt like hours of having Frankie pressed against her—lips and teeth and suppressed moans of each other's name. She all but expected the tremors, ache and release when Frankie's leg shifted a bit too high between her thighs and forced the zipper of her jeans down on that one spot that she didn't even know makes her lose it. In the dark, after that, it's a little too defenseless, especially when Frankie murmured, "It was pretty cool of your dad to come to the game. I know he's a busy guy."

Something inside Alex shifted, and she made a conscious effort not to move over, put some space between them. "How do you figure that?"

Frankie shrugged. "Billionaire hotel mogul and soccer Dad kind of seem mutually exclusive."

"Like world-class restauranteur slash executive chef, and soccer Dad?"

"Exactly."

One word, and the vulnerability in Frankie's tone wiped any hint of amusement right off Alex's face.

"Maybe that's why he never comes to see me play."

Alex frowned, angling her body to be more attentive, more open to whatever Frankie needed. "What about your mom?"

"Flying to a different city every night doesn't really make time for soccer games either."

"Oh," Alex muttered. "What does she do?"

"Pilot." When Frankie finally turned on her side to face Alex, she surveyed the space between them. "Guess it's better anyway. I played like shit tonight."

"Hey." Alex brought a hand to Frankie's chin. "You had an off game. But that doesn't mean you weren't good. I think you're just too used to making the rest of us look bad."

"Alex."

"No. I mean it. It was time we picked up some of the slack anyway."

The moment dragged. Frankie softened her gaze. "I should get kicked out of games more often. You did score a hat trick tonight. Maybe you'll finally realize how good you are."

"Not as good as you. Never as good as you. You're the best, Frankie. And it's your parents' loss not being around to see it."

For a while, they just stared at each other—conversation between their eyes as always—the buzz of the city faint beyond the walls along with everything else that scared Alex about moments like this. Frankie leaned in, lightly resting one hand on the left of Alex's face, slow, achingly soft when their lips touched. And it wasn't just outside that was scary.

They were equally palpable, Alex realized.

The fear of wanting someone she shouldn't, and the fear of losing someone who wasn't even hers.

Nothing had changed.

Not when Alex had left the confines of whatever she and Frankie had become to brave the cold of the city—fall and something else in the Manhattan air—to hop into the car her father had arranged, and stew on the ride home. Almost ten on a Friday night, but when she'd made her way into the penthouse and through the foyer, the light chatter and gentle clink of utensils drew her attention to her parents seated on opposite ends of the dining table. Ten o'clock at night but it was more common than not. Dishes of tenderloin and fish, salad and champagne laid out, and a well-groomed waiter standing nearby being punished with at least an hour of corporate dialogue.

"There she is." Alex's dad stood, wiping the corners of his lips with a cotton napkin before dropping it on the table. "Join us."

Alex shook her head, gaze wandering anywhere but the eyes of her father, let alone her mother. She was used to the post-Frankie guilt. Tonight, she had the perfect excuse. "I'm tired, Dad."

"You must be, after that game." He chuckled, resting a hand on her shoulder. Always caring, concerned, never overly affectionate. No hugs. No kisses on the forehead. I love yous found somewhere between the lines of taking afternoons off to watch her play, and insisting they have breakfast together at least once a week. "You were amazing out there."

Her mother all but scoffed, still eating her dinner, stake close to bloody just like she liked it. "Sometimes I think you forget she's the son you never had, Xander."

Her father shook his head. "I never wanted a son. He'd probably never be as good as you anyway." He laughed, ignoring the implication behind his wife's words. "Did you have fun? With your friends."

Alex nodded. "Yeah. I'm going to go to bed."

When she got up to her room, she stripped herself of clothes smelling too much like lavender and she went to the en suite. She wasn't sure why she reached for the razor in her cabinet. She wasn't sure why she curled up in her tub and chose a new spot high on her thigh. Maybe it had everything to do with thinking there was supposed to be some type of punishment for doing, *being*, something wrong.

So, she welcomed the sharp sting of dragging a blade across her skin—a familiar pain that never hurt as much as it was meant to—and she got lost in the red instead of her thoughts, succumbing to the cycle, the ambivalence.

Sanctity, purity, honor.

Blood.

It took another week of what had happened after the quarterfinal before Frankie found out. Another week of control within the walls of Trinity and losing it in the confines of Frankie's bedroom. Keyes the soundtrack to their muffled moans and sloppy kisses, Alex finally bold enough to be on top this time, in love with the feeling of Frankie's body beneath hers, high on the whine that left Frankie's lips when Alex dragged her teeth against Frankie's pulse point before soothing it with her tongue.

Frankie shifted her hands in search of a firmer grip, not presumptuous enough to settle on Alex's ass, just short. When Alex found that spot again, Frankie squeezed exactly where Alex had cut too deep last night.

The noise that left Alex's lips *wasn't* erotic.

Frankie pulled back—lips swollen and red, parted to allow her irregular breaths. "Sorry." She swallowed, both their composures out of reach. "Did I hurt you?"

Alex shook her head, leaning in. "No."

Frankie pulled away again, pushing on Alex's chest as she sat up. "Wait. What just hap—" She glanced down, and before Alex managed to adjust her shorts, Frankie drew her brows together. "Alex?"

Alex moved to fix her clothes. Frankie caught her hand, gaze still glued to the grid of healed and fresh scars on Alex's right thigh. Red and raw. Frankie pulled the hem of the shorts higher, slow, gentle, and Alex closed her eyes as she bit down on her bottom lip.

"What is this?"

Alex rolled off Frankie's lap, not experiencing anymore resistance when she stood and took a few paces across the room, fingers of her right hand tangled in her hair. "Nothing."

"Alex..." Frankie started slowly, a new edge to her voice. "Don't tell me that is nothing. You're—" She shook her head. "Are you hurting yourself?"

No answer. Just pacing and breathing and anything to not panic. Alex really, really didn't want to talk about this. It was more of an answer than she thought.

"Why?" Frankie asked, voice octaves higher.

Alex closed her eyes, dragging in a breath before she forced herself to meet the look on Frankie's face. "Can we not do this?"

"Do what, Alex? You're literally bleeding right now. Am I just supposed to ignore that?"

"I should go." Alex turned, suddenly confused about where she'd left her bag and books.

Frankie grabbed her hand and tugged so they were face-to-face again. "Tell me what's going on."

"I—" Her chest tightened. Had the room always been this small? "Frankie, *I can't.*"

"Why not? Why can't you just tal—"

"You're not my fucking girlfriend, okay?"

It just came out. Alex didn't know why, or where it'd come from. It just came out.

Frankie dropped her hand and stepped back, nodding. "No. No, I'm not, Alex." The silence dragged. "We just text any second we get, all hours of the night.

Kiss. I can't get enough of kissing you, and you know what? Sometimes I think you can't get enough of kissing me either, especially when you're hot and shivering under me, clawing at my bra with my name in your mouth. Especially"—she released a humorless laugh—"when you dry my tears in locker rooms and tell me how you're going to win games for me, lie in my bed hours later, and listen to me talk about missing my parents."

Alex swallowed, chest aching, lungs on fire, tears too, too close.

"But you're right. I'm not your girlfriend. If I had any idea what was good for me, I'd stop letting you role play whenever you fucking feel like it."

A single stream hit Frankie's cheek, forcing the pair on the rim of Alex's eyes to fall too, forcing her to regret her words that much more and take a step forward.

"Frankie..."

Frankie took one back. "Get out."

"Frankie, I—"

"Get the fuck out, Alex."

She'd never witnessed the look in Frankie's eyes before—pain and rage and darkness. Frankie had never talked to her in anything but the gentlest of tones, so nothing she said would work this time.

How does one fix something that had been built broken anyway?

This was new—Frankie being the one who didn't want to talk.

Alex couldn't handle it.

She couldn't handle the sleepless nights, eyes burning with exhaustion as she typed out *Hey* and *You up? Can we talk? Frankie...* only to receive nothing in return. When she did manage to close her eyes, she reenvisioned the tears on Frankie's cheeks, the hardness of her face, her lips when she asked Alex to leave, and Alex's own words would echo again. She'd tell herself she still didn't know why they'd left her lips with as much venom as they had, why they'd left her lips at all. But the shift was palpable. All those things Frankie had mentioned... Alex's inability to admit them wouldn't make them any less true.

Still, she couldn't handle making it more than covert texts, and glances, and after practice practices, just the two of them. Study-turned-make-out sessions in Frankie's bedroom, learning all the ways to make each other so soft and sensitive, and being naive enough to think the heart and body, feelings and feeling, were isolated.

She couldn't handle labels like *girlfriend*.

But being stuck inside the cafeteria because it was next to freezing outside, half the girls' soccer team sat in the middle engaged in something so interesting Frankie hadn't looked at Alex once, Alex couldn't handle that either. And all she felt was selfish. Selfish for wanting Frankie still. Selfish for still not wanting her the way she should.

"VK..." Dom lowered his phone next to the pizza slice in front of him, thumbs finally breaking from the back and forth texting that had ensued when he opted to have lunch with her instead of his not-so-secure girlfriend. "Why don't you just talk to her?"

Alex rolled her eyes—all her frustration over the situation way too close to erupting for her to deal with suggestions like that. "She *doesn't* want to talk to me. Have you been paying any attention?"

"Paying attention to what? All your silent seething?"

"Whatever."

"You miss her, VK."

Alex clenched her teeth. She did miss Frankie. Something about hearing the words out loud didn't process well anyway.

"Every time you guys do this, it drives you nuts. You're just too stubborn to admit it."

"She doesn't want to talk to me, Dom."

"Have you tried something worth hearing?"

Alex scoffed. "Like what?"

"Oh, I don't know, VK. The truth?"

There was Dom who supported Alex in all her whims and bullshit. And there Dom who called her out on it. It was something in the deep brown of his eyes—so free of humor and distraction, so brutally honest when he chose to be.

"Tell her everything you told me that night when your mom found her sleeping in your bed. Tell her how...you still get stuck on how gorgeous she is. Almost two years later and you can't help but stare. Tell her you love that she's pretty *and* smart, and you have no idea how she balances sports and AP but seeing her do it makes you think you can too. Tell her about how she pushes you, and you hate it, but you love it. Secretly, you can't get enough of how she coaches and cheers you on. And tell her how she's the only thing about this place"—he shook his head and glanced around the room—"that makes breathing easier and harder at the same time. You don't have to tell her all the dark stuff, VK. Just tell her even half the truth."

Alex swallowed, throat tight with words she'd choked out weeks ago, phone pressed to her ear as she sobbed on the edge of her tub. She closed her eyes and pushed back the memory. "*I can't*, Dom."

"Fine."

She reopened her eyes to find her best friend nodding, nothing but understanding at the end of it all. "Then how about you just start with I'm sorry?"

Alex was a wreck. Her mind had gone into overdrive, reliving everything she'd tried so hard to suppress—memories rushing in, pushing her toward something she wasn't sure she was strong enough to do. She hadn't been before, and no matter what Dom and Ry said, she wasn't sure four years had made an ounce of difference. Sitting in her car, across the street from Frankie's loft for the last twenty-six minutes all but proved as much.

The engine throttled quietly, the heat keeping her warm, gears at the ready for her to shift into drive and get out of there if she lost her nerve. The last thing she'd wanted was to hurt Frankie. Based on her conversation with Tan during their run-in at Brave, Alex had somehow managed to do that anyway. So why was she still sitting there?

Maybe, though this all felt too familiar, they weren't at Trinity, so Alex didn't know what to expect.

They weren't seventeen, eighteen, and kissing Frankie's tears away wouldn't work this time. They'd have to talk about all the things that were wrong. *Are* wrong. And that's what terrified her most. Hearing it all out loud. Not reliving a series of recluse dreams or nightmares in her head. Reality.

She grabbed her phone from the front passenger's seat and went straight to her messages.

Alex: Can I see you?

Frankie: What's up? Are you okay?

Alex: Yeah. I'm just outside your place. I'm not even sure you're home now that I think about it. But I'll wait. If that's okay.

Ellipses appeared on her screen. Based on the wait time, she figured Frankie must've been tapping out an explanation of why she wasn't home or why Alex couldn't come up. The bubble disappeared, leaving no trace of a response for a while. Then...

> *Frankie: Suite 9. Just give Freddy my name. He'll let you up.*

Whatever Frankie intended to say initially, she'd changed her mind. Alex could feel it. She switched off the engine and reached for the bottle of chardonnay she'd picked straight out of the winery back at The Van Kirk, then opened the door before she changed her mind. As she made her way across the street and into the lobby of the Wexmore, it occurred to her that she didn't even know if Frankie liked wine. She didn't know much of anything about Frankie anymore. She narrowed her gaze to the stout man standing by the door of the lobby, grey hair thinning but well-groomed to match his starched charcoal suit and black shoes. Freddy, announced the gold name tag on the right side of his chest.

"I'm here to see Frankie."

Freddy squinted. "I'm sorry. I don't believe there are any Frankie's at the Wexmore."

Alex glanced around the empty lobby, as if expecting Frankie to emerge. "Are you sure? Because I just spoke to her. Calvano?"

"Francesca!" The man grinned. "I'm sorry. Sometimes I forget how you young people are with names. Go by a million and one these days."

Alex smiled too, somewhere between genuine and just wanting to be polite.

Freddy bobbed his head toward the bottle in Alex's hand. "Bringing her a little pick me up?"

"Something like that." Alex started toward the elevator. "Have a good night, Freddy."

"You too..." he trailed off, eyes expectant.

"Alex."

"You too, Alex."

She stepped into the elevator and used the loft index as a guide for which floor to choose, suite nine being listed on the fourth floor. The ascent lasted a few seconds and she exited into a short hallway with cream accents and white doors. She slowed her steps as she got to Frankie's, the attempt to swallow all her anxiety failing, deep breath doing nothing to steady her climbing pulse. She brought the knuckles of her free hand to the door and knocked. When silence answered, her gaze shifted to her feet and she anxiously wiggled her toes around the pair of Garvani combat boots.

The door gently swung open and her head snapped up, eyes narrowing to the woman in front of her. Blonde hair a little messy, face makeup free, all tan skin and freckles lining the bridge of her nose, eyes blue—not so green today—dressed in a gray Henley and lounge shorts. "Hey."

Alex raked a hand through her hair. "I—uhm—I hope I wasn't interrupting anything."

Frankie shook her head. "Just watching *The Blind Side* for the millionth time."

Alex smiled. "I love that movie."

"I know."

A silence dragged out, just Alex standing there, afraid to look Frankie in the eyes too long, afraid of what she'll see if she does. She held the bottle in her hand tighter and lifted it in offering. "Not sure if you like wine, but I brought you this."

"Thank you." Frankie accepted the bottle, and Alex wasn't sure why, but she felt a little disappointed that the answer wasn't definitive. Not *I love wine, actually*, or even *It's not really my thing, but thanks anyway*. "Do you want to come in? I'm only at the part where Michael's walking in the rain."

She knew. Frankie knew there was more to Alex showing up at her door than to bring her a bottle of chardonnay she'd probably never drink. Always wanting to make things easier than Alex deserved, only to make them more difficult in the end.

Alex nodded. "Yeah. I'd like that."

*

They watched the whole movie in silence.

In fact, Alex spent the first twenty minutes barely watching at all, too distracted by the brick walls and stone beams in Frankie's loft. The beige and yellow of her sofa, soothing light blue accents and the glass partition separating living and bedroom, king bed robed in white and bluish gray. All contrasts of hard and soft, bold and subtle. So Francesca Calvano, with the exception of the copy of *Fifty Shades of Grey* next to the lamp on her nightstand. Interesting choice of reading material, but not very Frankie. At least, the Frankie Alex used to know.

Sometimes, after Alex had resolved to attempt to pay attention to the movie, she could feel Frankie's eyes on her even with all the space between them. Credits were going up the screen before she'd even faced Frankie once. She struggled to remind herself she was there for a reason. And this, whatever it was, wasn't it.

"You're reading *Fifty Shades of Grey*?"

Frankie shook her head, the look in her eyes resembling disappointment. "Tan brought it over weeks ago. I'm still on page one."

Alex nodded. Maybe she was still Frankie after all.

"Alex."

Definitely still Frankie, the way she mumbled Alex's name. All tenderness.

And pain.

"This is the part where you ask if I'm okay again," Alex whispered. "Then I lie, and you know it, but you'll let it go anyway because it's the only way we work. The only way we used to work. But..." She forced herself to meet Frankie's eyes. "I don't want to do that anymore. I don't want to do that to *you* anymore."

"Alex—"

"No." Alex shook her head. "Don't tell me *it's okay.* Don't make this easy for me. You're hurting." She closed her eyes, her sigh echoing the ache in her chest. "All I do is hurt you, and I may have missed it this time, but I want to fix it."

"There's nothing to fix."

"Frankie—"

"You can't fix it, Alex!"

Alex reopened her eyes at the shift in Frankie's tone. Rage and something else all twisted up in the words. Her eyes glimmered, tears already threatening to fall. Alex had expected at least this on the drive over. Yelling and tears. Expectations didn't make it any easier, sitting there. But she could never stand seeing Frankie cry.

Frankie got to her feet, shaking her head as she ran a hand through her hair. "Why are you doing this?"

"Frankie, I just..." There were no words. None that were enough. Wasn't that why Alex had always failed at using them back then? But things were different now. So much different. "I just want you to be okay."

Frankie released a humorless laugh as if she'd never heard anything more ridiculous. "You don't get it, do you?"

"Then make me."

She sighed, starting toward her bedroom. "Go home, Alex."

"No." Alex stood and caught Frankie's hand. Frankie paused, bottom lip pulled between her teeth as she glanced up at the high ceiling. Alex went closer, silently pleading for Frankie to face her. "Talk to me."

For a while, they just stood there—Frankie's back half-turned, Alex waiting for something already looming in the back of her mind. Then, Frankie faced her, jaw clenched, lips pursed. "It's not any fun, is it? Begging someone to let you in and just having them reject you over and over and over."

"I never meant for it to feel like that."

"Yeah, well it did. And you don't get to change that with a fucking bottle of wine, Alex!"

Alex nodded. "I know."

"You don't get to come here and tell me how you just want me to be okay when I haven't been okay since the day I laid eyes on you!"

"Frankie, I know."

"You don't get"—she took a step back, tears finally hitting her cheeks—"to tell me how much better I deserved, just so you can—" Her voice cracked, chest heaving as she squeezed her eyes shut.

Alex stepped forward, losing the battle not to cry too. She cradled Frankie's face and wiped at the tears with her thumbs. "Frankie."

Frankie opened her eyes—blue and red and tired—and Alex didn't hear the shatter, but she could feel

Frankie's heart break. If it was anything like her own, neither of them would ever collect all the pieces. And for a second, Alex wasn't sure, because now—twenty-one, twenty-two—standing in Frankie's loft, felt a lot like seventeen, eighteen, in a locker room at Trinity, especially when Frankie's gaze shifted lower and she started leaning in. Alex shut her eyes and her heart raced, overwhelmed by their proximity, the overload of lavender in her veins.

"Please don't," she begged.

Frankie brought both hands to Alex's hips and guided her backward before pushing her onto the couch.

"Frankie—"

She placed a hand on Alex's shoulder, straddling her as she brought her other hand to the nape of Alex's neck and she leaned in. So close to the old Frankie. But this wasn't her and it wasn't right. For more reasons than one.

"Look at me." She raised both hands to Frankie's face and dried more tears as they fell, searching for her gaze until Frankie finally opened her eyes. "*I can't.*"

"So she gets you at your best, and he got you at your worst, and I just—" Frankie closed her eyes, burying her face against Alex's neck, sobs echoing in her ear. "It's not fair. None of this is fair."

"I know."

"I loved you so much, Alex," she mumbled, breath hot against Alex's neck, tears soaking through her shirt. "I still"—she held on tighter, always so scared of Alex running after moments like this—"love you so much."

"I know."

Alex couldn't run even if she wanted to. Her walls had completely collapsed. Funny thing, how people tended to build those to keep things out. She was beginning to think hers had been formed very deliberately to keep something in.

"I've been in love with you since I was sixteen, Frankie. I was just never any good at showing it."

Chapter Twenty-Two

belvedere

Alex wasn't sure how long it had been since she'd all but picked up Frankie and adjusted on the couch—Frankie's head on her chest, body half on top of hers, arms and legs tangled in each other's. It didn't feel any less intimate than Frankie pushing her onto the couch and straddling her, but this is the most vulnerable they'd ever been.

What Frankie needed.

What they both needed.

"You're wrong," Frankie mumbled, voice so soft and tired from all their crying Alex almost hadn't caught the words.

Alex kept her eyes closed and their fingers intertwined, thumb stroking the back of Frankie's hand. "What am I wrong about?"

"You did know how to show it. I felt it every time we were together. The way you looked at me, the way you kissed me, the way every time you touched me it was like you were scared of breaking me and trying to keep me together all at the same time." A fresh tear soaked through Alex's shirt and she squeezed Frankie's hand a little tighter. "I didn't just feel your pain and torture, Alex. I felt it all. Especially the night of the finals. Almost every day after too."

It was fifteen minutes before the finals. Alex anxiously took shots from the spot while Greenfield worked at saving them. She still hadn't talked to Frankie yet. Two words. Two fucking words and she was already a week through not saying them. She shouldn't have even left the Calvanos' without apologizing that night. It would've been easier to say then. Frankie didn't want to hear it, but Alex should've sat outside her door and waited until she did. Maybe it would've been awkward trying to explain to Frankie's mom or dad why she was sitting there, tears on her face. Maybe she wouldn't have to since they were hardly ever home anyway. Either way, she should've stayed, should've fought.

"VK!"

Alex barely snapped out of her musing in time for the ball whipping toward her to miss her face. She blinked, turning in the direction it had come.

Tan glared at Alex from down the field—her jaw set, eyes not even the least bit remorseful. Then, she shrugged. "Guess my aim needs work."

Alex was so busy processing the implication, she almost didn't notice Frankie roll her eyes and start toward the side-line, leaving Tanaka alone in the center of the field.

She scored the first and last goal of the final. Frankie. After being suspended for the semis, she'd come back more of a leader than ever. No outbursts against illegal tackles or unfair rulings by the ref. Not when it came to Alex or anyone else on the team. Nothing but strength, responsibility and "Come on, guys! We've got this!" She never regarded Alex directly, never addressed her outside of generalizations to the team. So, it wasn't Alex's best game. Not by a long shot. The Doves killed it in the finals anyway and walked away with the game ball, player of the match and the championship.

And it wasn't that the realization hit Alex. She'd known the day she laid eyes on Frankie, been reminded of it every day since. Frankie didn't need her. Francesca Calvano didn't need anyone. She was some kind of whole all on her own. With her, Alex was broken at best. Without her, she was all the more broken still.

When Alex showed up to the postmatch chill at the Calvanos' later that night, it was the first time Frankie had even made eye contact with her since a week ago—the look unreadable, way too fleeting, and so much more than Alex deserved. But it was something. So, all night, she hung on to that single meeting of their eyes, and the fact that Frankie hadn't demanded she leave the second she'd set foot through the door.

It felt a little like last year all over again. A little like seeing Frankie for the first time and not being able to focus on anything but her even in a room full of people. Her voice over all the chatter. Her laugh through the roar of a joke Alex couldn't care for any less. The lavender of her skin though the air reeked of popcorn, pizza and punch that was more vodka than anything else. And her eyes. Blue-green and pure kryptonite.

Everything about Francesca Calvano still made Alex weak. What was the point in denying that if she was only going to bleed anyway? And she would... bleed. For as long as she was becoming more of something her mother disapproved, loathed even, she didn't know how she'd stop feeling all kinds of twisted up over it. Her sentiments of self-love and worth weren't meant to be so tied to someone else's opinion of her. But they were. She hated herself for not being the daughter her mother wanted almost as much as she did for not being everything Frankie deserved. They were mutually exclusive. Knowing that did nothing to stop her from wanting to be both.

So, watching Frankie be perfectly social with everyone but her did feel a bit like last year. Except, now that she'd gotten to know Frankie—mind, body, glimpses of her heart—it was impossible to stay away.

Midnight had struck by the time everyone cleared out. Alex tried to casually hang around under the pretense of stuffing a few stray cups into a trash bag. When Frankie reemerged in the living room—leaned against the archway, just watching—Alex pretended to not notice and resisted the urge to face her immediately. Her heart thumped against her ribs, finally catching up to the feeling of being alone with Frankie again. It didn't matter that they were fighting, not speaking at all. Her pulse always reacted the same way to having Frankie close.

"You should get going."

Alex paused mid-reach, heart stopping at the sound of Frankie's voice. For a second, she considered giving in to Frankie's words, to what she'd been telling herself all week. Frankie didn't want to talk to her. Instead, she followed through with picking up the stray napkin on the coffee table, a half-eaten pizza slice just inches away. "I will. Just...after I'm done here." It wasn't a very good excuse. Frankie always did most of the clean up after these parties, while her family's housekeeper, Jackie, did the rest.

"Alex." Frankie sighed. "It's late."

"I know."

"Don't—" She broke off, and without having a visual, Alex envisioned the tired shake of her head. "Don't worry about the mess. I'll take care of it."

There was nothing mean about the words. Hearing them hurt anyway. Hearing Frankie basically say she didn't want or need Alex's help for a second time in less than five minutes, hurt. Maybe Alex hadn't realized how easy Frankie had made it before for her to leave and just come back whenever it became too much. She never had to say she was sorry, or that she missed her, or even explain why she'd left in the first place. All it took was opening her eyes to Frankie's and letting them speak words she couldn't, and they'd be okay. For some reason, she didn't want it to be easy this time. She didn't deserve it.

She lowered the bag then turned for the door. "Okay."

"I'll walk you out."

Alex crossed the living room in silence and followed Frankie through the foyer. She grabbed her jacket from the coat rack and slipped into it, heart and mind still racing from Frankie's proximity and the words they weren't saying. Even fighting would be better. She'd take Frankie yelling at her for being inconsiderate and utterly in denial if it meant getting a glimpse inside Frankie's mind.

Alex opened the door opened and crossed the threshold into the fall night air, the city only relatively still behind her. She stuffed her hands into the front pockets of her jacket, awkwardly rocking forward. "You were great today."

Frankie nodded. "Thanks. I'm just glad we won after all the extra work this season."

"And now it's over."

"Yeah." Frankie glanced at her feet. "I'm never too happy about that, but I guess I could use the break."

"From the game..." Alex dragged out, her next words heavy on her tongue. "Or the team?"

"Neither." Frankie shrugged. "Both?"

Alex swallowed, waiting for Frankie to meet her gaze, telling herself if they just looked at each other—genuinely looked at each other—she'd get the words out.

"I don't know. Guess I'll figure it out," Frankie muttered, one hand steady on the handle of the door. "Good night, Van Kirk."

Alex's chest ached and she bit down on the correction wanting to leave her lips as she stepped back. "Bye, Frankie." She drew on all the will she had to turn around instead of having to see the door shut in her face, and she told herself that if this was what Frankie wanted, she'd have to accept it.

Three steps down the flight to Calvanos' front door, and Alex couldn't. She wheeled in the opposite direction and back up the stairs and she raised her hand to knock. The door swung open and Frankie stepped forward just long enough to grab the hem of Alex's shirt and pull her back into the warmth of the house, of her hands, her lips.

Alex dragged in a breath through her nose, forehead creased. "I'm sorry." The words got lost in Frankie's mouth. "I'm so sorry."

Frankie nodded as she wrapped her hands around Alex's waist to pull her closer. "I know."

"No." Alex shook her head and pressed one hand against Frankie's chest to put enough space between them. She wrapped both hands around Frankie's neck and she swallowed the tightness in her throat, squeezing away the prickle behind her eyes. "You don't. You *can't* know." She pressed their foreheads together to make her tears somehow less conspicuous. "I didn't mean it. I mean I did, because you're not my—Frankie, I want to tell you everything. I just—"

"Hey." Frankie raised both hands to Alex's cheeks and swept both thumbs across them. "I know." Slowly, she leaned in then brushed her lips against Alex's. "I'm probably not supposed to say this..." She paused, breath hot against Alex's lips, confusing her emotions, sending shivers straight to her toes. "But I really miss you."

She made it seem so easy to say the words, made it seem like the same ones hadn't been lodged in Alex's throat for weeks, months even, paralyzing her every time she so much as threatened to speak them.

"I shouldn't have gotten mad at you," Frankie whispered. "But when I saw it..." She closed her eyes, fingers barely brushing the scars over Alex's jeans, making her tenser. "You don't want to talk about it. I get that. I just need to know that this, us"—she pursed her lips and squeezed her eyes shut tighter"—has nothing to do with it."

"It doesn't."

A silence dragged out, both breathing each other's air, Alex's fingers lightly threading the golden strands at the back of Frankie's neck, Frankie's hands soft, hot, low on Alex's hips.

And then Frankie moved her lips against Alex's again. "You're lying."

"Frankie—"

"I've gotten pretty good at telling. And I—" She shook her head, taking a step back. "I can't do this if it means you have to hurt yourself, Alex. No matter how much I—No matter how much—" Her chest heaved, breaths quickening in a way that reminded Alex of Frankie crying in the locker room three weeks ago.

Alex closed the space between them. "Being with you is the only part that *doesn't* hurt." She licked her lips, ducking her head in search of Frankie's eyes. When Frankie looked up, Alex trailed the freckles on her cheek with her fingers and paused at her lips. "You were right. I can't get enough of kissing you, or having you close like this, having you nearby at all. I *want* to dry your tears—fuck, I want to make it so you never have to shed a single one. I want nothing but your laugh even if it completely paralyzes me, and the way you're so casually fucking incredible at school and soccer and just...everything." She swallowed, shaking her head. "God, Frankie, if you had any idea how much you—"

Frankie surged forward and pressed her lips against Alex's again so forcefully it sent them both stumbling. They managed to find a balance quickly with both of Frankie's hands on Alex's face and Alex's firm on Frankie's sides. Alex shifted Frankie's shirt to inevitably feel her skin.

It was a little like their first kiss—fast and wet and almost entirely in Frankie's control. Alex breathless from the way Frankie kisses her so... so... *Right*. No need for deliberation. No need to will her body to catch up or coax Frankie's lips to move in ways more accommodating, or less sloppy. Her hands moved higher, nails leaving crescents in their wake as she bit down on Frankie's bottom lip.

"Alex."

"Take me to your room."

Frankie shook her head. "No."

"Why not?"

"Alex."

Alex's toes curled, and she touched Frankie's bra-line, wanting more than anything to slip beneath it like she'd done for the first time a few weeks ago. She wanted the doubling of her pulse when her palm dragged over Frankie's breasts, nipples hard, grip tight on Alex's lower back. She wanted to know Frankie's body the way she'd been getting to know her mind before, between their kisses. She wanted to hear her name leave Frankie's lips breathless and weak and trembling, the way she felt every time her own body succumbed to having Frankie on top of her. "I want to kiss you."

"So kiss me."

"I want to feel you."

"*Alex.*"

The extra whine in Frankie's tone went straight to Alex's lower abdomen, making her want Frankie that much more. But she also sensed Frankie's hesitance, and she couldn't ignore it. Besides, though they'd obviously made up, she still had plenty to be sorry about. She forced herself to slow down a bit, planting her hands high on Frankie's ribs as she reluctantly pulled away. "Do you want me to go? Because I'll go."

"I don't want you to go."

Alex knit her brows. "Do you want to talk?"

"You don't want to talk." Frankie's eyes shone dark blue, all desire and apprehension when she brought her lips to Alex's. "Right now, I'm not so sure I want to either."

"Then what do you want?"

"You, Alex. Every fucking inch of you." She pulled away, brows furrowed, lips red and swollen and so sexy. "But I never know when you're going to stay or leave and I—" She released a heavy breath, angling her body away from Alex's. "I can't even look at you right now without—"

Alex got it. After everything she'd put them through the last few months? Rollercoaster didn't even begin to describe it. But things had been changing, even if none of them realized it. *Alex* had been changing. Maybe she'd still feel some of kind of wrong after it all—she didn't think that would ever go away—but at least, she wasn't so afraid to want it anymore. She wasn't afraid of the way her pulse reacted to Frankie's presence, or her body to Frankie's touch, or the way she was mind blown every time Frankie surprised her by being interested in sports *and* science *and* Shakespeare. She couldn't even begin to imagine what someone like Francesca Calvano could possibly see in her.

But that was a part of it too.

Frankie, while clearly aware Alex was an absolute coward, liar some days, perceived Alex as so much better than she truly was. Strangely, it felt like an ideal synthesis of acceptance and faith Alex didn't even know she needed. Francesca Calvano was everything Alex didn't know she needed. Even if the reverse wasn't true.

She intertwined their fingers and placed the gentlest of kisses on Frankie's lips. "Do you trust me?"

"You know I do."

"Then take me upstairs and show me all the words I make it too hard for you to say."

They kept it up for months.

Texting and laughing.

Breaking and building.

Sex and something so close to words Alex could never confess. She thought about it though. All through winter and spring. The night of her birthday when Frankie whisked her away from the always-too-elaborate party to the pool where they began a year ago. Leather jacket at the ready for the bite in the air, pure attentiveness when she turned to Alex and muttered, "You know what I've been thinking?"

Alex smiled, heart racing at their proximity, at the way the tips of Frankie's fingers constantly touched hers. "What have you been thinking?"

"That you should read me something. From your journal."

Alex furrowed her brows.

"It doesn't have to be tonight, and it doesn't have to be about me. I mean—" She cut herself off, shaking her head. "Assuming you even write about me because you probably don't. But it's okay if you do. Or if you don't."

"Frankie—"

"I just..." Frankie sighed. "I want to know what you write about."

The sincerity in her words, her gaze, hit Alex right in the chest. Actually, the way she looked at Alex always left her feeling light-headed and terrified and completely beguiled.

Frankie reached for the box next to her and handed it over, and she waited while Alex took her time in undoing the wrapping to reveal the pure leather, hand-sewed diary inside. "I know you already have one, but I also know you're pretty stressed about all those AP sciences next year. I don't think you should take them. Not if you don't want to. But if you do, just make sure you keep writing, okay? And when you're ready...to show me...I'll be here."

Alex thought about it all through the summer too, when the four of them—she, Frankie, Tan and Dom—road tripped from Manhattan to Miami because it's what Frankie and Tanaka wanted to do before they left for California. Frankie's leaving was the thing Alex hated to think about most, so she didn't. She focused on everything else until fall of her senior year when Frankie had been gone for over a month already, settling into a school which meant Alex neither saw nor talked to the girl she'd spent almost every day of the last two years thinking about. Well, she did. But it wasn't as frequent. It didn't feel the same.

And it kind of hit Alex out of nowhere.

It wasn't just soccer season that was different now.

Fall, winter, spring, summer...

All the seasons were ruined because of her.

And if Alex couldn't have Frankie in a way that hurt less than this, what was the point in torturing herself with dreams and possibilities she was sure to screw up?

Trying to be rid of it all reminded her of something she'd never been able to forget.

Being with Kason King could never compare to being with Francesca Calvano, even with him being older, more experienced now. But as a bonus, Alex learned something else too.

Regret is among the most potent of poisons.

Difficult to bleed from the body.

Even harder to bleed from the mind.

"I'll never forgive myself," Alex spoke up. She needed to say it. She needed to acknowledge how much she'd ruined them. "Sleeping with Kason..." Her throat tightened, closing in on the words. "God, I was such a fucking coward. I don't even get how you can look at me aft—"

"It's not like we were official, Alex."

"Stop."

"It's true. We never agreed we were exclusive." Frankie shook her head, sitting upright as Alex did too. "You weren't my..." She took a visible gulp, probably sending the word *girlfriend* straight to the pit of her stomach. Because last time, the only time it had come up, Alex had been painfully deluded, insistent on making it clear no matter how many times she fell asleep with Frankie's face behind her lids, cherry on her tongue, lavender on her skin, Frankie wasn't her girlfriend.

Frankie shrugged, something like resolve in her tone when she murmured, "You weren't mine, Alex."

"But I was." It's all resolve from Alex too. And maybe desperation for Frankie to understand just how much she meant to her, even if it was too little too late. "I *was* yours. And it scared the hell out of me. But it was also the reason I stopped running, why the last couple of months before you left were perfect. Because I stopped fighting." She licked her lips, drawing her brows together. "It was pointless anyway. I was never going to be straight. I was never going to want to be. Not as long as you looked at me like I was even close to deserving you. I was yours, Frankie. But then you left for USC, and it just wasn't the same. Trinity, my mom, *everything*...was hell."

She swallowed, letting the memories completely take over.

"It was your laugh in my head. The way your nose scrunched just a little and the corners of your eyes creased, always greener than blue when you're unbearably happy. It was the way your brows would stay furrowed all through homework and if they weren't, the assignment just wasn't challenging enough. Boring." She scoffed, and Frankie breathed a laugh, tears streaking her face. "It was the way I couldn't possibly wash your smell off my skin, random moments where I could feel that soft kiss you always left on my lips after we'd been making out for never long enough. In my mind, you were everywhere." She shrugged. "But in reality, you were gone, Frankie. And I *couldn't* breathe. I was still yours, but it didn't feel like you were mine. Not anymore."

Frankie squeezed her hand. "Alex..."

"I wanted to feel less."

Alex shook her head, mind flashing back to the campus visit to Cornell, the party, too much Belvedere, Kason using her drinking as an opportunity to get close for the first time since they'd broken up, and Alex just trying to use him period. Ten minutes of comparing the way he tasted, felt.

"I didn't want to feel anything."

And she didn't. It was supposed to hurt at least. Her first time with a guy. All she felt was numb.

When Kason rolled over next to her, chest heaving as if they'd been at it for hours, Cheshire cat grin on his face, her mind wrapped around her like barbed wire and bled the vodka right out of her veins. She barely managed to put her clothes on, Kason mumbling something about how she should stay before she threw up everything her stomach would yield.

Alex broke eye contact, chest, throat, whole body taut with the memory. "I'd give anything to take it back. But I can't." She forced herself to meet Frankie's gaze again, resolving to let the tears fall. "Just don't ever think I wasn't yours."

A part of me still is.

Frankie brought a hand to Alex's cheek and stroked it with her thumb, eyes roaming every inch of her face. "How do you expect me to not kiss you after that?"

"Because I don't trust myself to stop if you do."

Frankie shook her head. "I wouldn't want you to."

"But it wouldn't be fair to either of us."

A silence hung in the air. Frankie dropped her gaze to where she still had Alex's fingers intertwined with hers before focusing on the TV, though nothing was playing. "Because you're going back to her."

It was only half a question, and even though she said it without breaking—fearless, the only way Frankie said or did anything—the words slipped out like razors on her tongue. Alex had bled enough to know it wasn't always literal. And tonight, Frankie was bloody all over.

Still, all Alex managed to say was, "I love her, Frankie."

"I know." Frankie nodded, eyes back on Alex's. "I know you do, because if I know you, she's beautiful and smart, talented—maybe something artsy, like you—and she probably gets you in a way not a lot of people get close enough to. But is it crazy that I'm sitting here thinking, hoping, that everything you've said isn't just past?" She paused. "Am I crazy, Alex?"

"No." Alex shook her head. No matter how much easier things would be, she couldn't lie. Not after how honest they'd both been already. "It's not just past. I don't think it'll ever be just past."

"Then why is she the one who gets to have you?"

"Because..." Alex raked a hand through her hair, wracking her brain for any way to explain, and not hurt Frankie any more. "Because no matter how much this hurts right now, you deserve better, Frankie."

Frankie scoffed.

"No." Alex shifted closer, holding Frankie's face, looking her dead in the eyes. "It's like we keep saying. We're not them anymore. But especially after everything we went through, that *I* put you through, I'll never forgive myself for hurting you like that not once but twice. So if we ever get another chance at an *us*, it can't be like this."

She paused, desperate for the words to resonate. When she could see that they weren't, she sighed. "It can't be on the hinges of my relationship with someone else. I can't feel the way I feel about her and be with you too. And I know that sounds crazy because I'll be going back to her after confessing that I'm still in love with you, but it's not the same." She shook her head. "You're in me, Frankie. I spent years trying to bleed you from my veins and I failed. Which is how I know you'll always be there. It's just"—she swiped her thumb across Frankie's cheek—"not our time. Maybe someday it will be. Maybe we're star-crossed or something, but until then...I have to see where it goes with her."

Frankie nodded, cheeks rid of fresh tears, eyes glimmering with old ones. "I won't beg you to choose me. That's not the way I want your heart. Just..." She shut her eyes, the breath escaping her painfully resigned. "Don't go. We don't have to talk or anything. All I need is your arms around me tonight and caffè lattes in the morning, and somewhere in between I'll convince myself I'll be okay."

Alex adjusted to lie on the sofa again, zero hesitance when she pulled Frankie against her and pressed a kiss to her forehead. She wrapped her arms around her, desperate to comfort her without more inadequate words. But because they were so much a part of Alex, she couldn't help but whisper, "You will be okay, Frankie. I know it."

No answer. Not for a while anyway. Just both their gentle inhales and exhales, and a single night to bask in what could've been.

"Maybe I am crazy."

Alex tilted her head to look at Frankie. "What do you mean?"

"I think we are...star-crossed."

Epilogue

affogato

Goose bumps rose on Alex's skin, her heart wracking against her ribs. It had been like this, on and off, for eighty odd minutes already. She should've been used to it, but she wasn't. Not even close. She dragged her palms against her jean-clad thighs to dry them.

The Red Bull Arena was packed to capacity, crowd roaring at every mounting attack, outrageous tackle and blatant show of skill. Sky Blue FC led the Utah Royals two goals to one and looked well positioned to compound their lead, but Alex hadn't opened her mouth to cheer them on once.

Maybe it was nerves. Maybe it was anxiety over driving the last forty minutes alone with her thoughts, without announcing she'd be there that had left her too wired to function like an avid spectator. Maybe...seeing Frankie for the first time in almost eight months, especially like this—all drive and passion and raw talent— had Alex all but paralyzed.

Frankie used both hands to brush a few loose strands of golden hair out of her face, tan skin glistening, chest heaving with all the signs of how much she'd put into the game. Always her everything, nothing but enough to leave her breathless. And breathtaking. She readied herself as the keeper launched the ball in her direction, taking short steps to leave her just right for the drop despite the defender clinging to her back. She headed the ball off to their right-winger and turned for the run up-field. The Royals center-back they had on her was struggling. Had been all game. After ninety minutes of being outrun and out skilled, she was slow and tired and resorted to tugging Frankie to ground when the ball came back their way.

The whistle dinned, and she reached down to pull Frankie up, humbly accepting the yellow card shown her way. Frankie grinned as she accepted her rival's hand, and Alex couldn't help but smile a little herself.

This was the girl she knew. The one she fell for at sixteen.

That smile, those eyes, this game.

With three minutes left and an unremarkable free kick that flew over the bar, the game ended with the same score line. It was worth every second anyway. But as the field cleared and Frankie and Tanaka disappeared into the tunnel with the rest of their teammates, the feeling set in that being a spectator to ninety minutes of their fight was the only preparation she'd done for hers.

*

The race of Alex's pulse during the game didn't compare. She kept her feet grounded to the asphalt in the parking lot, turning her phone over and over in her hand. She stopped the motion when it vibrated again.

> Ryan: *Do you think she saw you?*

> Alex: *No. But I don't know if that makes me feel better or worse.*

> Ryan: *You guys haven't spoken since that night?*

> Alex: *We haven't. I guess I just figured we both needed space after everything, you know?*

They did need space. Alex didn't see how she could make things work with Dani otherwise, and she didn't see how Frankie would ever get over her if they were still spending all that time together.

> Ryan: *Why does it sound like you're second-guessing that now?*

> Alex: *Because I am.*

The main doors opened with a stream of chatter and a laugh Alex could never forget soaring in the midst of it all, searing through the walls of her chest. She willed herself to look up, and for a second, her heart stopped. Their eyes locked. Blue-green and brown, and so much unknown between them.

The contentment on Frankie's face faded slowly, morphing into something Alex couldn't identify. Her phone vibrated in her palm again, but instead of checking, she slid it into the back pocket of her jeans, eyes glued to Frankie as she turned to the three girls on her tail and told them, "I'll catch up with you guys later." A part of Alex was glad Tanaka wasn't among them because she if she was, getting Frankie alone wouldn't be easy.

Alex scoffed. How presumptuous.

Frankie hadn't agreed to talk, let alone go anywhere with her.

As Frankie descended the last few steps, it gave Alex a few more seconds to process the image of her—blonde hair wavy, still wet from her shower, fresh-faced, freckles dancing across her skin, eyes bluer than Alex had ever seen them. The blue tank and navy joggers were no adjustment—the memory of Frankie in Trinity's blue and white still occupied the forefront of Alex's mind—but the pair of slides on her feet were so fucking familiar, Alex's head was spinning. The hint of lavender in the air didn't help. Not even a little bit.

Alex dragged a hand through her hair, forcing herself to take a step forward. She opened her mouth. Nothing came out.

"Hi, Alex."

Her name uttered so gently, no hint of malice, was enough to get her mouth open again. "Hi, Frankie."

For a moment, a few moments, there was nothing else between them. Four words in the open, a million unsaid ones trapped in pit of Alex's stomach, questions in Frankie's gaze. The silence spread. Their last conversation had ended in a pointless declaration of I love you, bound in the memory of a night in each other's arms, and a morning marked by Alex carefully peeling her limbs away from Frankie's, desperate not to wake her when she left with a kiss pressed against her forehead.

It looped in her mind with the lucidity of yesterday.

The tremor of Frankie's lips when she declared, "All I need is your arms around me tonight, and caffè lattes in the morning, and somewhere in between I'll convince myself I'll be okay."

It was enough to get Alex to Brave and back to Frankie's with a latte in hand. She'd left it on Frankie's nightstand with a note that read *Always yours, if only in memory*, thankfully all before Frankie opened her eyes.

"Is everything okay?" Frankie asked.

"Yeah. No, of course. I just—" Alex licked her lips. She pulled her gaze away from Frankie's and glanced around them before looking at her again. "Can I uhm...Can I take you somewhere?"

Frankie drew her brows together. "Where?"

"I don't know." Alex shrugged. "Anywhere?"

"Alex."

"Wherever you want."

For a while, Frankie stared at Alex, processing the words, or working through her indecision. Then, she mumbled, "Okay," stepping past Alex and in the direction of Alex's car.

Always wanting to make things easier than Alex deserved, only to make them more difficult in the end.

*

They drove in silence, ten minutes tops, but wound up at a little Italian place near Frankie's apartment there in Jersey. It didn't surprise Alex. Italian cuisine had always been something Frankie loved ceaselessly, despite growing up on it. One of the things they never disagreed on. Their common ground. Their corner booth at Brave.

They both got amaretto coffee affogatos, neither in the mood for a big dinner, or food. The elderly man served them glass flutes with a wrinkled smile and offer that they stay as long as they like, despite closing soon. The grin Frankie returned along with the "Thanks Gio, but I know Rosa is waiting for you," told Alex just how well Frankie must have gotten to know the man, so instead of taking him up on his offer, they had their ice cream on the hood of Alex's car.

Stars gradually emerged across the darkened sky. More of them to see than in Manhattan. Alex spent half the time staring at Frankie anyway, hoping Frankie hadn't noticed and wishing she did all at once.

"So, you caught the game?" Frankie slipped her spoon from her mouth, leaving a bit of ice cream on the corner of her lips.

Alex tried not to stare at it, tried not to reach up and wipe it away with a swipe of her thumb or kiss of her lips. When she glanced down to her glass, taking another scoop on her own spoon as she answered the question, her throat tightened. "You were amazing."

Frankie scoffed. "You always say that."

"It's always true."

"Yeah, well, you've always been better at giving compliments than taking them."

Alex wouldn't argue with that, especially not coming from someone who knew her as well as Frankie did. "When's your next game?"

"The third. What? Is this going to be a regular thing now? Coming to my games."

"I don't know." Alex supposed it depended on how things ended between them tonight. If she was being honest, she missed watching Frankie play. She'd done near everything to not monitor Frankie's soccer career post-Trinity. Now that she'd put herself in a position to witness it again, she wasn't sure she'd be able go back to the bliss of ignorance. "Could it be?"

Frankie laughed. "It's not like I could stop you if that's what you wanted. They sell tickets to whoever will buy them."

It came with a smile, but the level of apathy in Frankie's answer bothered Alex more than it should have. Then again, she didn't have a right to be bothered, did she?

She stared at the drop of ice cream on the left corner of Frankie's lips again. "You have a little uhm..." She pointed in the direction, and Frankie wiped it away with the back of her hand. Alex realized she'd wanted Frankie to miss, wanted the opportunity to redirect her a few times, only to finally feel forced to wipe it away herself. They'd stare into each other's eyes—a little like they were now—and Alex wouldn't have to explain. Not yet. Maybe not ever. They'd both lean in, slow and hesitant, and they'd kiss. Everything would fall into place.

Frankie broke the eye contact.

They didn't kiss.

Pieces of what they were meant to be were still scattered in Alex's memory.

"We should probably get going." Frankie slid off the hood of Alex's car.

"Yeah."

Alex's chest ached as she got to her feet. Faint but potent. The feeling didn't warrant much attention. Not when it'd been there for years already.

*

The ride to Frankie's apartment was a lot like the one to Gio's diner. Just as quiet, only the faint melody of "Ocean" playing over the radio. Frankie didn't say a word, and Alex still hadn't found hers. None that were right or even okay, and the closer they got the angrier she became with herself for still being so bad at this, even when Frankie had gone out of her way to make it easy.

She parked along the curb outside a small apartment complex. Not as big as the Wexmore. Somehow equally luxurious.

"Walk me up?"

Alex nodded. "Sure."

Frankie reached for her gym bag and Alex opened her door then moved urgently to round the car and get Frankie's too. It didn't feel chivalrous. More than anything, it felt silly.

When they got to Frankie's apartment, Alex waited outside as Frankie fumbled around her bag for the key. Frankie pushed the door open and stepped over the threshold, dropping her bag before facing Alex again.

Alex was out of time. At least for tonight.

"Alex."

"So uhm..." Alex glanced at her feet, boots digging into the carpet. "I guess I'll see you."

"Alex." Frankie took her arm, forcing her to look up again, saying the words too softly when they left her lips. "Come here." And it was like she knew Alex had a hard time processing them, or the way she was gently being pulled forward. Frankie brought both her hands to Alex's face and confirmed her gaze. "I'm going to kiss you now."

Alex's mind blanked, and for a second, she was genuinely convinced her brain had short-circuited. "What?"

Frankie brushed her nose against Alex's then followed with her lips, leaving goose bumps all over Alex's skin. "I really want to kiss you now. But you have to tell me this is why you came here. You have to say yes—"

Alex took Frankie's bottom lip between hers, one hand landing on the nape of her neck as Frankie pulled her inside. The door slammed shut, and Alex's back collided with the wood, making her groan, making her grip Frankie tighter.

Kissing Francesca was every bit like coffee affogatos.

Bittersweet, warm chills down her spine.

Her chest heaved, her body heating up with the desire for something, someone it had taken every bit of her to deny. She couldn't breathe, but she didn't want to. She didn't ever want to take another breath if it meant she couldn't have Frankie's lips, hands, body against hers like this.

This was how they said it all.

"God, I missed you." Frankie breathed the words into her mouth, pushing the bomber jacket off Alex's shoulders. The racerback tank Alex wore went next. Strange, soothing, sexy how good Frankie was at this, how easy it was for Alex to give in, how she was so completely out of control in a way she'd never been with anyone else.

She wanted to say it back. That she missed Frankie too. That she'd been going crazy because of it. That she was sorry it took her *this* long to show up.

Frankie trailed the bare skin of Alex's sides down to her thighs and the instinct to wrap them around Frankie's waist overcame her.

Frankie turned and took blind steps further into the apartment as she joined their lips again. She lowered Alex onto her bed, and stood upright, eyes locked with Alex's as she pulled her shirt over her head and dropped it on the floor.

Alex swallowed as Frankie slipped out of her joggers. She'd always loved this part. How Frankie always made a show of getting undressed for her. Leaving the black Calvin Klein sport bra and panty combo she was wearing, she reached for the button of Alex's jeans. She pressed an open-mouthed kiss to Alex's stomach, tugging them off with more than a little urgency.

Alex took her hand and pulled Frankie on top of her as she moved further up the bed. Frankie kissed Alex's neck, using one knee to part her legs. She'd left both their underwear on, clearly having no intention of this being over quickly. She rocked forward, dragging her teeth against Alex's skin.

"Fuck." Alex's body tensed, coil tightening in her lower abdomen. She couldn't hold off what was coming. Her body had always responded the same way to having Frankie against her like this. It was either totally embarrassing, or a testament of exactly how she felt about her. Maybe it was both. "Frankie."

Frankie reached behind her, undid the clasp of Alex's bra and threw it across the room before getting rid of her own. She leaned in again and they both moaned at the feeling of their breasts against each other. "Is this okay?" Frankie asked.

"Yes. Just—" Alex tossed her head back. "Oh my God."

"Just what?" Frankie kissed the underside of her jaw, hips still in motion.

"If you keep doing that—fuck, Frankie."

"It's okay." Frankie pulled back and slipped one hand between them to press her fingers against Alex's clit over her underwear. She shook her head, locking their eyes. "Don't fight it."

Alex's body tremored with release. She wanted it to stop—it was too fast, and she wasn't *this* easy—but she also didn't. It felt too good. Frankie felt too good.

She kissed her way along Alex's chest, taking her nipples in her mouth one after the other, and all Alex could do was squirm and moan and fail at catching her breath. The aftershocks of her first orgasm weren't even close to being over when Frankie tugged her underwear down. She brought both hands to Alex's thighs and pushed them further apart as she kissed her way up, leaving Alex so completely open for her. Alex tried to close her legs just a little. Frankie held her firmly in place, wrapped her arms around Alex's thighs then dragged her lips over Alex's scars, whispering how she's "so damn beautiful."

The second Frankie's wrapped her lips around Alex's clit, she was about to crash again.

"Frankie..." In Alex's mind, there was something different in her tone this time. More than want or lust. Frankie took it as encouragement, reaching up to intertwine the fingers of one hand with Alex's as she moved her tongue in slower, more attentive patterns. Alex opened her eyes, parting her lips wider as the tremors in her body started. "Baby." She squeezed Frankie's hand and tugged as the prickle behind her eyes intensified. "Baby, wait."

Frankie pulled away, creasing her forehead as she hovered over Alex. She dragged a hand over her lips, freeing the one linked with Alex's to stroke her cheek. "Wha—You're...crying."

"I know." Alex swallowed, quickly wiping her face. "I'm sorry."

Frankie shook her head. "No. Don't apologize. Just..." She closed her eyes, bringing forehead to Alex's. "Please don't tell me it's nothing when I ask you what's wr—"

"I love you."

"Alex."

"No. Look at me." She swept a few strands of hair out of Frankie's face, waiting for Frankie to look at her. "I love you. And I'm sick of trying not to. This...the sex...the sex is nice. The sex is spectacular, but that's not why I came here. I came here to tell you that I want you. Not now. Not tonight. Forever. And that I know I fucked up. And then I fucked up again, but I'm ready to spend every day showing you how much I want this. Us."

"What about..." Frankie gulped. "What about Daniela?"

"It's been over for months. We tried. I tried, Frankie, but I—" She scoffed, her throat closing up at the words, tears so close. "I belong to you. I keep giving out bits and pieces of my heart because of that. Because with everyone else, I had to try. I admit, with Dani it was different. Easier. And I guess it's my fault for prolonging it, because she'd always say how she still felt like she didn't have me, like I wasn't hers yet, and I always thought it couldn't possibly be true, because I gave her so much of me. But she was right. I was never hers. Not really. And I could never be for as long as I was still yours."

"Alex..." Frankie rolled off her. "What are you saying?"

Alex propped up on one elbow then slowly pressed her lips to Frankie's jaw. "I'm saying I'm ready, and if you're not, that's okay. I'll be here when you are."

"So, you like..." Frankie beamed, one hand settling on the back of Alex's neck, weaving through her hair. "Love me, love me?"

Alex breathed a laugh, brushing her lips against Frankie's. "Yes, babe. I like...love you, love you."

"God." She studied Alex's face, eyes roaming every inch. "It took you long enough."

Alex's grin widened. "You just knew"—she took Frankie's lips in a languid kiss, moving to straddle her—"I was coming back to you?"

"Star-crossed, remember?"

"Cocky."

Frankie shook her head and kissed Alex before pulling away. "I knew I'd never feel the way I do about you for anyone else. I just hoped it was true for you too."

"It is."

"Good." She wrapped both hands around Alex's waist then flipped them so Alex was on her back again, both blissfully fucking happy. "Now..." She kissed a trail to Alex's right ear and took it between her teeth. Alex moaned, pulse racing all over again. "About that multiple orgasm you were about to have."

Acknowledgements

Say, thank you for your never-ending faith in me, your unbending love and support and your constant reminders that I could do this.

Lucy and Bryce, thank you for so easily becoming two of my favorite people, being there for my 300 hundred freak outs and always offering to help, even when you have fevers and colds.

Thanks to Dad Jobs for being the only writing group I could ever need.

And thank you to Cris, Stella, Mani and Sky for being there from the very beginning of it all.

Most importantly, a huge thank you to anyone who took the time to read this novel. You've brought my dream to life.

About the Author

Stephanie Shea is a self-proclaimed introvert who spends her days in corporate daydreaming of becoming a full-time novelist. Her favorite things include binging tv shows, creating worlds where no character is too queer, broken or sensitive, and snacks. Lots of snacks. Someday, she hopes to curb her road rage, and get past her anxiety over social media and author bios.

Email
stephaniesheawrites@gmail.com

Facebook
www.facebook.com/stephshea27

Twitter
@steph_shea27

Website
www.stephaniesheawrites.com

Also Available from NineStar Press

Connect with NineStar Press

www.ninestarpress.com

www.facebook.com/ninestarpress

www.facebook.com/groups/NineStarNiche

www.twitter.com/ninestarpress